MW00366791

"24 impressive storie something for any speculative fiction reader."

— *Publishers Weekly*

"Some of these stories explore a world that is fully broken, others are focused on when it just begins to crack. But what's clear above all is that the world breaks for some groups of people much earlier than others. An inclusive and adept anthology in which each story is a facet for a different perspective on where we've gone—or will go—wrong."

— Brian Evenson

"A thoughtful, diverse collection hewing closely to the themes of connection and devotion—tender reunions, heartbreaking partings, misplaced loyalty, friendship, romance, parenthood, these character-focused stories have it all."

— Premee Mohamed

"This anthology offers seriously admirable work. Highly recommended."

— Arley Sorg, *Lightspeed Magazine*

DREAMS FOR
A BROKEN WORLD

Book Two in the Dreams Anthology Series

Series Editor
JULIE C. DAY

Guest Editor
ELLEN MEEROPOL

Assistant Editor
CARINA BISSETT

Assistant Editor
CELIA JEFFRIES

Cover Illustration by
ANDY KEHOE

ESSENTIAL
DREAMS PRESS
NORTHAMPTON, MA
AN IMPRINT OF
RECKONING PRESS

Contents

Introduction

This anthology is about being broken and dreaming change. We imagine it as a written form of kintsugi, the Japanese method of "revising" broken ceramics with precious metals. "When the Japanese repair broken objects, they aggrandize the damage by filling the cracks with gold," writes artist Barbara Bloom. "They believe that when something has suffered damage and has a history, it becomes more beautiful."

Our literary version of kintsugi takes stories out of their comfort zones and threads them together to create a narrative about human connection despite differences. These stories come from diverse genres, from realistic and fantastical and magical and dystopian, from dark to playful, from speculative to activist. They offer opposing, sometimes contradictory visions, an intentional crossing of lines that, too often, not only divide us but also prevent us from even noticing the worlds which others inhabit. But they have much in common too, beginning with the awful mess our world is in. We created this anthology to break down barriers and call for change. As you read this book, we hope you notice the ways in which these stories connect, sometimes directly, sometimes more obliquely, to form an ensemble of voices that are stronger together and reach towards activism, community, and social justice.

This project started with Julie C. Day, whose own fiction resides in the liminal spaces and whose work, while noted for its range of tones and topics, is resolute in its focus on the private internal universes of her characters. She was editor-in-chief of *Weird Dream Society* (Reckoning Press, 2020), an anthology that represented both an attempt to present a more expansive definition of the term "Weird" fiction and just as importantly, an effort to raise funds. As the grandchild of Nazi war victims forced to give up their citizenship, displacement has had a profound impact on the trajectory of her own family. All proceeds from that book benefit RAICES, a nonprofit agency that promotes justice by providing free and low-cost legal services to under-served immigrant children, families, and refugees.

When she thought about creating a second benefit anthology in the *Dream* series, Julie decided to adjust both the creative and charitable focus. For this second book, she chose the Rosenberg Fund for Children (RFC), a non-profit public foundation that supports the educational and emotional needs of targeted activist youth and children of parents who have been targeted for their progressive activism. RFC grants can be used to attend summer camp, receive therapy, attend a dance program, take music lessons, and gather with other children with similar experiences. To thrive, as well as survive.

Julie invited Ellen Meeropol to serve as guest editor for this project. Ellen, who writes politically engaged novels, stories, and essays, suggested the title *Dreams for a Broken World*. A former pediatric nurse practitioner and lifelong activist, she began writing fiction in her fifties. Her characters live on the fault lines between political turmoil and human connection. Ellen's husband Robert (Robby) Meeropol was orphaned at age six when his parents, Ethel and Julius Rosenberg, were executed at the height of the McCarthy Era. Robby started the Rosenberg Fund for Children to help children who were experiencing the nightmare that he and his brother endured as youngsters. Ellen served as an RFC board member for over twenty years and has been intimately involved with the organization, now run by her daughter, Jenn Meeropol.

When Julie and Ellen decided this project needed more editorial help, Julie invited dark fiction and fabulism author, editor and teacher Carina Bissett, and Ellen lassoed editor extraordinaire Celia Jeffries, who writes literary fiction and memoir.

Not only do the four of us write very different sorts of stories, we also have diverse reading preferences. Julie refuses to claim love for just a few, though Angélica Gorodischer, Tanith Lee, Carol Emshwiller, Leena Krohn, and Kazuo Ishiguro are all authors who have inspired her. Ellen's literary heroines include Kamila Shamsie, Andrea Barrett, Paule Marshall, and Laura Hobson. Carina particularly admires Angela Carter, Kelly Link, and Aimee Bender. Celia's favorite reads include Maggie O'Farrell, Niall Williams, Margaret Atwood, and Elena Ferrante.

As you read these stories, try to imagine our conversations as we discussed such a wide range of storytelling styles. We can share that it was occasionally hilarious, often perplexing, but never boring. We invite you to put aside your previous ideas about what makes a short story compelling. Open your mind and heart to these wide-ranging tales of broken worlds and healing moments. Match these pieces together with gold and take them with you into your own dreams and efforts to repair our broken world.

How the Demon War Was Won

BY BENJAMIN PARZYBOK

Lauren sat up in bed, her head bowed, letting her long hair pattern across her legs.

She'd had nightmares. Not the nightmares of her youth, those filled with the big demons. *Lurking in dark shadows, harrowing escapes, the horror at looking down and finding part of your own body eaten away, your family members ravaged or devoured.* Those were the nightmares of wartime, which she still had on occasion. This was different. On the night before her first day as a Crosser, she dreamed of being out to dinner with her mother. Her mother had chatted incessantly across from her, about the fishing club she'd joined, about who said what, the neighbors, the things she was going to buy later that afternoon. But every time she looked up, her mother's appearance had altered. The eyes gone red with yellow centers; her mouth elongating with vicious double-rows of teeth; the nose curving upward to expose the nostrils, blackened and gnarled; a slick, licey, dark fur; ears that spiraled into evil points. Clearly a demon, but also her mother, who rattled on at her with inane banter. Lauren woke sweaty and confused and a little angry.

The anger had not diminished by the time she dropped by her mother's old farmhouse on her way to the gate. She'd meant only to say goodbye. A 'we-dare-not-speak-of-it, but-this-could-be-the-final-one,' goodbye. The truce, miraculously, had already lasted over nine months. Even now, babies were being born outside of wartime. Babies who may not, if all went well, spend every night afraid, as humans had done for the previous thousand years.

"I wondered if I'd see you before the big day." Her mother's gaze was intent, searching. She swung the door wide.

Impulsively, she relayed the entire dream to the older woman.

"Lauren," her mother said, one hand on her hip, the other gesturing defensively with a gaudy glass string of aquamarine beads interwoven between the fingers. The tone conveyed so much. A seed of indignant disappointment, a sprout of conde-scension planted among the vast field of muted grief, a gritty frustration at her daughter's inability to move past it all, to vault into the future.

Well, Lauren thought. Her mother wasn't the one doing the vaulting, was she.

"I know," Lauren said.

"Your father would have—"

"I *know*," Lauren said.

"Bless his soul. Just let me look at his hands."

Lauren held out her own hands, famously like her father's. Farmer's hands, strong and calloused, built for the plowing of fields and the planting of bounty. Her mother gripped each in one of her own, and then bent and kissed the open palm of her left hand.

"You and he can work wonders with these. But I tell you, I *have* joined a fishing club!" She released Lauren's hands and twirled backward. "We meet on the dock every Tuesday evening." Her mother gestured toward the corner of the room. Nestled between the wall bearing the history of her mother's hobbies—beads and pottery and watercolors and weaving—and the other, which bore photos of the many friends and family lost, a fishing pole leaned into the corner. "I'm not, as you say, turning into a demon. But *something's* going on up there." She pointed with her beaded hand at her own head, her hair coiffed miraculously above.

"Hm," Lauren said.

"Come here," her mother said, holding her arms wide for an embrace.

Lauren reluctantly let herself be held. Her mother's unflagging confidence and optimism, despite so many catastrophes, was an irksome comfort.

"You have always been a rock in the storm, the most steadfast of rocks. You have prepared and prepared. This is just a different storm. But you're still a rock. The best rock I've ever known."

"OK," Lauren whispered.

"OK?" Her mother said. Then in a moment of motherly fussiness notably absent for the last decade, she removed Lauren's Crosser's hat, re-coiled Lauren's long hair, and re-affixed the hat and its long sash with an aggravating tightness. Her mother, Lauren knew then, was also afraid.

————

She met Roger at their appointed gateway. A short, bearded, somewhat rotund man of sixty-something, shaped like a beet or a child's spinning top, and just as nimble. She stood nearly a foot above him, a carrot to his beet. His warmness startled her. She expected a hardened, 'you better toughen up' and 'get your mind right!' type of figure, like her trainer, like the other heroes of the war she'd met, not this smiling man with the tendency to rest his hands on his belly, as if sidling up to a bar.

He pumped her hand, told her how happy he was to meet her. She tried to grin through her terror. "I thought…"

"You thought I'd be taller. I get that a lot."

"No, it's just—" Yes, she realized, it was indeed partly that. He had a jagged scar across one cheek which descended into his beard, and belatedly she noted he missed two fingers on his left hand.

She stared down at that hand. Everyone knew that demons killed first, and ate after. The way they marked their kills was to bite off a combination of fingers.

He saw she was staring and held up the hand. "Guess they thought I was dead! That's why I feel like this, all this"—he gestured wide, to the gate behind him, to the human settlements in the distance—"is bonus time. You scared?"

She nodded. Seeing his hand certainly hadn't helped.

"There's nothing to it," he said. "Just think of your favorite food. It's waffles for me every time, smooth sailing."

"Smooth sailing," she repeated, but it came out inaudibly. He grinned again, made a hand gesture to indicate *onward*, and turned.

Smooth sailing was not at all guaranteed, she knew. In the early days of the truce, a few demons had succumbed to their appetites. The war had threatened to burble back into existence. The body of the last demon to do so˙was deposited on the human side of the gate, flayed and roasted. A gesture of their commitment to the peace, they had all supposed. And while this last bit had been troubling, for sure, it seemed very unlikely they'd see trouble from that individual demon again.

She thought of Jasper, who'd graduated just ahead of her. A slight young man who loved to play pranks and tell stories. When he went through the gate for the first time his mind had come unhinged. He sprinted away from his mentor into a canyon. He was missing for two weeks while tensions rose on either side of the gate, until two demons carried his thin body back through, not a nibble on him. They'd found him naked and stiff and curled into a tight ball, underneath an overhang twenty-five miles from the gate.

Roger led her up to the gate between worlds. It towered

above them, a great iron arch bathed in a sickly yellow glow. And just then, as if stepping forth from her own nightmares, an enormous demon strode through. Easily ten feet tall, chaos and claws.

"Rawwwgzher…" It said, with a rumbling, lisping accent.

Immediately and without thinking, she stepped behind Roger.

"G'Akath." Roger smiled. He reached his small hand out, and the demon his great clawed hand, and the two lightly brushed against each others' palms. The creature certainly fit the profiles of her nightmares, but the expression it wore was all new.

"Lauren, you've heard of G'Akath? One of the brightest scholars of demonic arts. G'Akath, please, gently if you will, good sir, meet my new Crosser-in-training, Lauren."

Lauren had been hand-picked because of her emotional stability, her calm in the face of danger, and because she'd studied most rigorously in their etiquette. But beholding this horrific, enormous demon in front of her, she found she shook with terror.

G'Akath bent one knee backwards. She swallowed. She knew her demon physiology, but the abstract knowledge in her mind refused to overlay on the reality. He lowered himself so that his head and horns were level with her. Then, slowly, he extended one clawed hand toward her. She stood unmoving, until she realized that he wished to brush palms with her, too.

She reached for his foremost claw, and then they touched. The contact was a shock. She could feel a great thrumming chaos surge through her, the scent of sulfur dizzying. Her head reeled, and she felt like retching. Then G'Akath abruptly ascended to his full height and stepped backwards. She could breathe again.

"G'Hegkongt," she squeaked out, as formally as she could.

"Nicely spoken," rumbled the demon and Roger grinned at both of them.

"Have yourself a good day, boss," Roger said, and saluted.

G'Akath nodded once more. "Gourd captain." Then he strode off, his giant wings nodding behind him.

"Boss?" she whispered.

"Just a pet term. He was my earliest student, you know. Now the little ingrate has three human pupils himself. Who'd have believed it. A real sentimental story, that."

"Where does he go?"

"They're building a school, would you believe it?"

She nodded numbly. Then they turned and strolled through the gate.

———

She had prepared to go through the gate for months. The mental exercises, the deep breathing, the lore and media, hearsay and fact, she had read all of it. The crossing specifically had been drilled into her.

Squint, for the air on the other side can burn at first, and the lightning scars the eyes if viewed in its entirety.

Hold within your mind a memory of stillness, and hold it fast. Practice this. On the other side, let that memory fade slowly.

Lauren centered on her mother's image of her, that unmoveable boulder in a swift stream.

Use your drape cloth, the five foot stretch of fabric attached to the top of your Crosser's hat, to cover ears, mouth, and nose. Like the eyes, the ears, mouth, and nose must be subjected slowly or risk permanent damage.

And so she went through blind.

No amount of training could have prepared her for this.

She removed her drape cloth slowly. The sky roiled redly, shapes swooped and materialized and then dissipated, as if the sky were made of writhing intestines or red snakes. The jagged mountains smoked, black or dark grey, and a hot wind howled around them, carrying the scent of sulfur and smoke.

"Welcome to D'Gaskak!" Roger said brightly. His drape cloth was nearly off, revealing the smile underneath.

She understood Jasper now. The sight and sound and smell were one thing, but it was the madness that swarmed her, a pervasive psychic chaos that she could feel chipping away at her. Her thoughts frantically slid away. Like falling into a pool amongst a feeding frenzy of eels. She reached one hand out, unbalanced, and Roger caught her arm and held her fast around the bicep.

"Hup! There you go, you're doing great. Just like a ship in a rough sea—more or less."

She bent over and retched, all the while tamping down the all-encompassing need to scream. It had been worse than they'd said, that much she was clear on. A rough sea! More like a psychic hurricane. She stared down at her fingers clasped around each knee, all ten of them, and took deep breaths of the harsh, smoky air. But even as she retched again, she could feel herself come together. Her mind hummed and stilled itself, she relaxed her shoulders and breathed a sigh of relief. She was no Jasper; she'd made it through. A rock in a stream, a melon in a field. Finally, purged of her breakfast, she came back to a stand.

"Well, I can see for a fact *you* didn't eat waffles. But see?" Roger said. "Come now, our guide is just ahead."

She stumbled alongside him, propped up by Roger's firm grip. It'll get easier, she told herself.

"You wouldn't believe how many I've had to push back through the gate," he said. "I was getting a bit worried we'd never get the program started, but hey, look at you."

"You mean—"

"Other apprentices." He shrugged. "In the first few seconds you see it. Jasper wasn't the only, you know."

———

G'Kelnkek, as she was introduced, was slightly less-evil looking than the scholar she'd met at the gate and the demons she'd seen in books.

A female demon, the four breasts bared, inspected Laura from her towering height.

Lauren performed the modern greeting, roughly translated to: 'The mind of my mind salutes the mind of your mind,' feeling some satisfaction that—at least to her—it sounded correct and was delivered with the proper etiquette. Her voice did not bely the inner tremors pulsing through her body. The more ancient greeting, spawned from the thousand-year war: "May you dine upon the flesh of humans" was thankfully retired and newly culturally inappropriate.

Lauren heard a deep rumbling and realized the demon replied. "G'Pleeeeezzz to meet. G'will show you your students."

"You know what they call us?" Roger whispered. They'd both noticed G'Kelnkek looking her over as if she were a farm animal she were considering buying, or, she swallowed, perhaps one she wished to eat. But in this profound inspection, she couldn't help but do the same. She watched how the wings heaved in and out with each breath of the smoking air, how about the crown of the head rested a type of bone structure, as if she wore a crown she could not remove.

"What?" she said.

"Rats. *G'ekskek*. The one animal that lives in both worlds. There are some that believe that when they first came through the gate, things were so bewildering that they thought rats and we were the same, just different versions of each other. Do we not both construct warrens?"

She shrugged.

"And are we not both delicious? To them anyway." Roger grinned. "I can just tell, you'll be fast friends. Let's head down to the fields. I'm hungry for melons."

"Melons it is," she replied.

———

For a thousand years, demons had come through the gates between worlds and attacked human villages, pillaging, eating their victims, engaging in horrendous acts of violence. But in retrospect, humans were no less evil. Lesser in stature and poorly outfitted for demon-to-human combat, they used far more devious forms of offense. Spies were created who snuck through the gates and poisoned whole demon communities. And humans, who could see better than demons at night, slaughtered demons in their sleep. Each side lived in a certain fear and hatred of the other for as long as any history could remember.

———

At the fields Lauren began to get her bearings. She felt the chaos peel back another layer or two, her mind almost entirely returned. The fields were not far from the gate, but in her mental map of herself, in her understanding of the whole of reality, they were right near the core of her. Growing plants were to her as walking was to others. She'd trailed after her father the moment she could walk, tending to the fields, learning his craft. Crossers were pulled exclusively off of farms, for this craft in particular was what had changed the war. Now, she saw immediately that the gourds were under-watered, that the rows were too far apart for maximum efficiency. She reached down and took a handful of soil and parsed through it with her thumb. There were foreign elements, or at least the lighting was foreign, but there was much she knew in that handful of earth. It would drain fine. In the fields she saw a young demon or two, awkwardly bent to inspect a gourd or tend to a plant. This, after eons of suffering and hatred, is how they had ended the war. That and the sheer exhaustion of tragedy. Gourds. Gourds for the demons, who had known nothing of farming and who loved them over even the taste of human flesh. In return, demons were teaching them the ancient languages, the lost languages. The demon lore that described the timeline of their worlds, that took them back a thousand, thousand years. Knowledge for knowledge. These were the stones that were building paths between their worlds.

———

From up the fields, she watched a demon come toward her, its wings partly unfolded, its ungainly strides through the field the stuff of every child's nightmare.

Even years from now, after she was the master and Roger had retired to a small village on the sea (where during visits he showed off his pet rodent and insisted on playing a most-awful piano for her, his home always teeming with exotic visitors from every corner) and after a statue of her would be built near this exact spot, and trade routes between the two worlds were opened, and even a few bondings, human-demon couples who'd decided to spend their lives together, and after she herself had taken a demon partner, and was lauded as one of the change agents of the peace, she would still remember this moment as the most profound of her life.

The demon moving up the long row of gourds finally reached her. In its ghastly claws, a small and sickly cantaloupe. The demon bowed his head, and Lauren knew what must be done. This was the moment she'd rehearsed a thousand times, with dread and excitement.

She dropped to one knee and asked, in the language of demons: "I ask the indulgence of your intellect and wisdom. May I be your teacher?"

The demon reached its arm down, its claws encircling her forearms, and raised her back up. "To be your pupil," he said, "would be my greatest honor."

The Drill

BY BREENA CLARKE

"Take the bus out 42nd Street—the crosstown bus, the M42—and get off at 7th Avenue. Then take the Number One train. Get off at 157th Street. Don't get off at 168th Street. Okay? When you're riding the Number One and you get off at 168th Street, you have to ride the elevator and the elevator is nasty. Also, there are too many homeless people on the platform at 168th Street. Anything can happen in that station. Don't get off at 168th Street. Take the Number One at Times Square and get off at 157th Street. Okay? I'll wait in the station at 157th Street. But if you don't see me, don't wait for me. Start walking up on the east side of the street, and I'll walk down on the east side, and I'll see you. So walk on the east side of the street."

She starts off a good ten minutes earlier than the earliest time he could have gotten to the station at 157th Street unless they got let out early. It's the middle of winter and has been dark for hours. She turns over in her mind the color of the cap he wore that morning and recalls what color the coat was. As if she needed clues to recognize him! She is absolutely certain that blindfolded and unable to hear or touch him, she'd be able to distinguish her son in a stadium full of fourteen-year-olds. She knows him in every cell of her body. But when you love someone, you memorize their clothes.

It's ten p.m. and she wishes she were reclining in front of the TV. She is playing and replaying in her head the tape of his itinerary from the deck of the docked aircraft carrier *Intrepid*, through the midtown streets, north on the subway, to the subway station where she'll meet him. "He can do it. I mean there is no reason to think he'll get lost or anything."

They'd struck a bargain. He wanted so badly to be independent and out after dark that he agreed to all her prerequisites. If she would agree not to go over there with him—after the first time—and stand around waiting for him to be finished and walk him home, he promised to follow the one and only agreed-upon itinerary and not make any unauthorized stops. She agreed he should have money for a slice and a Coke, or a hot dog and a Coke and some candy, probably. He agreed to travel quickly and prudently in the company of his new friend, Derrick. He would sit in the subway car with the conductor in it—only.

His smile when she was finally won over was triumphant. He exchanged a victory glance with his stepfather over her head as if they'd been together on a strategy against her. They thought she didn't catch it, but she could smell the testosterone in the air. She detected a difference in the house lately. Those two sharing a certain odor of complicity. Their hormones lined up against hers.

She is letting out the kite a little farther every day. She's giving it more string, exposing it to the wind, but holding her end tighter and tighter. The city closes in around kids nowadays and walking through the streets is like passing a gauntlet. Her husband thinks it's queer the way she leaps into the gutter to put her arms out a like a crossing guard when the three of them approach a street corner. "Look at all these people," he says sarcastically. "Most of them born and raised in New York City, and somehow they've survived as pedestrians without your help." This is not amusing to someone who regularly tests her own reflexes to be sure she's alert enough to charge in front of a raging bull of a car, driven by Lucifer's own taxi driver, careening directly toward her child.

Her letting him go by himself to the cadet practice way across town, his walking in a part of the city that's dark, his having to move through the gaudy neon swirl of Times Square, his traveling by himself on the subway at a dicey hour —this is all new.

He's had to memorize four different combinations for four different locks this year: his locker for coat and books, his locker for gym stuff, his swimming locker at the Y, and the lock for the chain on his bike. She bought him a bicycle, but they both know he better not take his hand off it unless he puts on the fifty-dollar lock with the money-back guarantee. When he had to replace a defective part on the bicycle, she put on jeans and a sweatshirt and rode with him and the bike on the subway. They're both glad he prefers his skateboard. It's easier to defend and cheaper to replace.

He's not a street child, but he's got pluck. He's not a fighter, but he's scrappy. He's tall, brown, with a sweet face, and she ruminates about what the cops will think if he reaches into his pocket for his gloves.

His wanting to join the cadet drill team is all tied up with the new friend, Derrick. They want to solidify their friendship with uniforms and syncopated walking. She disapproves of mumbling but likes this boy who mumbles shyly and respect-fully. He's got home training.

"Better to exit up this stairway than that because you'll be facing the right direction. Best to stand directly under the streetlamp so the bus driver will see you. Remember how we decided that standing well back from the edge of the platform is the best protection against an insane person pushing you onto the tracks in front of an arriving train? Keep your eyes and ears open, your mouth shut. Don't spend the transportation money on junk snacks and then try to get away with using your school pass after seven p.m. Don't jump the turnstile no matter what except in a case of being utterly stranded and having exhausted all other alternatives, including pleading with the token clerk."

Per the agreement, on the first night of the cadet program she went with him. She traced the route and discussed the idiosyncrasies in detail. She rolled her head from left to right and back again, surveying the street ahead—a walking defense mechanism picked up in the city. You let your eyes sweep broadly as far in front of you as possible. This way you can see certain crazies and drunks, and friends you're not in the mood for, before they see you. Leaving the *Intrepid*, standing with the two boys in the full bloom of the streetlamp, she was quietly annoyed with Derrick's people for not sending someone to accompany him. "He lives in the Bronx for chrissake!" Suddenly she was not sure if she wasn't overreacting to the perceived dangers. "Don't smother the boy." Even her father chimed in. Acutely sensitive to the Daniel Patrick Moynihan school of thought on pathological Black female emasculators, she checks herself. "No, they should have come. These boys are still too young to scrabble around New York City at ten o'clock at night."

They mounted the bus finally, and the driver was cheerful. She fought the impulse to ask him if he always drove this route and if it always rounded this corner at exactly this time. When the bus crossed 42nd Street between 8th Avenue and 7th, the boys stared out the window into the nine-hundred watt sex and sadism marquees. She saw some woman's tits and name lying across her son's cheek and *Terminator* and *Friday the Thirteenth* flickering across his blinking eyes. She really wanted to tell him not to look out the window but realized how stupid it would sound.

Most often she believes forewarned is forearmed, but once or twice she has surrendered to an overwhelming desire to pretend that some things don't happen if you don't ever see them happening. One time she surveyed the street ahead of them as they walked together and caught sight of a man pulling down his disgusting pants and bending over and tooting his ass over a pile of garbage right on the corner of 50th Street and 8th Avenue. She reached around and put her hand over her son's eyes. It was a simple reflex, but he pouted a long while because he knew he'd missed something interesting.

Tonight she walks down the east side of the street but sweeps the whole thoroughfare with her eyes, in case he didn't do what he was supposed to do. One of the pillars of maternal wisdom: after you've drilled into the child's head what he must do, you try to imagine what will happen if he does exactly the opposite. You've got to be prepared.

She waits at the turnstiles. She can see the platform. There is only one way to exit the station. If he's sitting in the car with the conductor, he'll be in the middle of the train. As each train enters the station, she looks at the middle first, then fans out to scout the front and back. Three trains come through and he doesn't arrive. She is sick of looking at the token clerk and annoyed that he is looking at her. She walks back toward the stairs. He's the kind of bullet-headed clerk who thinks the Transit Authority is paying him to scout fashion models rather than sell tokens. Out of his line of vision, she reads the subway map, traces grimy tiles with an index finger, and wipes her finger with a tissue.

He's not on the next train. She's getting angry and mutters to herself. She's getting scared. "Walk to the bus stop, ride across 42nd Street, get off at 7th Avenue, catch the uptown Number One, sit in the car with the conductor, get off at 157th Street. Simple."

Her stomach is not quiet. One hundred and thirty-eight pounds. The last time he went to the doctor's that's what he weighed, one hundred and thirty-eight pounds. She thinks

that's accurate. Five feet eight inches tall. Half an inch taller
than she. She can feel the brush of the bird's wing—the bird
who brushes his wing against the mountaintop and in an eternity will have worn it to a pebble. This tiny bird of worry that
brushes his wing against the soul of a mother and thus
shortens her life by minutes, hours, days.

A throng of people come out of the next train, and he is
not among them. She sits disconsolately on the crummy steps
next to a plaque about the Jumel Mansion and silently begs
whoever is listening to give her a break. "Let him be on the
next train. Please!" All the while knowing that personal
prayers don't alter events already in motion.

A train pulls in. She leaps to attention at the turnstile,
leans over. Looks anxious. She searches the windows. He
bounds out of the middle of the train, poised for fussing but
begging with his eyes for her to be calm. "They let us out late
and the bus took forever." His voice is trembling. Words dam
up behind her front teeth. She takes his hand silently and
climbs the stairs behind the exiting crowd. At street level, he
tactfully disengages his hand to show her the badges that have
to be sewn on the sleeve of a white shirt. She stands looking at
the knit cap he wears fashionably above his naked ears.
Worried about the cold, she pulls it down. They walk home.

Faith

BY AIMEE LIU

On November 17, 1997, retired career intelligence officer Dean Shaughnessy died of natural causes at his home in Greenwich, Connecticut. Mr. Shaughnessy's sole survivor, his son Ben, discovered the following statement among his father's papers. He has contributed this document to the Millennium Asia History Project, for publication in its entirety.

I was one of her nighttime customers in Hong Kong during the fall of 1941, just before the evacuation. We relied on her services. SOE and OSS agents passed her notes in cypher, scripted inside SenSen wrappers, stuffed into discarded condoms. Some of her customers were the enemy, and she would pick their pockets for useful details, names, addresses, shopping lists. Hours later, we came to complete the relay— she called us her morning customers, no matter what time we saw her.

I never slept with her. I may have been the only one who didn't. "Why not?" my counterpart from the SOE, T. L., used to nudge me. "She loves us. We're not the enemy."

Maybe. But maybe not. In any case, I found her too beautiful, in a shipwrecked sort of way. She reminded me of a figurehead with her defiant, sea-sprayed pride intact but stripped of all color and gloss. I admired her and, yes, desired her more than I probably admitted even to myself. But what I loved about her was something entirely different.

I loved the way she picked up her child, squatting first in the corner like a peasant, plucking him out of his padding. She would lift him into the crook of her elbow, swaying just so slightly, that wobbly head of thick black hair feathering her naked arm.

The baby was three months old and slept in a brown wicker basket in the same soulless room where she serviced her customers. One night she told me, "He knew we would have a son." I asked her to tell me her story.

She asked if she could trust me.

I gave her my promise.

———

The ruse was old, familiar, continues to this day. Her family was war-struck in Korea, father and brothers all vanished, she, her mother and sisters subsisting on rainwater and roots. Faith was not her name then, but she acted on it, nonetheless. When she was fifteen, the rumor passed around her village—strong girls could make good money doing factory or domestic work for the Japanese. Her mother and sisters would have one less mouth to feed. She could send her good money home.

She stood in the bed of a truck with twenty other girls from the village, not one of them waving goodbye. A neighbor man she had known her whole life drove the truck to the port. The girls were herded onto a black-painted ship and shut into rooms like prison cells. No windows, air, or water. The sea was rough, and many sickened. They could not tell day from night, which direction or how far from home they traveled.

When they were finally allowed on deck, the ship had docked in a large, bustling city which, they were told, was

Shanghai. Another truck took them from the pier to a big house that looked like an image from the British picture books Faith remembered from the Catholic school she attended until she was nine.

She could read, you see. She was not stupid—only poor and trusting. In the picture books, the British houses had wide green lawns and chimney pots, square windows and pitched roofs and vine-covered walls. Inside, they had great rooms with polished floors and chairs that looked like soft, panting animals, beds that floated high off the floor under tents the nuns called canopies. The house to which she was taken in Shanghai looked just right on the outside, but inside, the great rooms had been sliced into cells even smaller than those on the ship. Some of the walls were of wood, some merely fabric partitions. There were no chairs or floating beds, only thin cotton mattresses flat on the floor. A sign above the door read in Japanese: *Comfort Station.*

———

Faith was placed in one of the partitions and raped the first night by four young sentries taking turns until she fainted. The next morning, she was slapped awake at six a.m. and fed a breakfast of gruel by an elderly Chinese man who whispered that she would be bayoneted if she tried to escape—he promised he had seen it happen.

At nine, Japanese soldiers formed queues outside the partitions. Each held a ticket and a condom. The first to come told her he loved her. She spat in his face, and he broke her jaw. He and forty others used her that day. Each ticket entitled them to fifteen minutes. Sleep was the first basic function she missed.

———

She stopped fighting. She was not allowed to speak to the other girls, but she knew when one of them died. Some of the soldiers gave them opium. The girls would save it up until they had a lethal dose, then swallow it whole. Some hung themselves in the toilet or stole the soldiers' knives. One killed two soldiers before a third shot her.

On days the soldiers returned from the battlefields, they would take the women from behind, call them pigs and pin their arms, refuse to use the condoms. But on the nights before they fought, they would fall on the women as if already wounded, holding them tenderly, desperately, clutching. Then they would stroke Faith's cheek and ears and eyes, weeping over her beauty. They would beg her to pray for them, tell her they loved her. They would knead her lips with kisses.

———

When she was deemed docile enough, she was taken by car certain evenings to entertain Japanese officers at another house. There, she lay in beds and rooms like those she had seen in the nuns' picture books. But it was still not the same. She could no longer recall the nuns' faces, or her mother's or sisters'. She forgot her Korean birth name. She was seventeen when Colonel Taro first slept with her. He was more than twice her age, and he kept her with him all that night.

The next week, Taro told her, his company was to be sent several hundred miles east. The girls from the comfort station would follow. They belonged to the company now, he said. The women would service the men within smell of the fighting. Outside their hut, wild dogs would carry off corpses, and the streams in which the girls were expected to bathe might run red with blood. When he asked if she loved him, she told him she did. Then she accompanied him to war.

As her reward, she did not have to share the mud hut with the other girls but remained all day and night in the governor's yamen that had been seized for the use of officers. Taro was no different to her than the other soldiers, but she knew how to make him feel that he was. In exchange, she could sleep—in his arms. Dreams, she had long since abandoned.

———

By the spring of 1940, Faith had belonged to Taro for half a year and was pregnant with his child. Then Taro was wounded. A bullet through the calf left him so hobbled that he was ordered back to Tokyo to await reassignment. His eyes when he looked at her clouded with tears. He spoke in clichés she despised, comparing her skin to that of a peach, her eyes to stars and her hair to silk. She had learned the secret of becoming a wall on which he could paint his fantasy.

He loved her, he said. He could not take her to Japan, because he was married, but he would send her to Hong Kong, where she could wait for him in safety at the home of a friend. He confided that soon, within months or weeks, Hong Kong would fall into Japanese hands. He would take his reassignment there, and they would be together again with their child—a son, he knew it would be a son.

He put her on a sampan with invented papers, the disguise of a fisherman's widow, and he told her to be brave. She noticed as the boat pulled away that he had an unusually large nose for a Japanese, with a bony bridge and eyes too closely set together. His ears were almost completely flat along the sides of his head. She thought this must be the first time that she had ever truly looked at him. His homeliness surprised her.

———

She meant to get rid of the child as soon as possible, but Hong Kong changed her mind. It was a city still brimming with life. The evacuation of westerners had begun. Boatloads of white women and children were leaving for India and Australia, but for the rest, these days seemed deceptively normal. The streets were filled with Communist and Nationalist propagandists, Western sailors, soldiers, and marines. And, through them, opportunity.

She did not go to Taro's friend, but instead took a job at a bar on the Kowloon side of the harbor. Her belly was big, but her face was good, and she was tall and had strong arms, so the proprietor told her she could work behind the bar until the child came, then go out front when her body returned. As if, she thought, my body itself is an occupied country.

———

Upstairs from the bar, there were rooms where the other girls took their customers. One night, a Hong Kong Chinese with a British accent asked if she had any Bombay gin. She raised her arm in the mirror-tinted gloom and traced a finger across the labels. Gilbey's, Tanqueray, there was Bombay. The owner was a connoisseur of labels, whatever the bottles might actually contain, and he charged accordingly.

The customer, who called himself Tom, watched her closely and commented on her ability to read English. She told him she was once taught by nuns, a long, long time ago. Tom finished one drink and another, continuing to chat with her when she was free of other customers. When her shift ended, he asked if she would take him upstairs. She stood on tiptoes to show him her belly, thinking him daft for not noticing. He whispered, he'd pay her fifty Hong Kong dollars. She took him upstairs.

Tom had figured her out. She was just what the SOE needed. Men would come to this bar, he told her. Chinese, Filipino, even Sikhs and Muslims would ask for "a taste of Bombay." She would lead them upstairs for whatever was her customary amount of time. When they paid her, the fold of bills would contain a slip of paper. It might look like an ordinary sales invoice—a flat of canned lychees, so much. A tin of coffee, a crate of tea. Sometime later she would receive an American or British officer who'd call her by a code name, and when he paid, she would return the slip with his change. In exchange, she would be paid more than double her normal rate, and her child would be taken care of.

She would also have to entertain any other men who wanted her, or else it would look suspicious. But, Tom asked, wasn't that what she intended to do, in any case?

When he finished this proposition, she found herself sitting on the end of her bed. A mirror hung on the facing wall. She stared at her reflection, but all she could see was her lover Taro, gazing back and laughing.

Yes, she answered. Yes, of course, that was what she intended. Would Tom pay her extra for information she picked up from those other customers? Japanese, for instance? That depended, said Tom, on the value of her intelligence.

My intelligence is good, she shot back.

He grinned, slid a hand through his shiny black hair. "Prove it," he challenged her. "Pick your code name."

"Faith," she said promptly. Only, she pronounced it "Fate."

———

I met her not long after this, but it took several months before she would talk about Colonel Taro, and even then, I was not entirely sure I believed her. She never returned his affection, she told me. Though she was a good actress, she hated the Japanese with such venom that she would give her life to defeat them.

She had not thought she could love Taro's child, either, but she took too long to kill it. Once it started moving, she saw that to destroy the invader she would have to destroy what little good was left in herself.

My tour ended just a week before what would be the fall of Hong Kong. At the last minute I figured out a way that I might take her and the baby to America.

The night I proposed this escape, she sat holding the child on her lap. I watched her nurse him. The lamplight in that room was the color of a ripe apricot, and it made them both look warm, though in fact the whole building was unheated, and a cold rain was falling outside. The infant sucked with such greedy intensity that he seemed intent on swallowing her soul. Her skin and his mouth glistened with milk. The whole room smelled of it, sweet and thick. She didn't answer my proposal, just shifted the baby after a time onto her other side. The used nipple hung distended like a handle from the globe of her breast.

Faith made no attempt to cover herself. Her life had rid her of modesty. I was ashamed of admiring that.

The child fell asleep still attached to her. She gently pried open his jaws, replacing her nipple with her forefinger. He sucked with unconscious vigor.

"Carry a small vial of syrup," she said. "If he cries, coat your finger with the sweet and place it in his mouth."

Without waiting for my startled reply, she stood up, tucking the white of her blouse back into her skirt. Before returning her baby to the basket, she wrapped him like a parcel in his pale blue wool blanket, a present from one of her other OSS officers. "I have studied all of you," she said. "You are the only one I know to keep the secret."

For several seconds she went on leaning over the bassinet, staring at her child, addressing me without looking at me. "Give him a name. I must not know it. Never tell him, or anyone, who are his parents. You are his father now. Your wife his mother."

All I could think to say was, "I don't have a wife."

She turned. "Take one."

"You, then."

I withered under the look she gave me. It was like a ray of sunshine magnified through glass to the point of combustion.

She hoisted the basket onto her hip and gestured with her chin toward the door. I opened it. She put the basket into my arms with one last glance at her son. When I started to speak, she shook her head. Her eyes were glassy as an opium addict's, though I was sure she didn't smoke. Yet.

"I promise," I said anyway, as the door swung shut. "You can trust me."

Outside, the wind slanted rain into my face as I looked back up to her window. I expected to see her looking out, silhouetted by that apricot glow, but the room was dark, a black rectangle set into the damp gray wall. If she watched, I couldn't see her. I bought a bottle of cane syrup on the way back to my flat, a case of formula for a considerable fortune before boarding the ship the next morning.

I named the baby Ben.

———

On Christmas, the day Hong Kong fell to the Japanese, I landed with Ben in Calcutta. It took another two months to negotiate the rest of our journey home and nearly a year after that for my adoption of Ben to be legalized. When I married, the following year, my bride understood that I'd found the child, abandoned, in the ruins of a Kowloon factory. She was a nurse from Poughkeepsie, willfully oblivious to race, and said she saw in me the gentle father her own dad never had been.

In 1943, T.L. turned up in Washington. We met at a bar on Dupont Circle, and I asked if he knew what had happened to Faith. Neither of us mentioned her son.

T.L. said she'd been arrested within weeks of the fall of Hong Kong. The Japs had caught her with one of the SOE's

Communist agents. They found the cypher message in a bill for baby clothes. The two were tortured with electric prods. The Communist agent was eventually shot. Faith died in custody, which I hoped meant that she'd committed suicide.

I went home and brought Ben into bed with us that night. "You adore him, don't you?" my wife asked.

Two years old, he still smelled of sweet milk. "I do," I said.

I will always believe, though I have no proof, that Faith had two executioners. One was Colonel Taro, her savior, her protector, and her lover. The other rescued her son.

————

Ben Shaughnessy today is an optical engineer living in La Canada, California, and working for Jet Propulsion Laboratories. Mr. Shaughnessy declined The Millennium Asia History Project's invitation to contribute a postscript to his father's story.

MAHP March 13, 2000

The Vaporization Enthalpy of a Peculiar Pakistani Family

BY USMAN T. MALIK

1

The Solid Phase of Matter is a state wherein a substance is particulately bound. To transform a solid into liquid, the intermolecular forces need to be overcome, which may be achieved by adding energy. The energy necessary to break such bonds is, ironically, called the *heat of fusion.*

On a Friday after jummah prayers, under the sturdy old oak in their yard, they came together as a family for the last time. Her brother gave in and wept as Tara watched, eyes prickling with a warmth that wouldn't disperse no matter how much she knuckled them, or blinked.

"Monsters," Sohail said, voice raspy. He wiped his mouth with the back of his hand and looked at the sky, a vast whiteness cobblestoned with heat. The plowed wheat fields beyond the steppe on which their house perched were baked and khaki and shivered a little under Tara's feet. An earthquake or a passing vehicle on the highway? Perhaps it was just foreknowledge that made her dizzy. She pulled at her lower lip and said nothing.

"Monsters," Sohail said again. "Oh God, Apee. Murderers."

She reached out and touched his shoulders. "I'm sorry." She thought he would pull back. When he didn't, she let her fingers fall and linger on the flame-shaped scar on his arm. So it begins, she thought. How many times has this happened before? Pushing and prodding us repeatedly until the night swallows us whole. She thought of that until her heart constricted with dread. "Don't do it," she said. "Don't go."

Sohail lifted his shoulders and drew his head back, watched her as if seeing her for the first time.

"I know I ask too much," she said. "I know the customs of honor, but for the love of God let it go. One death needn't become a lodestone for others. One horror needn't—"

But he wasn't listening, she could tell. They would not hear nor see once the blood was upon them, didn't the scriptures say so? Sohail heard, but didn't listen. His conjoined eyebrows, like dark hands held, twitched. "Her name meant a rose," he said and smiled. It was beautiful, that smile, heartbreaking, frightening. "Under the mango trees by Chacha Barkat's farm Gulminay told me that, as I kissed her hand. Whispered it in my ear, her finger circling my temple. *A rose blooming in the rain*. Did you know that?"

Tara didn't. The sorrow of his confession filled her now as did the certainty of his leaving. "Yes," she said, looking him in the eyes. His eyes looked awful: webbed with red, with thin tendrils of steam rising from them. "A rose God gave us and took away because He loved her so."

"Wasn't God," Sohail said and rubbed his fingers together. The sound was insectile. "Monsters." He turned his back to her and was able to speak rapidly: "I'm leaving tomorrow morning. I'm going to the mountains. I will take some bread and dried meat. I will stay there until I'm shown a sign, and once I am," his back arched, then straightened. He had lost weight; his shoulder blades poked through the khaddar shirt like trowels, "I will arise and go to their homes. I will go to them as God's wrath. I will——"

She cut him off, her heart pumping fear through her body like poison. "What if you go to them and die? What if you go to them like a steer to the slaughter? And Ma and I—what if months later we sit here and watch a dusty vehicle climb the hill, bouncing a sack of meat in the back seat that was once you? What if. . ."

But she couldn't go on giving name to her terrors. Instead, she said, "If you go, know that we as we are now will be gone forever."

He shuddered. "*We* were gone when *she* was gone. We were shattered with her bones." The wind picked up, a whipping, chador-lifting sultry gust that made Tara's flesh prickle. Sohail began to walk down the steppes, each with its own crop: tobacco, corn, rice stalks wavering in knee-high water; and as she watched his lean farmer body move away, it seemed to her as if his back was not drenched in sweat, but acid. That his flesh glistened not from moisture, but blood. All at once their world was just too much, or not enough—Tara couldn't decide which—and the weight of that unseen future weighed her down until she couldn't breathe. "My brother," she said and her voice shook. "You're my little brother."

Sohail continued walking his careful, dead man's walk until his head was a wobbling black pumpkin rising from the last steppe. She watched him disappear in the undulations of her motherland, helpless to stop the fatal fracturing of her world, wondering if he would stop or doubt or look back.

Sohail never looked back.

———

Ma died three months later.

The village menfolk told her the death prayer was brief and moving. Tara couldn't attend because she was a woman.

They helped her bury Ma's sorrow-filled body, and the rotund mullah clucked and murmured over the fresh mound. The women embraced her and crooned and urged her to vent. "Weep, our daughter," they cried, "for the childrens' tears of love are like manna for the departed."

Tara tried to weep and felt guilty when she couldn't. Ma had been sick and in pain for a long time and her hastened death was a mercy, but you couldn't say that out loud. Besides, the women had said *children*, and Sohail wasn't there. Not at the funeral, not during the days after. Tara dared not wonder where he was, or imagine his beautiful face gleaming in the dark atop a stony mountain, persevering in his vigil.

"What will you do now?" they asked, gathering around her with sharp, interested eyes. She knew what they really meant. A young widow with no family was a stranger amidst her clan. At best an oddity; at her worst a seductress. Tara was surprised to discover their concern didn't frighten her. The perfect loneliness of it, the inadmissible exclusion—they were just more beads in the tautening string of her life.

"I'm thinking of going to the City," she told them. "Ma has a cousin there. Perhaps he can help me with bread and board, while I look for work." She paused, startled by a clear memory: Sohail and Gulminay by the Kunhar River, fishing for trout. Gulminay's sequined hijab dappling the stream with emerald as she reached down into the water with long, pale fingers. Sohail grinning his stupid lover's grin as his small hands encircled her waist, and Tara watched them both from the shade of the eucalyptus, fond and jealous. By then Tara's husband was long gone and she could forgive herself the occasional resentment.

She forced the memory away. "Yes, I think I might go to the City for a while," she said and laughed. The sound rang hollow and strange in the emptiness of her tin and-timber house. "Who knows I might even go back to school. I used to enjoy reading once." She smiled at these women with their sympathetic, hateful eyes that watched her cautiously as they would a rabid animal. She nodded, talking mostly to herself. "Yes, that would be good. Hashim would've wanted that."

They drew back from her, from her late husband's mention. Why not? she thought. Everything she touched fell apart; everyone around her died or went missing. There was no judgment here, just dreadful awe. She could allow them that, she thought.

2

The Liquid Phase of Matter is a restless volume that, by dint of the vast spaces between its molecules, fills any container it is poured in and takes its shape. Liquids tend to have higher energy than solids, and while the particles retain inter-particle forces they have enough energy to move relative to each other.

The structure therefore becomes mobile and malleable.

In the City, Tara turned feral in her pursuit of learning. This had been long coming and it didn't surprise her. At thirteen, she had been withdrawn from school; she needed not homework but a husband, she was told. At sixteen, she was wedded to Hashim; he was blown to smithereens on her twenty-first birthday. A suicide attack on his unit's northern check post.

"I want to go to school," she told Wasif Khan, her mother's cousin. They were sitting in his six-by-eight yard, peeling fresh oranges he had confiscated from an illegal food vendor. Wasif was a police hawaldar, and on the rough side of sixty. He often said confiscation was his first love and contraband second. He grinned when he said it, which made it easier for her to like him.

Now Wasif tossed a half-gnawed chicken bone to his

spotted mongrel and said, "I don't know if you want to do that."

"I do."

"You need a husband, not—"

"I don't care. I need to go back to school."

"Why?" He dropped an orange rind in the basket at his feet, gestured with a large liver-spotted hand. "The City doesn't care if you can read. Besides, I need someone to help me around the house. I'm old and ugly and useless, but I have this tolerable place and no children. You're my cousin's daughter. You can stay here as long as you like."

In a different time she might have mistaken his generosity for loneliness, but now she understood it for what it was. Such was the way of age: it melted prejudice or hardened it. "I want to learn about the world," she said. "I want to see if there are others like me. If there have been others before me."

He was confused. "Like you how?"

She rubbed an orange peel between her fingers, pressing the fibrous texture of it in the creases of her flesh, considering how much to tell him. Her mother had trusted him. Yet Ma hardly had their gift, and even if she did, Tara doubted she would have been open about it. Ma had been wary of giving too much of herself away, a trait she passed on to both her children. Among other things.

So now Tara said, "Others who *need* to learn more about themselves. I spent my entire childhood being just a bride, and look where that got me. I am left with nothing. No children, no husband, no family." Wasif Khan looked hurt. She smiled kindly. "You know what I mean, Uncle. I love you, but I need to love me too."

Wasif Khan tilted his head back and pinched a slice of orange above his mouth. Squeezed it until his tongue and remaining teeth gleamed with the juice. He closed his eyes, sighed, and nodded. "I don't know if I approve, but I think I understand." He lifted his hand and tousled his own hair thoughtfully. "It's a different time. Others my age who don't realize it don't fare well. The traditional rules don't apply anymore, you know. Sometimes, I think that is wonderful. Other times, it feels like the whole damn world is conspiring against you."

She rose, picking up her mess and his. "Thank you for letting me stay here."

"It's either you or every hookah-sucking asshole in this neighborhood for company." He grinned and shrugged his shoulders. "My apologies. I've been living alone too long and my tongue is spoilt."

She laughed loudly; and thought of a blazing cliff somewhere from which dangled two browned, peeling, inflamed legs, swinging back and forth like pendulums.

———

She read everything she could get her hands on. At first, her alphabet was broken and awkward, as was her rusty brain, but she did it anyway. It took her two years, but eventually she qualified for FA examinations, and passed on her first try.

"I don't know how you did it," Wasif Khan said to her, his face beaming at the neighborhood children as he handed out specially prepared sweetmeat to eager hands, "but I'm proud of you."

She wasn't, but she didn't say it. Instead, once the children left, she went to the mirror and gazed at her reflection, flexing her arm this way and that, making the flame-shaped scar bulge. We all drink the blood of yesterday, she thought. The next day she enrolled at Punjab University's B.Sc program.

In biology class, they learned about plants and animals. Flora and fauna, they called them. Things constructed piece by piece from the basic units of life—cells. These cells in turn were made from tiny building blocks called atoms, which themselves were bonded by the very things that repelled their core: electrons.

In physics class, she learned what electrons were. Little flickering ghosts that vanished and reappeared as they pleased. Her flesh was empty, she discovered, or most of it. So were human bones and solid buildings and the incessantly agitated world. All that immense loneliness and darkness with only a hint that we existed. The idea awed her. Did we exist only as a possibility?

In Wasif Khan's yard was a tall mulberry tree with saw-like leaves. On her way to school she touched them; they were spiny and jagged. She hadn't eaten mulberries before. She picked a basketful, nipped her wrist with her teeth, and let her blood roast a few. She watched them curl and smoke from the heat of her genes, inhaled the sweet steam of their juice as they turned into mystical symbols. Mama would have been proud.

She ate them with salt and pepper, and was offended when Wasif Khan wouldn't touch the remaining.

He said they gave him reflux.

3

The Gaseous Phase of Matter is one in which particles have enough kinetic energy to make the effect of intermolecular forces negligible. A gas, therefore, will occupy the entire container in which it is confined.

Liquid may be converted to gas by heating at constant pressure to a certain temperature.

This temperature is called the *boiling point.*

The worst flooding the province has seen in forty years was the one thing all radio broadcasters agreed on.

Wasif Khan hadn't confiscated a television yet, but if he had, Tara was sure, it would show the same cataclysmic damage to life and property. At one point, someone said, an area the size of England was submerged in raging floodwater.

Wasif's neighborhood in the northern, hillier part of town escaped the worst of the devastation, but Tara and Wasif witnessed it daily when they went for rescue work: upchucked power pylons and splintered oak trees smashing through the marketplace stalls; murderous tin sheets and iron rods slicing through inundated alleys; bloated dead cows and sheep eddying in shoulder-high water with terrified children clinging to them. It pawed at the towering steel-and-concrete structures, this restless liquid death that had come to the city; it ripped out their underpinnings and annihilated everything in its path.

Tara survived these days of heartbreak and horror by helping to set up a small tent city on the sports fields of her university. She volunteered to establish a nursery for displaced children and went with rescue teams to scour the ruins for usable supplies, and corpses.

As she pulled out the dead and living from beneath the wreckage, as she tossed plastic-wrapped food and dry clothing to the dull-eyed homeless, she thought of how bright and hot and dry the spines of her brother's mountains must be. It had been four years since she saw him, but her dreams were filled with his absence. Did he sit parched and caved in, like a deliberate Buddha? Or was he dead and pecked on by ravens and falcons?

She shuddered at the thought and grabbed another packet of cooked rice and dry beans for the benighted survivors.

———

The first warning came on the last night of Ramadan. Chand raat. Tara was eating bread and lentils with her foundling children in the nursery when it happened. A bone-deep trembling that ran through the grass, flattening its blades, evaporating the evening dew trembling on them. Seconds later, a distant boom followed: a hollow rumbling that hurt Tara's ears and made her feel nauseated. (Later, she would learn that the blast had torn through the marble-walled shrine of Data Sahib, wrenching its iron fence from its moorings, sending jagged pieces of metal and scorched human limbs spinning across the walled part of the City.) Her children sat up, confused and scared. She soothed them. Once a replacement was found, she went to talk to the tent city administrator. "I've seen this before," she told him once he confirmed it was a suicide blast. "My husband and sister-in-law both died in similar circumstances." That wasn't entirely true for Gulminay, but close enough. "Usually one such attack is followed by another when rescue attempts are made. My husband used to call them 'double tap' attacks." She paused, thinking of his kind, dearly loved face for the first time in months. "He understood the psychology behind them well."

The administrator, a chubby short man with filthy cheeks, scratched his chin. "How come?"

"He was a Frontier Corps soldier. He tackled many such situations before he died."

"Condolences, bibi." The administrator's face crinkled with sympathy. "But what does that have to do with us?"

"Sometimes these terrorists will use the double tap like a magnet and come after more civilian structures."

"Thank you for the warning. I'll send out word to form a volunteer perimeter patrol." He scrutinized her, taking in her hijab, the bruised elbows, and grimy fingernails from days of work. "God bless you for the lives you've saved already. For the labor you've done."

He handed her a packet of boiled corn and alphabet books. She nodded absently, charred bodies and boiled human blood swirling up from the shrine vivid inside her head, thanked him, and left.

The emergency broadcast thirty minutes later confirmed

her fear: a second blast at Data Sahib obliterated a fire engine, killed a jeep-full of policemen, and vaporized twenty-five rescuers. Five of these were female medical students. Their glass bangles were melted and their headscarves burned down to unrecognizable gunk by the time the EMS came, they later said.

Tara didn't weep when she heard. In her heart was a steaming shadow that whispered nasty things. It impaled her with its familiarity, and a dreadful suspicion grew in her that the beast was rage and wore a face she knew well.

4

When matter is heated to high temperatures, such as in a flame, electrons begin to leave the atoms. At very high temperatures, essentially all electrons are assumed to be dissociated, resulting in a unique state wherein positively charged nuclei swim in a raging 'sea' of free electrons.

This state is called the Plasma Phase of Matter and exists in lightning, electric sparks, neon lights, and the Sun.

In a rash of terror attacks, the City quickly fell apart: the Tower of Pakistan, Lahore Fort, Iqbal's Memorial, Shalimar Gardens, Anarkali's Tomb, and the thirteen gates of the Walled City. They exploded and fell in burning tatters, survived only by a quivering bloodhaze through which peeked the haunted eyes of their immortal ghosts.

This is death, this is love, this is the comeuppance of the two, as the world according to you will finally come to an end. So snarled the beast in Tara's head each night. The tragedy of the floodwaters was not over yet, and now this.

Tara survived this new world through her books and her children. The two seemed to have become one: pages filled with unfathomable loss. White space itching to be written, reshaped, or incinerated. Sometimes, she would bite her lips and let the trickle of blood stain her callused fingers. Would touch them to water-spoilt paper and watch it catch fire and flutter madly in the air, aflame like a phoenix. An impossible glamour created by tribulation. Then again we were all glamours, weren't we; so as the City burned and her tears burned, Tara reminded herself of the beautiful emptiness of it all and forced herself to smile.

Until one morning she awoke and discovered that, in the cover of the night, a suicide teenager had hit her tent city's perimeter patrol.

———

After the others had left, she stood over her friends' graves in the twilight. Kites and vultures unzipped the darkness above in circles, lost specks in this ghostly desolation. She remembered how cold it was when they lowered Gulminay's remains in the ground. How the drone attack had torn her limbs clean off so that, along with a head shriveled by heat, a glistening, misshapen, idiot torso remained. She remembered Ma, too, and how she was killed by her son's love. The first of many murders.

"I know you," she whispered to the Beast resident in her soul. "I know you," and all the time she scribbled on her flesh with a glass shard she found buried in a patrolman's eye. Her wrist glowed with her heat and that of her ancestors. She watched her blood bubble and surge skyward. To join the plasma of the world and drift its soft, vaporous way across the darkened City; and she wondered again if she was still capable of loving them both.

The administrator promised her he would take care of her children. He gave her food and a bundle of longshirts and shalwars. He asked her where she was going and why, and she knew he was afraid for her.

"I will be all right," she told him. "I know someone who

lives up there." "I don't understand why you must go. It's dangerous," he said, his flesh red under the hollows of his eyes. He wiped his cheeks. "I wish you didn't have to. But I suppose you will. I see that in your face. I saw that when you first came here."

She laughed. The sound of her own laughter saddened her. "The world will change," she said. "It always does. We are all empty, but this changing is what saves us. That is why I must go."

He nodded. She smiled. They touched hands briefly; she stepped forward and hugged him, her headscarf tickling his nostrils, making him sneeze. She giggled and told him how much she loved him and the others. He looked pleased, and she saw how much kindness and gentleness lived inside his skin, how his blood would never boil with undesired heat.

She lifted his finger, kissed it, wondering at how solid his vacant flesh felt against her lips.

Then she turned and left him, leaving the water and fire and the crackling, hissing earth of the City behind.

Such was how Tara Khan left for the mountains.

————

The journey took a week. The roads were barren, the landscape abraded by floodwater and flensed by intermittent fires. Shocked trees, stripped of fruit, stood rigid and receding as Tara's bus rolled by, their gnarled limbs pointing accusatorially at the heavens.

Wrapped in her chador, headscarf, and khaddar shalwar kameez, Tara folded into the rugged barrenness with its rugged people. They were not unkind; even in the midst of this madness, they held onto their deeply honored tradition of hospitality, allowing Tara to scout for hints of the Beast's presence. The northerners chattered constantly and were horrified by the atrocities blooming from within them, and because she too spoke Pashto they treated her like one of them.

Tara kept her ears open. Rumors, whispers, beckonings by skeletal fingers. Someone said there was a man in Abbottabad who was the puppeteer. Another shook his head and said that was a deliberate shadow show, a gaudy interplay of light and dark put up by the real perpetrators. That the Supreme Conspirator was swallowed by earth soaked with the blood of thousands and lived only as an extension of this irredeemable evil.

Tara listened and tried to read between their words. Slowly, the hints in the midnight alleys, the leprous grins, the desperate, clutching fingers, incinerated trees and smoldering human and animal skulls—they began to come together and form a map.

Tara followed it into the heart of the mountains.

5

When the elementary particle boson is cooled to temperatures near absolute zero, a dilute 'gas' is created. Under such conditions, a large number of bosons occupy the lowest quantum state and an unusual thing happens: quantum effects become visible on a macroscopic scale. This effect is called the macroscopic quantum phenomena and the 'Bose-Einstein condensate' is inferred to be a new state of matter. The presence of one such particle, the Higgs-Boson, was tentatively confirmed on March 14th, 2013 in the most complex experimental facility built in human history.

This particle is sometimes called the *God Particle*.

———

When she found him, he had changed his name.

There is a story told around campfires since the beginning of time: Millennia ago a stone fell from the infinite bosom of space and plunked onto a statistically impossible planet. The stone was round, smaller than a pebble of hard goat shit, and carried a word inscribed on it.

It has been passed down generations of Pahari clans that that word is the Ism e-Azam, the Most High Name of God.

Every sect in the history of our world has written about it. Egyptians, Mayans. Jewish, Christian, and Muslim mystics. Some have described it as the primal point from which existence began, and that the Universal Essence lives in this nuktah.

The closest approximation to the First Word, some say, is one that originated in Mesopotamia, the land between the two rivers. The Sumerians called it *Annunaki*.

He of Godly Blood.

Tara thought of this oral tradition and sat down at the mouth of the demolished cave. She knew he lived inside the cave, for every living and nonliving thing near it reeked of his heat. Twisted boulders stretched granite hands toward its mouth like pilgrims at the Kaaba. The heat of the stars they both carried in their genes, in the sputtering, whisking emptiness of their cells, had leeched out and warped the mountains and the path leading up to it.

Tara sat cross-legged in the lotus position her mother taught them both when they were young. She took a sharp rock and ran it across her palm. Crimson droplets appeared and evaporated, leaving a metallic tang in the air. She sat and inhaled that smell and thought of the home that once was. She thought of her mother, and her husband; of Gulminay and Sohail; of the floods (did he have something to do with that too? Did his rage liquefy snow-topped mountains and drown an entire country?); of suicide bombers, and the University patrol; and of countless human eyes that flicked each moment toward an unforgiving sky where something merciful may or may not live; and her eyes began to burn and at last Tara Khan began to cry. "Come out," she said between her sobs. "Come out, Beast. Come out, Rage. Come out, Death of the Two Worlds and all that lives in between. Come out, Monster. Come out, Fear," and all the while she rubbed her eyes and let the salt of her tears crumble between her fingertips. She looked at the white crystals, flattened them, and screamed, "Come out, ANNUNAKI."

And in a belch of shrieking air and a blast of heat, her brother came to her.

———

They faced each other.

His skin was gone. His eyes melted, his nose bridge collapsed; the bones underneath were simmering white seas that rolled and twinkled across the constantly melting and rearranging meat of him. His limbs were pseudopodic, his movement that of a softly turning planet drifting across the possibility that is being.

Now he floated toward her on a gliding plane of his skin. His potent heat, a shifting locus of time-space with infinite energy roiling inside it, touched her, making her recoil. When he breathed, she saw everything that once was; and knew what she knew.

"Salam," she said. "Peace be upon you, brother."

The nuktah that was him twitched. His fried vocal cords were not capable of producing words anymore.

"I used to think," she continued, licking her dry lips, watching the infinitesimal shifting of matter and emptiness inside him, "that love was all that mattered. That the bonds that pull us all together are of timeless love. But it is not true. It has never been true, has it?"

He shimmered, and said nothing.

"I still believe, though. In existing. In *ex nihilo nihil fit.* If nothing comes from nothing, we cannot return to it. Ergo life has a reason and needs to be." She paused, remembering a day when her brother plucked a sunflower from a lush meadow and slipped it into Gulminay's hair. "Gulminay-jaan once was and still is. Perhaps inside you and me." Tara wiped her tears and smiled. "Even if most of us is nothing."

The heat-thing her brother was slipped forward a notch. Tara rose to her feet and began walking toward it. The blood in her vasculature seethed and raged. "Even if death breaks some bonds and forms others. Even if the world flinches, implodes, and becomes a grain of sand."

Annunaki watched her through eyes like black holes and gently swirled. "Even if we have killed and shall kill. Even if the source is nothing if not grief. Even if sorrow is the distillate of our life."

She reached out and gripped his melting amebic limb. He shrank, but didn't let go as the maddened heat of her essence surged forth to meet his. "Even if we never come to much. Even if the sea of our consciousness breaks against the shore of quantum impossibilities."

She pressed his now-arm, her fingers elongating, stretching, turning, fusing; her flame-scar rippling and coiling to probe for his like a proboscis. Sohail tried to smile. In his smile were heat-deaths of countless worlds, supernova bursts, and the chrysalis sheen of a freshly hatched larva. She thought he might have whispered *sorry*. That in another time and universe there were not countless intemperate blood-children of his spreading across the earth's face like vitriolic tides rising to obliterate the planet. That all this wasn't really happening for one misdirected missile, for one careless press of a button somewhere by a soldier eating junk food and licking his fingers. But it was. Tara had glimpsed it in his nuktah when she touched him.

"Even if," she whispered as his being engulfed hers and the thermonuclear reaction of matter and antimatter fusion sparked and began to eradicate them both, "our puny existence, the conclusion of an agitated, conscious universe, is insignificant, remember. . . remember, brother, that mercy will go on. Kindness will go on."

Let there be gentleness, she thought. Let there be equilibrium, if all we are and will be can survive in some form. Let there be grace and goodness and a hint of something to come, no matter how uncertain.

Let there be *possibility*, she thought, as they flickered annihilatively and were immolated in some fool's idea of love.

———

For the 145 innocents of the 16/12 Peshawar terrorist attack and countless known & unknown before.

Belly of the Beast

BY JOY BAGLIO

It's Saturday night, and the beast has swallowed my husband. One minute he was there, the next, gone—just a shout, half smothered, as the creature engulfed him. I didn't see the actual swallowing. I arrived seconds later, in time to see the wolfish thing licking its jowls. It's not like anything you've ever seen: eyes small and black like papaya seeds, hispid hair covering its limbs, claws like small sickles. Tongue: long and leathery. I would have attacked it, grabbed a fire iron or my husband's reenactment sword if I had been feeling heroic, but there was something about the way the creature sighed, tired after its work consuming him, that made me pause and watch. It sank onto the bed, where my husband had been lying only moments before, whimpered like something lost, and seemed to take no notice of me.

When I whisper to my friends over the phone of what has happened, they reiterate the stories we've all heard of women in our neighborhood whose men have disappeared: the retired teacher whose husband vanished ostensibly nearby, so close that she sometimes catches glimpses of him in their driveway, at the corner store, on their street; the three young mothers whose men stay out later, later until one night they don't return at all; the wife who claims hers was spirited away by a herd of deer. At least you know what happened, my friends say. And of course, this is true: I knew this was coming. I'd seen the creature skulking in the yard all month yet did nothing, refusing to believe it could harm us. Last week it was outside our door, and yesterday, I found its dark hairs all along the bedside. What does it mean that I saw the warning signs and did nothing but pray they'd go away, that I was somehow mistaken?

Later that day, I hear what sounds like crying, loud and guttural, and I think, if anything, the creature must be thirsty. So I creep near it with a coffee tin full of water, leave it on my husband's nightstand, and sleep on the couch that night, one eye open, wide awake at the slightest sound. The next day, the beast still seems sleepy, so I let him stay undisturbed. I'm not surprised to find that he understands speech quite well and can answer back: mostly barely intelligible words in the deepest growl, but sometimes so like my husband that it stops my breath, sets every molecule in me spinning. Perhaps he's stolen my husband's voice, I think; breathed it in, preserved it, and I don't know if this is more comfort or horror. Still, I bring him water and soup, ask if there's anything else he needs. Is he sick? Sleep deprived? Depressed? No, he shakes his bestial head, he isn't any of those things.

After a week, a strange thing happens: I'm creeping around the creature where he's standing by the bedroom windows, when I glimpse my husband's face behind the whorls of dark fur. It shocks me to see it because, for days now, I've contended with the creature alone. It's almost as if a light is shining from somewhere inside the beast itself. The thick tangles of hair that cover the creature are illuminated, and my husband's face flashes, barely perceptible, as if just behind a layer of skin and fur. I cry when I see it and sink down on the bed, much to the bewilderment of the beast, who prowls into the next room, growling, no patience for such emotion.

Later, I tell myself it was a trick of the light. The westerly sun often stabs through our ground-level windows, brightening all in its path. But the next day, I'm sitting on the foot of the bed while the beast—propped up on a pillow—guzzles a salad I made, and I see my husband's fingers moving inside the creature's mouth, as though he has simply fallen into some large, black costume, a well of fur and teeth and claws.

"John?" I whisper. Then louder, shouting as if he is across some mile-wide chasm, not just an arm's length from me. My husband's hand stretches out like a second tongue emerging from the maw of the beast, and without thinking, I grasp for his fingers, clench and hold his hand that is warm and wet and solid and still alive.

"John!" I shout. And then the snap of jaws, the quick flight of both our hands.

———

One friend, a woman whose own husband was taken by wolves, brings me a long spear. It's not the kind of thing you'd see someone carrying around, and even now, I wonder how she came upon it. She lives two doors down, in a house set back from the road. When her husband was around, they had been into outdoor activities: fishing, hiking, camping, survival. I remember her laughing as she told us about her husband's skill with a bow drill, the fire he'd made for her on their first camping excursion. Now, her eyes are filled with a wordless ferocity as she hands me the spear. She doesn't want to say it, but I know what she's offering.

"Sometimes there are no good choices," she says.

I hold the spear in both hands. It's smooth, heavy,

perfectly sanded hardwood with a black metal tang and a serrated tip, like a modern arrowhead.

"Thank you," I say, knowing she's trying to help.

I leave the spear in the hallway and invite her in for tea. We talk about other things: about the end of summer, the failure of trash collection on our street, fall festivals we will both attend.

That night, I slip the beast the strongest sleeping pill I have, and I enter the bedroom and stand in the doorway, spear in hand. The silence is heavy, deep, and I can almost feel the texture of his dreams through his breathing. I wonder if they are fused with my husband's, if my husband is somehow still there, in the belly, fighting to survive. I wait minutes, then I crumple with guilt and tiptoe outside, into the yard, where I hack the spear to pieces.

Inside, I begin to weave a rope. I braid it out of our bed sheets (I've shredded them); my husband's childhood blanket; the quilt I made seven years ago; my own hair that I snip in long strands and bind to the rope like thread. I've Googled "how to make a four-strand rope that won't break," and I work late into the night. When I finally finish, I return to the sleeping beast, use all my strength to heave his bulk up on the pillows, wondering if he'll wake in a rage, the pills I gave him hardly enough. I sing as I work, the same song my mother used to sing to me as a child, when she would sit by me at night to say prayers, to rub my back as I fell asleep. "There's nothing to fear," she'd say. "All those monsters, you know, they're just sad, afraid." I think of this as I sing—the little melody pushing through all that is dark and terrifying—think of it as my hand hovers over the sleeping jaws, as I lower the rope down the beast's throat and pray that my husband has the strength to grab on.

Flag Bearer

BY AVA HOMA

When his grandpa, Bapir, drew a yogurt mustache above Alan's lips, the boy dissolved into giggles. Picturing himself with real whiskers thrilled Alan, who thought that facial hair might make up for being shorter than the other boys in his class.

"Your laughter woke me up, you cheeky monkey!" Uncle Soran, youngest of the six uncles and the only one awake, tousled Alan's hair as he came onto the patio that opened to the yard. They sat around a nylon cloth spread atop a crimson handmade rug to eat breakfast.

Alan laughed again. "Bapir, I want handlebars, please."

With a chapped finger, Bapir curled the ends of the yogurt mustache on either side of Alan's puckered-up lips and planted a dab of the stuff on his nose too. Alan collapsed into laughter.

That June morning in 1963, Alan decided that Bapir was the most amusing person on Earth. Perhaps he was the reason Alan adored older people and loved to listen to their stories of maama rewi, the trickster fox. It hurt Alan that most people with gray hair weren't able to read or write, that their backs hurt and their papery hands trembled; his dream was to read stories into a loudspeaker for hundreds of elders while they relaxed in a large meadow filled with purple and red flowers.

Grandma brought out more naan, the thin, round bread she had baked in the cylindrical clay oven dug into the basement. Alan made his own "bulletproof" sandwich: fresh honeycomb mixed with ghee. "After I eat this, I can run faster than the bullets," he said.

"Our monkey is growing up, and yet we all treat him as if he is a young child!" Uncle Soran said, making his own bulletproof morsel.

"One's grandchild is always young. That's just how it is." Bapir brushed crumbs from his lap. He winked. "If I were you, Alan, I would make it so I never grew up."

"Growing up is a trap," Grandma agreed, nodding.

"But I like the future," Alan said.

They laughed. Bapir splashed a kiss on Alan's face. "Something a six-year-old would say."

Still wearing his yogurt mustache, Alan frowned. "I am seven."

They cackled.

Father had come to Sulaimani to publish an article he'd written with Uncle Soran illustrating the suffering of the working class in Kurdistan and the rest of Iraq. Kurds had settled in the Zagros Mountains three hundred years before Christ was born, but now Alan's people had no country to call their own. When the Western Allies had drawn the map of the Middle East, they had cut Kurdistan into four pieces, dividing it among Iran, Iraq, Turkey, and Syria.

To visit Bapir with his father, Alan had to ace Kurdish spelling. But Kurdish was not a subject taught at school; Arabic was the only language used there. Father had been trying to teach him and his three brothers to write in their mother tongue, something Alan saw no use for. That morning, Father had skipped breakfast to search the city for a contraband typewriter.

Across the yard, Grandma was watering the pink roses and white lilies. A pounding on the wooden gate in the cement wall that surrounded their plot of land shattered her concentration. She dropped the hose.

"I'll get it." Alan ran across the yard to save her the trouble, but before he reached the gate, six men in Iraqi army uniforms, their faces hidden by striped gray scarves, broke the lock and directed their Kalashnikovs at Grandma's face.

"Where are they?" the shortest one demanded.

Bapir froze, a morsel still in his open mouth. Alan turned to see Uncle Soran leaping over the wall and clambering onto the neighbor's roof. Somebody—Grandma—grabbed Alan and backed him toward the house.

Nestled against her bosom, Alan watched the soldiers invade the house without waiting for an answer. All six uncles were pulled from their beds or hauled from the bathroom, the basement, a closet, and off the roof next door. Alan wiped off his white handlebars with his sleeve and tried to make sense of the chaos, the jerky movements, the incomprehensible noises escaping people's throats. If only his eyes would give him weapons instead of tears!

His uncles were dragged by the neck, screaming and struggling, like animals to slaughter. Bapir's questions and prayers, Grandma's cries and pleas, the neighbors' screams and curses —nothing had the slightest effect on the soldiers, who conducted the raid without a reply.

Alan's uncles, some still in undershirts, were marched out at gunpoint to army trucks carrying hundreds of Kurdish boys and men between the ages of fourteen and twenty-five. Alan peeled himself from Grandma's arms and ran to the street. The men were told to squat in the beds of the trucks, to place their hands on their heads, and to shut their mouths. Alan looked back at Bapir, who remained next to his smashed gate, head bowed.

Along with other children, women, and elderly, Alan

chased after the lumbering trucks, their huge rubber tires kicking up clouds of dust as they carted away the men amid the anxious cries of the followers. The older men, unarmed and horrified, searched for weapons and ran up the mountains, asking the Peshmerga to come down to the city to face the armed-to-the-teeth soldiers.

Alan trailed after the truck carrying his uncles as it traveled up the hillside at the city center. His heart had never beaten so fast. The truck finally stopped at the top of the hill, and prisoners were shoved out. On the hard soil, the captives were each given a shovel and ordered to dig.

"Ebn-al-ghahba," spat the soldiers—Son of a whore. The angry bystanders were ordered to stand back. People obeyed the AK-47s.

Dirt sprayed over the prisoners' bodies, hair, and eyelashes as their shovels cracked the earth open. Sweat dripped down their faces, and tears ran down over hands that muffled sobs. Alan looked at the pee running down the pants of a boy next to him; at a woman behind him clawing her face and calling out, "God, God, God"; at an older man shaking uncontrollably, his hand barely holding onto his crutch. Alan did not seem to be in possession of his own frozen body.

Once the trenches were dug, half of the prisoners were ordered to climb down into the ditches, and the rest were forced to shovel dirt up to their friends' and relatives' chins. Bapir had finally made his way to the top of the hill; he had found Alan in the first row of spectators, gnawing his thumbnail as he watched. Alan begged his grandpa to stop the cruelty.

Bapir hugged him. "They will be released in a few days, these young men." He pressed Alan's head to his chest. "They will be sent back home, bawanem, maybe with blisters and bruises, but they will be all right. Pray for them." His hands trembled as he squeezed Alan's. "May it rain before these men die of thirst."

Alan searched through the crowd to find Uncle Soran lifting a pile of dirt with his shovel. Soran's grip loosened when he looked into the eyes of his brother Hewa, whose name meant "hope." Hewa stood in the hole, waiting to be buried by his closest relative, a man whom he'd play-wrestled as a boy and confided in throughout his life.

"Do it, Soran," he said, his eyes shining up from the hole. A bearded soldier dressed in camouflage saw Soran's hesitation. "Kalb, ebn-al-kalb!"—Dog, son of a dog—he barked, and swung his Kalashnikov at Soran, the barrel slicing the skin under his left ear.

Soran growled, almost choking, as he turned. With his shovel, he batted the Kalashnikov away so that the gun hit its owner in the head, cutting his scalp. Alan flinched. Bullets rained from every direction. Soran crumbled. His blood sprayed over Hewa, who was screaming and reaching for the perforated body, pulling him forward, pressing his face to the bleeding cheek of his brother.

Crying out, Bapir tried to run toward his sons, but dozens of guns pointed at his chest, dozens of hands held him back. The shower of gunfire wouldn't cease; it struck the hugging siblings, painting them and the soil around them red.

His uncles, still in each other's arms, were buried in one hole. Half of the prisoners were still covered up to their chins with dirt. The remaining ninety-five men were sent down into the other trenches, and the soldiers buried them up to their heads. Alan stared at the rows upon rows of human heads, a garden of agony.

Intoxicated with power, the soldiers kicked the exposed heads of the prisoners, knocked some with the butts of their guns, and jeered at them. At the top of the hill, Bapir sobbed with such force that his wails shook the earth, Alan felt. He clutched Bapir's hunched shoulders and felt impossibly small.

A sunburnt man and a neighbor with shrunken features

hugged Bapir, then placed the old man's trembling arms around their shoulders and walked him down the hill.

"Where are my other sons?" Bapir gasped for air.

"Let's get you home," the neighbors told him.

Alan wanted to go with his grandpa, but he was afraid to move. If he took a step, the nightmare would become real. He scanned the hill for his other uncles, who were perhaps buried in some distant trench and unable to move. He couldn't see them. Even Bapir was no longer in sight.

The hubbub was dying down. The strangers who'd witnessed the scene were bound by their dread, their exchanged looks the only solace they could offer each other. Their heads seemed to move in slow motion, as if everyone were suspended underwater. Alan breathed in the atmosphere of quiet horror, of paused hysteria.

Suddenly people cried out in terror. From the road below them, several armored tanks were approaching. Gaping in disbelief, Alan staggered back, holding a hand to his mouth. He could neither run away nor slow his hammering heart, which was now threatening to explode. When the panicking crowd pushed forward, guns fired into the air to hold them back.

The tanks advanced.

Alan's mind couldn't process the scene before him. Screams. Curses. Pleas. The devilish laughter of the soldiers. He felt an invisible piece of himself drop away and melt into the ground. He was not Alan anymore.

It took an excruciatingly long time for the tanks to pulverize the heads of the prisoners.

The metallic stench of blood, of crushed human flesh and skulls, the foul odor of death made its way into the spectators' nostrils and throats. The lucky ones threw up. Alan did not.

While the giant metal treads ground his family and the other Kurds into nothingness, Alan sucked in shallow and unhelpful breaths.

Bapir lay in bed at home, tossing in anguish, a hand still on his aching chest. By his bedside, Grandma shed silent tears. Although they had not witnessed the crushing of their sons, they collapsed that day of broken hearts, one after the other. Someone went to find a doctor.

Father arrived at his parents' home oblivious to the tragedy, having taken an unusual road to safeguard his treasure. His typed article was tucked under his shirt. The joy of achievement and hope for his people glowed in his eyes. Then he found his parents on their deathbed. In bits and pieces, the neighbors told him of the massacre, how Ba'ath soldiers—ordered by President Aref and Prime Minister Al-Baker—had punished the Kurds for daring to demand autonomy.

Father ran to the hill, where bewildered children gathered and clung to each other. Beside them, a group of adults wailed and cried, threw dirt into their hair, and beat their faces in terror.

"The British bastards armed Baghdad to kill us. Their tanks, their planes, their goddamn firebombs and mustard gas that killed Iraqis forty years ago are now killing us," Father said to no one in particular.

Then he just stared with unseeing eyes at the gory mound of his pulverized people, his brothers.

Seeing his father's dazed reaction, Alan finally allowed the sobs he'd held in since he first saw the soldiers to burst forth. Other children followed suit. Tears and snot rolled down the dusty faces of the boys and girls who'd been abandoned by the living and dead alike.

Alan ran to his father and held on to his leg. "Baba gian, Baba!" he cried. It took a couple of moments before his father noticed him and hugged him close.

"We will leave Iraq. We won't live here any longer." A wild urge to be anywhere but here tugged at Alan's gut too.

Some stoic women and a few elderly men tearlessly buried the unidentifiable remains. They laid down uncarved stones in row after row and asked Alan and the other children to pick wildflowers and pink roses from the slope of the hill, placing them in rows too.

Alan sucked on the blood dripping down his index finger, torn by the rose thorns.

"Alan!" cried a woman whom Alan did not recognize. Three other boys turned when she called; one ran to her. Alan was a popular name, meaning "flag bearer." It testified to what was expected of the children of a stateless nation, who had to fight against nonexistence.

Author's Note: As a secular Kurdish female author, a minority within a minority, I feel I have seen the end of our broken world. My childhood memories are tinged with the screeches of the air-raid sirens, the stampedes while running to underground shelters. And yet I have witnessed, cherished, and documented moments of defiance and resilience. So many like me try to escape the unending horrors. Relying on education, asylum, family, investments or other means, Kurds in droves have attempted to find a home elsewhere on this planet, mostly to no avail, stuck in a ping-pong between domestic tyrannies and Western demonization. Many of us carry our homelessness on our backs, can't belong anywhere, and end up sitting on a hyphen of our complicated identities. Nonetheless, for me being a Kurdish-Iranian-Canadian writer is about rebirth and resistance. I continue to write stories of people who find and employ agency in the face of tyrannies.

And Then the Rain Will Come from the Mountain

BY INNOCENT CHIZARAMA ILO

I

This is how Papa paints.

In the evenings, when air collects at people's feet in chilly, invisible spools, he gathers his painting things to the balcony and sits in front of a rotting canvas. The numb fingers of his right hand grip the paintbrush, and the aluminium paint tray sways on his quivering left palm. Papa starts by making a whorl at the top left edge. He twirls and twirls the paintbrush, concocting a riotous mesh of colours. It does not make sense. Mama has always warned me never to disturb Papa when he is painting, but still I linger, hiding behind the torn brocade curtain in the parlour.

They call Papa 'Agozie, the Finder.' Many years ago, before I was even born, people used to flock to our house and beg him to draw maps for them. Nobody comes to our compound anymore, unless you count Mama Odera, who comes to buy Mama's vegetables, and the fishmonger who haggles all evening with Mama until he decides to part with some fish for the paltry sum Mama can offer.

It was two weeks ago when Mama finally agreed to tell

me about Papa's painting. "We'd just got married then and those people came in and out of this house as if they owned it." Mama had laughed and cocked her head sideways when she said this. "'Please draw me a map' they'd say. 'I want to find my wife's box of jewels'; 'my grandfather's favorite sheep wandered off last night'; 'my husband needs to find a perfect seed-shop in the market, the planting season is around the corner'; 'My favorite sickle got lost in the woods.' Ahhhhh."

"How does the map work?"

"You have to let the map guide you, see its destination with your heart and not your mind. Something like that."

"What?" I was confused.

"That's what your father used to say before gifting someone a map. I don't understand the man I married."

"Why did they stop coming?"

The house grew more silent, as if it too wanted to know why people stopped swarming in and out of it, why it has been misremembered: hollow and forgotten.

Mama paused and cleared her throat. "You know some of the people who came to your father never reached their destination. Some wandered off the edge of the map and disappeared. But Mama Alo was different. She'd asked for a map to find her son who went missing on the night of the Great Whirlwind. She'd followed with her heart. When she couldn't find Alo, something inside your father died. He packed up his things and stopped painting, even though people begged him to continue; that one failed map wasn't enough to blot out all the good work he had done. But then you came. He started painting again in the evenings, though now he scrubs the canvas clean when he's finished."

Today, the painting is almost done. From my hiding place behind the brocade curtain, it is clear now that Papa is painting a mountain. He has perfected the blue of the mountain's peak, and what looked like spilt milk yesterday is now snowcaps. He is darkening the brown-brown skin of the elephants and buffalos grazing at the foot of the mountain.

"Papa, come inside and eat," I say.

"Who are you?" he asks, baring the remains of his chequered teeth.

"I live here," I tell him because I don't have the muscle to remind Papa that I am his son.

"So we are like neighbours." Papa sets the paint tray on the floor. "You remind me of my son, Zim. He's thirteen. Do you know him?"

"Yes. We're good friends."

"My boy has started making friends. They grow up so quick, you know."

"What are you drawing?"

"Mmili Mountain."

"The same one as in the bedtime stories mothers tell little children?"

"Yes. There is a wispy line between bedtime stories and reality."

"So it's real. Where is it?"

"Not just where, *when.*" Papa gestures me closer. "There was a time when the entire town used to go there when the rains failed to come. The rains haven't failed in centuries, so everyone has forgotten: deep inside these peaks, an endless stream of water flows." He runs his right middle finger along the painting, carefully skipping the portions where the paint is yet to dry. "Come, touch it."

I obey.

"Do you feel the water strumming beneath your finger?"

I do not feel anything, but I nod my head.

"Let me tell you something." Papa's voice dims to a whisper. "The rains are going to flee from the clouds, and they are going to take the waters away from you. When they do, this map will guide you to Mmili Mountain." He pauses to scratch off the paint flakes in his hair. "You have to let the map guide you—see its destination with your heart and not your mind. Such a smart boy. No wonder you're friends with Zim."

Papa grips my hand and pulls me closer. His pupils look like a swirling, blue sea has been trapped inside.

"Now you must listen, and tell Zim all I am going to say. The rains will retreat from the clouds in Selemku when the one who keeps it safe goes to the mountains for his eternal rest. It is Zim's duty to seek the rains at Mmili Mountain and convince them that he is worthy to protect them like I did."

Midnight. Papa calls Mama and me to come and see his finished painting. He never shows anyone his painting when he's done, we normally wake up in the morning to find out that he has wiped the canvas clean. He struggles and fails to keep his hands, his entire body from trembling. The wind puffs up his jalabia, and he tries to keep himself from falling. When did he become so shrunken?

Papa's face has a ghostly glow as he talks about dying. His voice is barely above a whisper as he settles into his easy chair.

"By morning, I will crawl into the canvas and return to Mmili Mountain."

Mama and I gather beside him, chewing our tears.

"We all came from the mountain and must go back there someday," Papa mutters before he grows cold.

II

The drought sets in a week after Papa's funeral. By the end of the month, the horizon casts a dry purple hue on Selemku, as all the rains evaporate from the clouds. Wells start to run dry; the River Bambu becomes a pool of ash mingled with cow dung, and Tutukele Spring reeks of scorching death.

Neighbours whisper to each other behind closed doors, "It's Town Council that is taking all the water away from us; they did something to the clouds. That's why they hiked the taxes for the new reservoir. Greed." Only people who can afford the one thousand buzas per day get daily water rations from Town Council.

Mama and I leave our water cans on the rooftop at night to collect morning dew. But we always find them drier than before. We give up. Mama puts an extra lock on Papa's cellar where we hide our water tank. People have started burgling and ravaging other people's houses in search of water. As Mama says, "We can never be too safe." Her words don't stop there.

"Always have a ready excuse for why your lips aren't chapped; say you always smear them with groundnut oil," Mama's voice resounds in my ear. "And hiccup from time to time when you're in the midst of people. Once they know we have water, they'll come here and steal it."

The dreams that come at night, just before the barn owls retreat into their nests, are the only things I look forward to these days. The first dream occurs on the night after Papa's funeral. It begins with soft music prodding me and tickling my feet until I see myself many miles away from Selemku and at the foot of Mmili Mountain where Papa is riding on the back of an elephant. The path to the mountain is so warped, I do not remember the route when I wake up. Lost even in my dreams.

"It's time for you to accept your quest and bring back water to Selemku," Papa says in a second dream.

"Papa, you know it's only heroes that go on quests," I reply. "Look at my hands and legs—very feeble, like twigs. Boys like me are not heroes."

Papa laughs, the sound filled with grainy warmth. "You don't have to be a hero, Zim. The map has chosen you."

III

It is Mama Odera who raps on our door early in the morning to remind Mama and me about the meeting at Town

Council Hall. Mama double-checks the locks on the front door and the cellar before we leave the house. "We can't be too careful," she states once again.

The hall is already jam-packed by the time Mama and I arrive. Townsfolk have been talking about the meeting for days now. We have to squeeze and push our way through sweaty bodies to secure a seat. Mama and I struggle to hear ourselves over the din. Everybody is talking at once, demanding that the members of the Town Council come speak to us. We wait and wait some more. Mama fans herself with the loose end of her lappah.

"Zim, listen. If the crowd becomes rowdy. Make sure nobody pushes you to the ground."

You don't have to be a hero, Zim. The map has chosen you, Papa's words begin to echo at the back of my head. Is it enough to avoid being trampled to death? Map chosen, means I am now Selemku's guide. So many in this hall are thirsty...

"I know how to bring water back to Selemku!" A voice thunders across the hall. The din dies down and everyone turns to the source of that voice—me! The voice is deep, like a thousand rushing mountain winds, something that is alien to my thirteen-year-old tongue.

"It's a boy. A silly, little boy." A man in the crowd bawls.

"Let him speak, unless you know how to solve this prob-lem." The woman sitting next to Mama snaps back at the man. Then she turns, nods in my direction. "Go ahead. Speak."

"My name is Zim, the son of Agozie, the Finder." Again, the strange voice possesses my tongue. "Before my father died, he told me about Mmili Mountain."

"So your father is the man who couldn't help Mama Alo find her son." The first man who spoke snickers.

"Mmili Mountain only exists in the bedtime stories women tell children," another person says.

"The map has chosen me," I say, trying and failing to ignore the person's words. The crowd is starting to get restless.

"What does he think he's talking about?"

"The map—" I start to reply.

"Zim, enough," Mama hisses. She grabs my hand and begins to drag me out of the hall.

"Let the boy speak!" Someone yells from the front.

Mama shoves and pushes people aside to make way until we are out of the room. "Stop giving people false hope with the things your father told you. Ah, I warned you not to bother him when he painted in the evenings. Why don't you ever listen?"

"Mmili Mountain is real."

"No, Zim."

"I've visited it so many times in my dreams. Papa is there."

A line of tears breaks out of Mama's right eye. She wipes them away and forces out a smile. "Just like Agozie, you don't know where fantasy stops and reality begins. I don't want to hear of this nonsense again."

People have started trooping out of the hall. It is way into the afternoon, and they are tired of waiting for Town Council members to come and talk to them. They point at me as they walk past.

"Look at him; he thinks he is the water carrier."

"Ah, so full of himself to think the gods have chosen him to save us."

IV

Our front door is unlocked when Mama and I get back home. She dashes into the house, towards Papa's cellar. By the time I catch up with her, she is sprawled on the cellar's wooden floor beside our now empty water tank.

"Who could have done this to us?" Mama asks no one in

particular. "Where will I get one thousand buzas for Town Council's water rations?"

Wails are also emanating from other compounds. "Our water!" "No." "We are lost."

Like us, their homes have been broken into, and their water reserves have been stolen.

Mama rises to her feet and reties her lappah. She storms out of the house, and we join a crowd gathering at the end of the street. Someone from Town Council is addressing the crowd. He is holding a megaphone above his head, preventing the woman in front from snatching it away.

"We have exhausted the water in the new reservoir. Town Council has decided to collect water from people who are hoarding it in order to refill the new reservoir. The real enemies of the people are those who are hoarding water while the rest of us die of thirst."

"Hear! Hear!" Someone yells at the back.

No sooner has the man from Town Council finished talking than men in forest-green uniforms circle the crowd and start making arrests. One of them grabs Mama's arms and twists them backwards.

"Run!" A voice cries before pulling me away from the crowd.

I am running without looking back, without pausing to breathe, teardrops dripping onto my dusty feet, Mama Alo at my side. Images of the men in forest-green uniforms snatching Mama up flash across my eyes. Where will they take her? What will become of Mama? *Mama...* We turn left at the end of Onwuhafor Street and hide inside an abandoned warehouse.

Mama Alo sinks down on an empty wooden crate. "What you said at Town Council Hall today... Did your father really draw you a map to Mmili Mountain?"

"Y-yes..." I manage to stutter.

"Then you must follow the map."

"You... you believe me, how? Papa's map failed to lead you to your son."

"Your father's map took me to Ana Mmuo, the Land of the Spirits, where I found Alo. I came back to Selemku too heartbroken to say he is dead. I let them believe that your father's map couldn't help me."

Tears well up behind my eyes. "Why?"

"My heart wanted to believe he was still alive... For a time it almost worked."

"But...Papa. He stopped believing—"

Mama Alo lurches forward and clasps my mouth. She pulls me down and, with her free hand, gestures towards the crack in the wall. One of the men in forest-green uniform is patrolling beside the warehouse. She releases her hand over my mouth when the man takes the left bend to the next street.

"Papa was so—"

"I did a terrible thing many years ago. Zim," Mama Alo interrupts, "and I am sorry for that, but please... You can save us all."

"I am no hero," I say, thinking of Papa. What are the promises of a map when I have no water, no food? Mama still reminds me which streets are safe to walk after dark. I may be young, but I know there is a vast difference between knowing a location and being able to reach it.

Mama Alo stands up and walks towards the door. She turns toward me and sighs. "I cannot go with you."

I want to rage at this old woman, but what would be the point? She isn't lying. She's too old to make it up the mountain.

"But I can offer your family one final payment," Mama Alo continues. She yanks a tuft of hair from her afro and ties it with one of the silver strings wrapped around her wrists. "Take," she says, throwing the tuft of hair on the floor.

"Why?"

"It is my promise." Her face looks so old in the dim light

of the warehouse. Sunken. Lonely. "I will tell the truth about Alo and the map."

I pick up the length of hair and stash it in my back pocket. "Truly?"

"You have my word."

A shadow creeps into the warehouse. It is one of the guards. He looms over Mama Alo in the open doorway.

"Run... Run! I'll keep him here as long as I can," Mama Alo says, as she hurls the wooden crate at the man.

I escape through the back door.

V

In all the stories Mama has told me about people saving a town, they were always *special* and chosen at birth by a prophecy. A prophecy that sometimes dated back to long before they were born. Boys, girls, men, women, all dubbed *the chosen one*, set off on their quest fully prepared, their backs turned on a bunch of hopeful townsfolk they are about to save, a bag of food and a water flask slung across their shoulder, their palms gripping a sword or a magic wand. These people are certainly not a barefoot thirteen-year-old boy wearing a khaki shirt and shorts, with nothing in his pocket save for a tuft of hair and a painted map.

I am outside the town's rusty gate now; this is the first time I have gone through it. Mama used to point it out, the few times she took me uptown. My legs hurt from all the running. My feet burn on the blazing ground. I wish I had worn my sandals when I left the house to join the crowd with Mama. I want to stop to find food or water, but my feet keep on walking like they have a mind of their own. They stop walking when I get to an oak tree where a human-like figure is hunched over some dried leaves.

"Ah, it's you, Zim," the figure says.

"How do you know my name?" This is not a voice I recognize.

The figure turns to face me. An orange scar runs along the length of its chipped nose. "He's inquisitive. I like this one." It giggles, and the leaves on the oak rustle back. "It's been a long time since Agozie sent someone our way. Why did he take so long? Did the people of Selemku forget the old ways? After we led Mama Alo to her son, we waited and waited for another person to come."

"Who are you?"

"We're Nduga. We will guide you to wherever the map is taking you."

"I'm going to Mmili Mountain."

The figure frowns. "That's not a place for a young boy. Agozie couldn't find someone bigger?"

"He's…"

"He is dead. You think we wouldn't know? And now you are here—small and untried. How will you be able to pass the Trail of Voices without looking back? How will you know which of the roads to take when you confront Anansi at the Great Crossroads?" Nduga shook its head. "Despite all that, you are the one Agozie sent, so who am I to disagree? Come here, Zim, sit. We have a lot to talk about."

Nduga makes a small fire and cooks mushroom soup over it.

"Eat up. Eat up," it says, setting the soup down.

The soup bowl is small but refills itself after each scoop until I am filled up. We sit and talk.

By nightfall, Nduga and the oak have disappeared. In their place, a calm nestles beside me. It is so soothing I press my hand against the pocket with Mama Alo's hair. I do not remember when I fall asleep.

VI

Noon. I can see the Trail of Voices before me. It is a winding path that seems to go on forever.

"Walk through it, don't stop, don't take a step backwards, and don't look back, no matter who you think is calling you." Nduga's words replay in my head. "Follow the map's path, or at least, try." And then, as though to themselves, "Perhaps that will be all you can do."

I brace myself before taking a step forward.

"Zim," a voice behind me calls. "It's Papa." A warm hand rests on my shoulder. "Come, let me show you something I painted."

I hasten my pace. The voice becomes insistent, gnawing at the insides of my ear. It is crying now, howling.

"Don't you want to see my painting? Nobody wants to see my painting, Zim." The voice sniffles. "Just a look. It's right behind you. Do it for Papa."

The distraction causes me to miss the tree stump in front of me. I slam my right foot against it and let out a scream, forcing myself not to step backward. Forcing myself to take another step.

"Is that you, Zim? It's Mama."

Mama? It can't be… I feel a sharp pang of longing in my chest, then remember where I am. I close my eyes for a moment, feel the air fill my lungs. This is only the second voice.

I hear someone breathing heavily and running towards me. I have to force myself not to turn back and look.

"Zim, you're bleeding. Let me tend to it. Just stop for a minute and listen to your poor mother."

"I wonder where he gets this stubbornness from?" the first voice asks.

"We may never know," the second voice replies—not

Mama, no matter how she sounds, I remind myself. I am walking alone.

I ignore the voices and continue up the mountain. The dust rises from my footsteps, settling on my legs and the nearby grasses.

The end of the trail is so near, I can almost touch the arched udala tree at its exit.

"I won't tell the townsfolk that I lied about your father's map," a third voice says.

I stop frozen in my tracks.

"And when you bring back the rains to Selemku, nobody will ever believe that you did it and that your papa's maps actually worked. They will always remember him as he was when he died. Confused. Foolish. Barely a man at all."

I try to take a step forward, but my legs are as heavy as lead.

"You think I'm bluffing because I sealed my promise with my hair? Are you that naive? Foolish like your father? Where is the hair, Zim?"

I rummage through my pocket. The tuft of Mama Alo's hair is gone.

"Give it back," I say, without turning round. I can feel my hands shaking.

"I dropped it behind you."

My head becomes a sea of voices, as I manage another step.

Don't stop, don't take a step backwards, and don't look back.

Listen to your Mama, Zim. I need you.

It's right behind you, Zim. Just turn and pick it up. Don't you want the townsfolk to know I lied about your father? Or do I have it wrong? Perhaps you want them to see him as a foolish broken man?

The voice of Nduga rises up, drowning out the others, as I reach the end of the trail and cross beneath the arched udala tree. I feel in my pockets again and bring out the tuft of hair and hug it close to my chest. I sit on the ground and burst into tears. When I have emptied out all the tears inside me, I dust myself off and continue my journey.

Evening. The clouds are darkening and a distant rumble of thunder looms above. I need to find shelter before it starts raining. Quickly, I begin to scour the area for a suitable place to rest. The rain is already pouring down from the sky. I can barely see but I continue running until I slip and fall, muddying up myself in the dirt. I am too tired to stand so I lie there, hoping the rain will stop.

But the rain does not stop. Its watery strumming lulls me to fitful sleep. Darkness surrounds me.

VII

"Not many people have come this far. Welcome to the Great Crossroads, Zim. The rain has led you here."

My clothes feel damp against my skin. The scrapes on my feet and lower legs throb. I blink twice to make sure the voice is not a dream. "Who—" I say before deciding on silence.

A man is standing beside me. He has jet-black skin and is wearing a shiny black suit, making it hard to tell where the suit stops and his skin begins. His teeth glisten in the warm morning light. The nails of his fingers are so long they are grazing the ground. I remember Nduga's words. I know who this man is.

"Who am I?" The man tilts his head to one side, his gaze intent. "I am Anansi, the Trickster. Nobles would pay a fortune to have me riddle their guests in their halls but I've chosen to guard the Great Crossroads."

He offers his hand. I grab it and pull myself up, carefully avoiding the fingernails. We are standing at the intersection of two roads.

"It is time. Choose your path," Anansi says. "One leads to Mmili Mountain; the other leads one back to your home."

I believe Nduga. Anansi knows which road is which. But

he cannot be trusted. His truth and lies sound the same, though everyone knows he tells the truth and lies alternately.

"Zim, son of Agozie, the Finder, you may proceed to Mmili Mountain, but only by facing the sharp wit of Anansi. Only I know the way. Without me you will surely be lost."

"I—"

Anansi cuts me off. "You may want to think deeply before you ask any question, for Anansi can only grant one answer to each traveller he meets at the Great Crossroads."

That was surprisingly honest. Nduga had not told me what to ask at the Great Crossroads. It had only told me not to be quick to ask Anansi the obvious.

"Zim," Nduga had said that night, "think and think and think until your head hurts, before you pose a question to Anansi."

Now, standing before Anansi, I hold onto my silence.

Anansi chuckles. "Take your time." He stands too close to me. I can see the veins running the length of his curling fingernails.

I think long. I think hard. I remember the riddle games I would play with my friends. My feet still ache. I feel thirsty despite the evening's rain. I shouldn't ask the obvious. I shouldn't ask the—

"I want to know which road you pointed at for the last traveller going to Mmili Mountain."

Anansi points right.

"Thank you. You have been most helpful," I say and start walking towards the left road.

"Wait, where are you going?" The Trickster sounds confused.

"To Mmili Mountain." I pause and turn to face my unwilling guide. Anansi's teeth are far too prominent.

"How sure are you that's the right way?"

"Anansi," I say, "if you lied to the last traveller and you are telling me the truth now, that means the left way is the way to

Mmili Mountain. If you're lying to me now but spoke the truth to the last traveller, that means the left road is also the way to Mmili Mountain."

"That's not possible... How did you... ? How could you ... ? Someone has rivaled Anansi. I thought I was the wisest. Go away little boy, I underestimated you." He breaks down and starts sobbing.

I wave him goodbye and disappear up the left road.

VIII

I am at Mmili Mountain. It is as magnificent as Papa's painting. The mountain's peaks almost nudge the clouds. My feet still hurt. My stomach grumbles its hunger. I do not know what I am supposed to do now. Neither the map nor Nduga gave me the slightest clue.

"Zim, you made it." The voice is Papa's. I can see him now, sitting among the elephant and buffalo at the foot of the mountain. "Now you must go back and bring the rains to Selemku."

"But Papa, how?"

"You came here, Zim. You walked through the Trail of Voices and beat Anansi at his own game. Zim, you *are* the rain. Now it is time for you to go."

IX

Anansi is still sobbing when I get back to the Great Cross-roads. I pay him no heed and follow the right road, leading me straight to the town's gate. The town is quiet, as I walk through it.

"Where is everybody?" I ask a little girl sitting at the feet of an old woman in front of an unpainted bungalow.

"They are at Town Council Hall. The water in the new reservoir has run out," the girl says. "Mama says I'm too small to go with them, that I have to look after Grandma."

"Thank you." Perhaps Mama will be at the meeting. Perhaps Mama Alo will be there, as well.

"Wait. Who are you? Oh, I know... You're the boy Mama Alo says will bring back the rain. She has been telling everybody, but no one believes her. You're back. It's still so dry. Have you brought the rain?"

"I need to get to Town Council Hall, and fast." I run off before the little girl can ask me more questions.

I hear them before I see them. Town Council Hall's entrance is besieged by a sea of bodies. The concrete stairs tremble under their feet. They bang their balled fists against the hall's closed iron doors.

"Give us water from the reservoir we paid taxes for!" The townsfolk shriek, voices packed full of gravel.

My desperation drives me forward. I manage to wriggle my way to the front.

"Stop," I say in the voice of a thousand rushing mountain winds.

A hush falls on the crowd.

"That's him, that's the boy Mama Alo says will bring back the rain," they murmur.

"I have journeyed to the ends of the earth where no one has been," I continue, stretching my hands out to the sky. The voice comes from deep within me; it is not my own. "I have fought and overcome the trepidation in the Trail of Voices. I have unraveled the mystery of the Great Crossroads, a mystery Anansi the Trickster has guarded for centuries. I am Zim, the son of Agozie, the Finder. I am the rain!"

A flurry of words rises from the great crowd.

The clouds darken and the sky begins to rumble. Within a moment rain pours down in quantities no one has seen since the beginning of time. It rains and rains and rains, softening the parched ground, filling the waterholes, the River Bambu, and Tutukele Spring. It rains so much Town Council puts up notices on our doors saying they are willing to pay people to use the water at the new reservoir. It rains so much the months of drought wash away from our memory. And I smile each time I look to the sky because I know Papa is somewhere behind the blue horizon, smiling back at me.

X

This is how I paint.

In the evenings, when air collects at people's feet in chilly, invisible spools, I gather my painting things to the balcony and sit in front of the rotting canvas. The fingers of my right hand grip the paintbrush and the aluminium paint tray sits in my left palm. I start by making a whorl at the top left edge of the canvas. I twirl and twirl the paintbrush on the canvas, concocting a riotous mesh of colours. It does not make sense. It does not make sense at all. No one can tell what I am painting until I am done. Mama peeps out from behind the brocade curtain in the parlour, although she never admits it.

"You have to let the map guide you, see its destination with your heart and not your mind," I say, as I show the map to whom it has chosen in the morning.

For Papa, wherever he may be.

Mt. Washington

BY CAI EMMONS

People often laugh upon meeting Lanny and Bronwyn together. What they see is a snapshot of an unlikely pair. Lanny, a high school gym teacher, is six feet tall and burly; she clips her hair short. Bronwyn is five-foot-two and slender, her long wavy dark red hair a defining feature. Next, people notice their contrasting behavioral traits: Lanny's boisterousness and lack of a verbal filter, Bronwyn's public reserve. It is clear to everyone that theirs is a friendship born of complementarity.

But what is not visible is the long history that holds the friendship together, their knowledge of each other's families and of the private pains of the past. Bronwyn was there in early high school when Lanny's parents went through an ugly divorce. Lanny knows how difficult it was for Bronwyn to grow up with a frightened and often bitter single mother. They both remember Lanny getting her first period in seventh grade math class, blood pooling over the seat. They remember Bronwyn's broken arm from a ninth grade bicycle accident. Bronwyn attended most of Lanny's high school basketball games, and Lanny came to Bronwyn's science fairs. After Lanny got her license she would often borrow her father's car and take Bronwyn on road trips to the shore, or the Delaware

River. Sometimes they took the bus into the city and wandered around the West Village. Lanny liked shocking people. She was the first among their classmates to get a tattoo, not a delicate one, but a dragon breathing fire that spiraled around her left arm. For almost an entire year in high school she wore the same pair of neon orange cargo pants and a red paisley shirt. But in certain arenas Bronwyn and Lanny's tastes have always been identical. They have always liked the same junk food (nachos above all else), and they are both hooked on the same old movies (*Gone With the Wind*) and old TV shows (*Seinfeld* and *The X Files*). Though tough on the outside, they are both closet romantics. Bronwyn has no idea how she would get through life without a friend like Lanny, though they go through long periods when they're out of touch.

Now they sit in low camp chairs at their campsite overlooking the Swift River, sipping bottles of beer, mesmerized by the river's pell-mell rush over the rocks, bathing them in its negative ions. Chipmunks and nuthatches dash here and there. The light is a delicate damask; the air gloves their skin, a temperate seventy. Nature could not have engineered a more perfect situation for soothing a human being.

The sun slips behind the trees, dimming the air, imparting a contemplative mood to the landscape. Lanny wants to climb Mt. Washington tomorrow. Bronwyn is game as long as she gets a solid sleep. She hopes she's in good enough shape for such a climb. They prepare a dinner of spaghetti with meat sauce and salad, and are in their sleeping bags by 9:00 p.m.; the tent flaps open to the last embers of light. Night critters are venturing out. A bat circles. An owl hoots. Tree frogs bleat. She and Lanny breathe in unison, as if entrained.

When the birds awaken her before 5:00 a.m., Bronwyn takes measure of herself. A good sleep has swept away apprehension. She feels surprisingly rested, ready for adventure, and eager to kick the Reed chapter of her life into history. She stares at Lanny, still slack-jawed in sleep, and slathers her friend with love as if spreading her with a thick layer of honey. Lanny knows her better than anyone in the world and will always be her best friend.

It's cold—high thirties, maybe forties—and geodes of frost still linger in the patches of shade. But it's mostly clear, a few high clouds to the west that Bronwyn deems unthreatening. Once the temperature rises a little it will be a perfect day for hiking. She tugs Lanny awake, pulls on some clothes, and begins scrambling eggs. Within forty-five minutes they're packing small backpacks with sandwiches and nuts and chocolate and two full quarts of water for each of them. They have rain gear and extra clothes, a first aid kit, compass, flashlight, map. Though it's been a while since Bronwyn has made an expedition like this, she knows the protocol: be prepared for all eventualities, and know, above all, that the weather can change.

"I won't be able to keep up with you," Bronwyn says. "You're in much better shape than I am."

"I'm not as fit as I look."

"Last night I dreamed you were wearing those orange cargo pants and that paisley shirt."

"Oh god, what was I thinking back then? I should have kept those pants as a souvenir of my youthful stupidity."

Sunlight bristles over the picnic table and the day charges forward, calling them to action. At 6:03 a.m. they're on the road in Lanny's Subaru. The eastern sky is clear. A few stringy cirrus clouds, not of particular concern, laze high to the west. Temperatures are in the low fifties now and rising. Spectacular weather for the White Mountains, spectacular weather by any standards. Climbing a mountain seems like such a pure and uncomplicated thing to do, and it gives Bronwyn a satisfying sense of purpose.

Bronwyn squints through the windshield and holds her hand out the open window.

"What're you doing?" Lanny asks.

"Sizing up the day."

"Highly scientific, I see."

"Actually, it *is* scientific. Observation is where science begins. You establish norms and departures from norms. But it all begins with looking and noticing."

Lanny laughs. "Always calculating, aren't you?"

They set out on the Jewell Trail at 7:20 a.m., Lanny in the lead taking long aggressive strides. The trail, ascending along Mt. Washington's western ridge, is the longest but most gradual trail to the summit. It will take them four to five hours to reach the top and another three or four hours to descend. Allowing an hour for lunch and rest breaks, they estimate they'll be done by 6:00 p.m., safely back at the campsite before nightfall.

The first part of the trail slopes gently uphill through a deciduous forest, underfoot a soft bed of leaves and earth, moist from spring rain, muddy in some places. The air is still cool, but sunlight, yellow and sweet as butterscotch, speckles the forest floor.

Lanny sings. "I'm happy when I'm hiking, pack upon my back. I'm happy when I'm hiking, along the beaten track..."

Lanny has a child's talent for sinking into the moment and plumbing it fully. Bronwyn herself speculates too much about the future, effacing the present. When you situate your mind in the future you do not feel the soft loam giving way as each boot hits the ground. You do not hear your knees creak, or feel the sweat slithering down the back of your neck, or see the garter snake making his quick getaway. You do not hear the birdcalls or revel in the sunrise. You scarcely hear yourself breathe.

When the trail crosses a brook they stop for a break and sit on rocks, snacking on walnuts and raisins, sipping their water. They do not speak, and the silence seals their bond.

"It feels like it's going to rain." Lanny peers up through the canopy to the few chips of visible sky.

"It won't rain," Bronwyn says.

"If you say so. You'd know, I guess."

"I'm paid to know." But in fact she hasn't checked the National Weather Service. She has consulted only her own instinct today, reports from her pores.

They allow a foursome of twenty-something men to pass them, and Bronwyn feels a twinge of envy for their youth and fitness. Thirty isn't old, but it's getting there, and something about the springy sinewy calves of those men brings this home acutely.

A series of switchbacks take them up the side of the ridge, and by mid-morning they emerge above the tree line. The air is noticeably cooler and windy, and though blue sky still predominates, a posse of dark-bellied nimbus clouds rolls in from the west. After so much time under the trees, the massive stretch of sky is disquieting. Light but dark. At once revealing and undisclosing. They've lost their protection. Lanny was right, rain is all but certain now. Bronwyn should have known better than to think they could reach the summit without some weather to contend with. Nevertheless, the clouds are still high enough to permit an impressive view of the Presidentials: Mt. Jefferson, Mt. Adams, and Mt. Madison preside like a receiving line to the north. *We're here, we're always reliably here,* they seem to be saying. Ahead, along a ridge directly in front of them, stands the peak of Mt. Washington, still a fair hike away. A sudden gust of wind kicks up from the west northwest and careens into Lanny, so she teeters, almost falls.

"Jeez, that was rude!"

"You should put on your raingear to break the wind," Bronwyn says.

"Yes, Mom."

"I know, I'm sorry—" Bronwyn can't stand this cautionary

role of hers, but she plays it well, as she always has. They both take out their jackets and put them on without speaking.

"Good to go," Lanny shouts over the wind.

The trail now requires extra caution as it ascends over boulders. Ahead of them hikers dot the mountainside like a herd of colorfully jacketed goats. Bronwyn is highly alert, highly focused, shifting her attention between monitoring Lanny's uncertain progress over the rocks and scrutinizing the advancing front which is clotted with black pannus clouds, a sure sign of precipitation to come. She tries to estimate the speed of the front's approach and surmise what it will deliver. The winds are gusting at thirty to forty miles per hour, she guesses, which makes talking almost impossible. Worse, it makes the mountain unfriendly, even sinister. She hates this job of trying to forecast when the data are incomplete. There is so much about which she cannot be sure. Ahead of her Lanny marches on, apparently unperturbed. Is Bronwyn crazy to think they should quit? Yes, the summit is in sight, but it will take them at least another hour to get there.

"Maybe we should turn around," Bronwyn suggests, yelling over the wind.

"You've got to be kidding. I'm not giving up now. Not when we're so close to the top."

"It's farther than it looks."

Lanny makes a face. Bronwyn vacillates. It isn't clear who's in charge. But Bronwyn feels Lanny's intransigence, and it would be foolish to separate. Bronwyn gives a slight nod and they continue.

———

Because Bronwyn is who she is—because her body is earth-sentient and she has spent her life thinking about weather—she feels the updraft before it manifests, warm air rising, smashing into the cooler air above. She pictures the fracas of colliding molecules overhead, imagines she hears them.

"I don't like this," she says.

Lanny either doesn't hear, or chooses not to respond.

The clouds have assumed the steely look of military tanks; they knock against the sky's boundaries. The cog railway, chugging uphill, emits noxious black smoke that rises like a feisty runt to test itself against the storm clouds. Sheet lightning explodes, whitening the sky, as if to erase all memories, making a clean palette for itself. It pixelates everything, illuminating Lanny and making of her a hallucination. *One one thousand, two one thousand.* Thunder detonates. They both jump. Rain follows, sudden, hard, cold, slicing the air at a sharp angle, obscuring everything.

"Stay there," Bronwyn shouts to Lanny, leaning into the wind, bent at the waist, eyes slitted. She reaches Lanny, grabs her arm, tugs. Lanny, taller than Bronwyn and much heavier, resists. Then, without warning she yields, allowing herself to be guided to the nearest boulder where they both crouch under a ledge. Lanny says something made unintelligible by the tumult. She leans closer. "We're going to die," she says directly into Bronwyn's ear.

Bronwyn shakes her head, an emphatic *no*. They aren't safe here, but it's better than venturing into the open in such low visibility to make grounding rods of themselves. She thinks briefly of Reed, how he would react to hearing she has died in an electrical storm on Mt. Washington. Would he feel remorse? Would he think his rejection drove her to recklessness?

Rain is everywhere, petulant, soaking her waterproof jacket, running in full-blown rivers down her torso. Lanny, famously always-warm Lanny, shivers. Bronwyn pulls her close to help them both preserve heat. What fools they are. Bronwyn should have steered them away from this mountain whose weather lore she knows so well. There are plenty of other mountains they could have climbed with far less fickle weather. They should have turned back at the first sighting of storm clouds. She shouldn't have relied on her own instinct, should have investigated the weather reports before they set out.

An aura surrounds them, cool and merciless. The beckoning arm of Death. It is so senseless to die this way, accidentally, beneath Nature's fist. She is overcome with fury, with a wish for things to be different than they are, furious for all the things she cannot change, beginning with this moment and bleeding back into everything else, Reed's disinterest, her mother's negativity. Another flash blanches the sky, stealing all dimensions but two. Scarcely a second passes before thunder cracks.

Rain turns to hail, vitriolic and personal, each pellet hard as a falling doll head. Her rage spikes. Her brain seems to pucker and roll inside her skull. Her head is on fire. Her vision wavers. She sloughs her backpack and pushes herself to standing.

"What're you doing?" Lanny shouts.

Entangled in something, Bronwyn can hardly speak. "Stay there," she croaks.

Gripped by the storm, enshrined in its clamor, she turns west to its source and folds herself into the symphonic chaos. Her chest throbs. She strains to keep her lids apart. Hail batters her cheeks. Red fills her vision. Clouds swirl around her, malevolent evaporating tongues. She summons all her will, heaving with the effort, with rage and need. She hurls forth the volcanic heat in her brain, her eyes like rapiers jousting with the crazed molecules. She slides through a portal and is sundered from any sense of self she has known, wholly devoted to some other entity, hearing only her own strained breath, life at its limit.

———

The mountaintop is still. Hailstones litter the rocks. The sun glistens. The sky is blue; the air, gilded. There isn't a breath of wind. Bronwyn scans the Presidentials, etched in perfect clarity against the guileless, cloudless blue. Where exactly is she? Who is she? A warm presence at her side. A human body. A woman. Her old friend Lanny, churning out sound that could be laughter.

"My god. What just happened?"

Bronwyn pants. The laughter comes at her like a raucous Greenland Piteraq. She shakes her head, sits on a rock, cradles her head, sniffs the post-rain ozone and petrichor.

"Bronwyn, talk to me. That was wild. If I didn't know better, I'd think you did something to call off that storm."

Bronwyn reaches for words, but they're sealed in a remote part of her body. Even if she could find them, they could not touch or express her experience of what has happened.

More laughter rolls from Lanny, then stops abruptly. "I *do* know better and I *still* think you did something. You made that storm go away. I watched you. I swear to god you cast some spell."

Bronwyn remains motionless, replaying what just happened, the heat that overtook her, the energy that coursed through her whole body, the sense of power she felt. Lanny is right—she did the impossible.

Finding Ways

BY ZIG ZAG CLAYBOURNE

His mother fit in a box. A sturdy plastic box. Black. Meant to be dignified. When they gave it to him, he had no idea what to do with it. They mentioned urns, which seemed suffocating, and vials on necklaces, which baffled him because he had no intention of wearing his mother as bling.

But they'd prodded his indecision. "Perhaps a simple, base-level, inexpensive urn. Or any selection from our catalog of keepsakes. For your family?"

The family was scattered around the world, a world experiencing a worldwide illness. A very quiet virus, one that pretended it wasn't there then assumed ownership as though intent on remodeling.

The Gentrification Virus, the internet called it. It hadn't killed his mother. What it did was effectively close off the world. Borders. Airlines. Bridges. The family had never been close; now, following a funeral where only Benjamin and three others were allowed to attend—Mother's friends being old, he'd pled with them to remain home—there was literally no intimate family opportunity to grow closer. One sister was stationed in an active war zone, the other in near permanent quarantine in a part of the world too attractive to the world's truest disease—the type that always found a way to spread where unwanted: the affluent.

Inside the box: a bag of ashes. He trusted them when they said they were Mother's last remains. He trusted them when they'd repeatedly assured him they were "taking care of" Mrs. Clara August every time he called prior to the memorial service to make sure there was nothing more he needed to do.

He'd seen her die. She'd fallen. He hadn't been able to take care of her at that moment in any way, nothing outside of sitting slumped with a racing heart, waiting for the ambulance to arrive, park, shut its driver and passenger doors, come up the stairs, knock, and bring officiousness in with the winter chill.

Questions. Questions which he'd answered numbly, the same as he had the police who arrived, the same as every "Yes, "No," "She didn't smoke," "No medical issues," "I have her insurance information," "Autopsy?" Benjamin August *knew* himself to be alive, but Ma's death made him invisible to every system and function Death engineered.

"So sorry for your loss" was not the hug of an obeah from back home. It wasn't the power of a human body poured into another human body which had lost more than another's physical shell.

In this country, at this time, it had to do.

Mother's box had a white sticker on it. The cremation company's name first, because commerce always, then printed in plain type, "THIS TEMPORARY RECEPTACLE CONTAINS THE CREMATED REMAINS OF," with Ma's name, the date of cremation, and a number. Ma's secret number. 25290. As though she were an agent her entire life, entirely unbeknownst to her family. "NOTE:"—the sticker ended—"For perpetual security, a permanent receptacle or urn should be provided."

Well, one wasn't.

They were for sale.

He had no money.

He had a small bungalow that she shared with him in her old age. They enjoyed grocery shopping together. Ever since arthritis had made the use of her left hip a random thing, it was really the only time she got out, hobbling to the car, complaining about having to use the store's electric scooter, using it anyway as he trailed her, ready to reach things on high shelves, ready to try suggested new meats when they were on sale.

For some reason he thought the ashes should remain cool, so the box now sat atop his refrigerator. He knew the refrigerant didn't leak upward, but it seemed as if it should, which was enough. It was important that things seem to make sense.

When he opened the box, there was a plastic bag, a thick filmy one. The bag had a metal tag with that same number.

25290.

He and mother loved science fiction movies. She was forever Unit 25290 now.

Indestructible. Invulnerable.

But only because she was dead.

Even that word had died in him. Where was its terror, where was its dread? When he cried in the shower his tears flowed at her being dead but not at the word *dead*. Which felt odd. She'd taught him his first words of English in her heavy Trini accent. Words had been important.

The word "dead" had as much energy today as a plastic box.

How could a rectangle no bigger than a large bag of sugar contain all of his mother?

And if that *was* all of her, what to do?

The box sat atop his refrigerator. Far to the back. Seen only when standing. The funeral had been in February. It was April. He hadn't even apportioned the amounts of ash for the eventual vials he knew he had to find. His sisters, though distant, loved and trusted him enough not to worry him with queries about delivery.

People started to ask if he had lost weight.

"Yes," he said. "A bit. I'm trying."

"You look good," was the usual response, hoping it was a bolster.

"Thank you," he said, never "It's because I've been avoiding the kitchen."

By May, when plants were on everyone's minds, even at the grocers that placed rows of houseplants for sale at entrances, a feeling hit. He couldn't quite call it an idea. A feeling that was vague, certain, perfect, and ridiculous. Which to him felt full and complete. There'd be no burial of the bag or scattering to the wind. At their favorite big box store he purchased a large clear vase of thick hearty glass with a diameter wide enough for him to put his entire arm inside. At two-feet tall it was expensive and heavy, but worth it.

He bought a plant meant to thrive well in or out of soil. He bought a smaller vase, gourd-shaped with a wide lip, again clear. Out of a wire hanger he fashioned a holder for the smaller so that it would sit suspended within the larger. He filled the glass gourd with water. The plant—a bamboo shoot of some type—already had small roots. He inserted the plant into the vase, imagining the water must have felt comfortable to its delicate fibers, and placed the smaller inside the larger in a sunny spot beside a bookcase in his living room. Books had been the family joy since his earliest memories of arriving in the US.

"Books are smarter plants," she might tell him.

Or, closer to Halloween, gleefully: "Books are death masks!"

Or at Christmas: "If the book is good I've given you several presents at once!"

The day he sat the vase-within-a-vase down, he also sat to read, actually in the sun as well. He'd done neither for a while, but now that there was a companion in that inviting space, it would be rude otherwise.

The feeling now felt like a plan. Plans helped immensely.

The roots had grown to nearly a foot long by August. He changed the water often enough that the glass remained pristine. It was like having an undersea farm. He loved the air bubbles that formed on each root, putting him in mind of ecosystems and dependable cycles. Each time he freshened the water, and sometimes even the roots themselves—which would accumulate brownish gunk easily washed down the drain with the kitchen sprayer—the roots seemed eager to grow another inch. They knew what they were ultimately growing toward. He imagined it so, and in imagining knew it to be truth.

Benjamin wasn't happy. He imagined his mother was. On a hot August day, the plastic box on the counter—always dusted, always clean—sat out of reach of the spray, a large garbage bag spread under it. A scoop sat nearby, as well, but he didn't know if he could use it. Maybe. He'd see.

He didn't think Ma would mind being dripped on.

He cut a circle of plastic the diameter of the smaller vase's lip from a jug of grape juice, cored a hole in the center of that circle the thickness of the bamboo shoot, fed the shoot with its wet dangling roots through the hole, then tested the apparatus for fit. The shoot held snugly a few inches below the larger vase's lip. The plastic circle sat securely atop the original wire hanger, and he could easily spray the roots with the water bottle placed by the side of his bookcase. The plastic circle acted as a moisture seal. A terrarium within a terrarium was a beautiful thing. Bright, airy, and full of life.

He let it sit—he let *both* sit, Ma and the terrarium—on the counter overnight. It wouldn't take Ma long to get acquainted. He would know in the morning if she had.

By morning it didn't feel like a weight had been lifted when he entered the kitchen. Didn't feel like a bright new day. Instead, it felt like Sunday.

It hadn't felt like Sunday in months: breakfast in the nook, sun through the golden curtains, and food that wasn't entirely displeasurable to eat. His first thought wasn't of the plastic box anchoring his kitchen. It was of who was in the box.

He ate cereal. He spoke using his thoughts. His mother, he imagined, agreed.

No need for the scoop. Ma would prefer the sliding joy of a straight pour, which was exactly what Benjamin did. He lifted the five pounds of his mother from the plastic box, removed the spy tag, unsealed the bag, and slowly, mindfully, poured her into the large vase, now emptied of its plant guest. Even pouring slowly, dust whorls formed inside as though training to be a genie. He made sure to keep his face far from the pour. It would be disrespectful to breathe her in. When the only thing left in the bag was enough for his sisters, he stopped. He re-tied the bag, replaced the metal tag, tucked the bag in the box, and set the hard box back atop the refrigerator.

He left the remains to settle in the vase, the dust to dissipate, and his mother's soul to cry out her relief in peace.

Sunday.

He planned to fill the kitchen that afternoon with the scents of a grand dinner.

———

"Are you well?" his sister Penelope asked. This from a war zone. He didn't hear bombs going off and bullets, yet he felt them nearby. It didn't matter that she said she was nowhere near the front line. Death traveled.

"I am," he said.

"You eating?" his sister Sara asked.

Their faces within their squares on his computer monitor were as tired as his, their expressions mirroring his concern.

"I cooked oxtails a month ago," he said.

"Not Ma's recipe?" said Penelope.

"No," he said.

"Good, 'cause Ma's was shit!"

They all laughed. It was true. Ma oversalted tails each time. Everything else she cooked? Perfect.

The children paused to reflect on this.

This was how the rare conversations ended. The virus hadn't abated. "I love you" would follow a pause. "Love you." "Love you, brother." Then the hard finality of *This video call has ended* coming from Sara's end. She was the only one who actually had a paid video conferencing account. Turks and Caicos was an affluence-hell that paid even better than war and freelance editing.

————

The roots hadn't reached the sand of Ma's remains yet. He lifted the shoot—as he did every three days—and spritzed the roots. They were close though. It was like the two wanted to reach each other. He'd tell his sisters about the vase-within-a-vase arrangement when that happened. They'd smile then but not likely before.

He left a small votive candle burning by the vase during the day. It felt right. At night, just after shutting out the living room light, he'd open the curtains so that all the night and each of its stars—however meager the city allowed—could pour in to fill his Ma's vase with dreams.

It didn't take long after the last video-conference for the roots to tentatively touch the crown of Clara Louisa August's head.

Benjamin felt the change while dreaming: an acquaintance he had known for years kissed him in an elevator whose doors never opened nor closed. He knew that odd fact in the dream. Had no idea how the two of them had even gotten in, but it was a sweet dream. A human dream.

Hadn't been those for quite a while.

In the dream his scalp tingled. He scratched. The kiss broke. Imani studied his face. The dream shifted.

It shifted to a song. Less than that, a frequency, one that modulated into a repetitive melody.

A humming.

Like an old woman humming.

When he woke to start the day's work he was well aware that Ma would hum when focused on something or particularly happy, but everyone hummed. Even he did.

He did so while he worked that day.

When he finished work, he made dinner. After dinner, shower. After shower, bed—the best part of his day.

He dreamed there.

The leaves atop the shoot had gotten quite large. He held them gently whenever he dusted them. They didn't feel like skin but he enjoyed the contact. He imagined they did too. He imagined a lot as Christmas rolled around. A California Christmas didn't mean cold temperatures. As a child he'd asked why they couldn't move somewhere with an actual winter Christmas. He wanted to see snow. "Bean, you don't move *toward* inconvenience!" she'd said.

Enough of it will find you, he'd later realized.

Death and taxes and failure and too many types of unrequited love…but mostly death.

Death was fucking inconvenient.

He wanted that on a T-shirt he would never wear anywhere.

Now that the roots had reached the sand, the perforations he'd made in the plastic a month ago would serve as a watering mechanism. Ma was surely acclimated to the moisture by now. A little extra water wouldn't faze her a bit. Benjamin kept watch for signs of mold, rot, human slime, or whatever else might come of such basic constituents of the universe mixing under the powers of both day and night.

That was god stuff. That was ancestor stuff. He didn't consider himself playing with it.

He considered himself respecting it.

He'd been stuck at home for a year. He'd been stuck inside death for a year.

Inconvenience will find you. He knew that to be true.

"Counter it," Ma had said, and conspiratorially showed him what a middle finger meant, "with this."

———

He was dreaming. "Plant me in the sun," Ma said. He was sure it was her. He knew that if he touched the plant in the morning he would hear the same.

He did. And he did. The connection of skin and leaf. Her voice humming within his mind.

He left the bungalow, locked the door and even the gate—just in case someone decided his home was a valuable thing—and Benjamin took a very long, very tearful walk.

Plants communicated. He knew that. Everything communicated. Water. Earth. Invisibilities humans would never comprehend.

Everybody knew that.

At a certain point everything had a voice—or found one.

He returned home just as the dusk sky went from gray and pink to smoky purple.

After closing the curtains and turning on the lights, he poured himself a glass of fruit water, sat on the floor in front of the vase, and touched the bamboo.

He listened. He waited. He shifted uncomfortably. He pulled the vase closer to his reading chair, sat, and let a hand dangle in contact with a leaf.

And eventually tears did what tears are meant to do. Drained, he slept.

And dreamed.

The dreams Benjamin had now were dreams of potlucks and graduations, of being scared witless walking the new San Diego neighborhoods, and dreams of Benjamin and his sisters attempting to fool Ma and being found out.

And then there were Mama's dreams, full of tears and regrets and worry.

He slept through the night and half the morning. The plant sat quietly nearby. Waking, he cleared his eyes, reached to touch the plant—and then let himself breathe slowly. Ma had said her peace.

———

There was a section along the side yard that got good light and plentiful water from a seam in the gutter that hadn't been repaired in three years. Benjamin dusted dirt from his pants and poured a glass of water onto the newly turned soil. This was the perfect spot. Now over a foot tall, sunlight turned the bamboo's leaves into lime candy, its stalk into the beginnings of an ancient tree.

The shoot would grow for as long as Benjamin needed it, neither inconvenient nor silent. Its sunshine-fed voice never lost.

La Gorda and the City of Silver

BY SABRINA VOURVOULIAS

I

I was born on a Wednesday, in middle of a chapuzón.

The sudden squall of sky water bears little resemblance to a thunderstorm—it's more like a vertical flood, though very brief.

I considered Chapuzón for my luchador name—I had poured out of my mother with the same fulminating relentlessness and washed her into the hereafter—but fate took a hand, and the name is still available to anyone who wants to design its mask and come up with some signature moves.

Fate always takes a hand and leads us where she will. Fate is not funny, although she thinks she is as she laughs at us. When I meet her face-to-face, I intend to talk to her about it. Maybe I'll body slam her while I'm at it.

But until then I'm stuck with the name she set out for me when I packed on weight on my way to adolescence: La Gorda. The Fat One.

It's okay. I *am* fat, though not compared to the luchadores in my father's company. But they're men and are allowed to be corpulent. They're also allowed to be luchadores in the ring and on the screen and in the cantina—where they swallow their tequilazos through the mouth holes of their masks because otherwise no one would recognize them, and they'd have to pay.

There is no ring for me, and no movies, because women are not luchadores. That's what El Patojo and El Súper Fly and El Diablo Colorado tell me when they come to my father's house for the Sunday tamalada. I make the tamales, of course, and after they've eaten their fill, my father gets out his camera and films another one of their episodic adventures right in our backyard.

A week later, I see them up on screen, in the packed Zone 7 movie palace some five blocks from our house. El Diablo Colorado is the villain, of course, since his name has the word "devil" in it. And his mask is red with flames, with a puckered hornlet near each temple. He's the only luchador with a three-dimensional component to his mask, and he's very proud of this innovation. People hate him and love him at the same time, and when he's wrestling in the ring they throw things at him: bags of mango slices coated with flaked chile; packs of Payaso cigarettes (reputedly made from the tobacco scavenged from discarded butts collected off the streets); and week-old lottery tickets with sad, unwinning numbers.

When the night is over, I help clean up. We toss everything but the mango slices. We aren't rich, and the mangoes are good eating. Sometimes, if we're particularly tapped out, El Súper Fly keeps the Payasos, too.

El Súper Fly is the hero of my father's movies and lucha libre events, and El Patojo is his young sidekick. Nobody throws anything at them, though I think this will change now that El Patojo has turned from gangly to cut, and the girls have started squealing when he gets tagged in. I think someday there'll be underwear in the ring for me to clear away.

They are all my godfathers, this company of good and

evil, and I love them even without their masks. But they are not smart, and they don't know the first thing about women. The more they tell me no, the more I think yes, and one of these days La Gorda will show up in the ring and blow them all away.

I already made her mask.

II

Maybe when the builders named Ciudad de Plata they intended the rich would be fooled and move into the neighborhood. Fate again, laughing. City of Silver, the neighborhood in Zone 7 where the Guatemalan luchador movies get made, is more or less lower middle class and mostly a decent place to grow up. The houses have a patch of yard in front and back, and a concrete patio in between, with a rough lava rock pila where we scrub our clothes and hang them to dry.

If you're up to your elbows in suds and look up from the pila across your patio, you'll see your neighbor's pila, and the pila in the lot beyond that, and so forth until the block comes to an end.

This is where La Gorda first tags in.

I'm wringing out sheets when I hear Elena crying. She is six and as skinny as I am fat. We've stopped playing together now that I'm fifteen, but that doesn't mean anything. I'm still her friend, and I know the sobs aren't frivolous. She didn't cry when her mother died of cancer two years ago. In fact, I don't believe I've ever seen tears glaze her dark eyes.

I shake the soapy water off my arms and walk to the chicken-wire fence that separates our houses. "What happened?" I ask when I finally sight her up in the first big branches of a tree we call eucalipto but may or may not bear any resemblance to a real eucalyptus tree. It's like that here— we take the proper Spanish name for something and give it to something else altogether, and so we have melocotones, which aren't peaches as they are elsewhere in the Spanish-speaking world but a type of squash.

Elena shakes her head at me, doesn't answer, keeps sobbing.

I stick my feet into the holes of the chicken wire and climb over. I'm so heavy I bend the fence. So much the better—less height to deal with. I go to stand under the tree where my friend is roosting. If I could haul myself up to her I would, but all my strength resides in my legs and midsection; my arms would better fit a skinny girl.

"Come down," I call up.

"No."

"Why're you crying?"

She shakes her head again, but I don't go away.

"A bad man," she says finally.

"Did someone hurt you?"

She nods.

"What did he do to you?"

I expect a slap, a knocking down, a vicious arm pull—for these are the ways adults get angry and careless with children. What I get is an earful of six-year-old words that, when properly strung together, amount to something much, much worse.

"Who?" I ask. "Describe him to me." And if the demand comes out sounding harsh it is because I know this is not the ring where the villains are in truth nice guys who sell pork cutlets when their masks are off. No, like those words that are the same but really name vastly different objects, villains outside the ring are evil, masked in ordinary, and the damage they do is often permanent.

When she tells me, I convince her to climb over the chicken-wire fence with me. Then I carefully bend the fencing back so it looks as it did before it bore my weight. I take her to my room and teach her how to set the lock. Then I take off my apron and go find my father and godfathers.

They will do nothing—because he is Elena's sole guardian.

In their eyes, it is worse to leave a child alone in the world than to leave her in bad company.

Perhaps there is some right in their thinking. Perhaps there is even heroism in the pact they make to distract the stepfather with nights out at the cantina and free tickets to the lucha events—after all, not a one of them has a quinto to spare, and it represents a commitment to monetary loss as well as time spent in the company of a man they can now do nothing but abhor.

Perhaps there is even a bit of creativity in their thinking. They discuss tailoring one of their movies to shame the man into desisting his predation—though El Diablo Colorado refuses to even pretend to be that kind of villain.

Perhaps. But to me their plans sound exactly like their nos to women luchadoras—senseless.

So I go back and write a note for Elena's stepfather, telling him she'll be staying with us the next couple of nights to help me with a project. Then I go home and wait for night to fall.

The mask is tight to my face, as all luchador masks are, and yellow like butter. There are chocolate-colored spirals on each cheek, and on the back, where my tucked-in hair lumps at just the right spot, is an image of the pot-bellied gorda—a Pre-Colombian find from an underground site that sits right on the edge of City of Silver.

Since only the huge belly survives, there is a lot of argument about whether the stone idol was supposed to represent a fat man or a pregnant woman, but I know it is neither. There's a reason for the stylized ears of corn that fill the belly, and for the knotted strings that are carved where the belly button should be. I tie my apron in exactly the same configuration, and so does every woman and girl in City of Silver. We learned it from our mothers at the same time we learned to grill ears of corn in their husks and then turn them into the chuchitos and paches that so often fill our bellies.

There is one thing all City of Silver residents agree on: the fat and ancient stone person found on our border is one of us.

After I've gotten the mask just right, I bind my breasts with the Ace bandages my father keeps around for when my godfathers hurt themselves during filming. Then I pull on the shiny, stretchy brown catsuit and super-high-top yellow sneakers that complete La Gorda's outfit. I've been hiding the outfit since I made it, at the bottom of a chest full of women's things where my father will never think to go. At the last minute I add a tablecloth—it has a cheery papaya popsicle print—as a cape and secure it with one of those hair elastics that has decorative plastic balls strung through it.

When I look at myself in the full-length mirror I see a luchador. A hero.

There is a moment when I wish I could unbind and show what I really am—a luchadora, a heroine with a name handed down by fate and moves learned at my father's knee—but then I realize it doesn't matter. I'm behind the mask anyway.

I climb over the chicken-wire fence and employ El Diablo Colorado's skulking walk to carry me to the back door. It's locked, but I know where there's a spare key Elena uses to let herself in when she gets back from school. I open the door quietly, and although there is no light on, I find my way through the house without bumping into anything. All of the houses on the block are identical. I stand a few moments at the threshold of the biggest bedroom.

Elena's stepfather is sprawled on his back on the bed, snoring softly with his mouth open. The moonlight travels weakly through the sheer curtains and pools around his body. He's dressed still, though the waistband of his pants are undone and his zipper's down. I consider returning to the kitchen and finding a knife to slice off what is behind the dingy white briefs that peek out, but that's not a move worthy of a luchador. So I calculate, as I've watched El Súper Fly calculate so many times in the ring.

I land solidly on his chest, and to say I drive the air from his lungs is to understate. I think I hear a rib crack under my massive knees. He tries to cough. Then he tries to speak, but I tear my cape off and ball it into his mouth. He struggles to breathe.

I borrow El Patojo's gravelly growl to issue my threat. After Elena's stepfather nods his agreement, I knock him into tomorrow with an illegal blow my father made me learn so I'd always recognize it. He won't let his luchadores get near any wrestlers who attempt to bring it into the ring, and I've had to flag him once or twice so he knows a particularly unscrupulous one has tried to slip it by our notice during a match.

But this is no show ring, and there's no one around to ban La Gorda for nastiness, so I don't regret using it.

Sometimes you just have to fight dirty.

III

Legends have a date of birth.

The legend of El Panzón is born the year Elena's stepfather goes on a bender he never comes back from, and El Diablo Colorado and his wife adopt the girl.

Everyone gets the gender and the name of the new hero wrong, but no matter. As a luchador he does one thing and one thing only—he makes City of Silver safe for women and girls.

He's never been seen in the ring, or up on screen, but he has a local following anyway. The itinerant street vendors sell ingenious mini masks to slip over a thumb for thumb-wrestling —and El Panzón's replica is every bit as popular as El Súper Fly's or El Diablo Colorado's. Only El Patojo's sells more.

I buy a set of each for Elena and me, and when we play our thumb lucha libre, my godfathers gather around to cheer us, and themselves, on. I make sure La Gorda always wins.

In my twenty-first year I discover that the age difference

between El Patojo and me has miraculously become insignificant and, after the first time he kisses me, I no longer think of him as my godfather.

Women still throw their panties at him because he has, as I always hear them declare during the ring matches, "a body by God." But under his mask, El Patojo's face is goofy and shy, and I couldn't love it any better.

We marry, and although he won't wear his wedding ring at the same time as he wears his mask—it would hurt the box office—he comes home every night and revels in my generous body.

Los Enanitos, our tag team of boys, are born; and then La Princesa. We teach them all the best wrestling moves, and when a girl finally has a role in one of my father's lucha libre movies, it is my five-year-old Princesa.

There is only sporadic need for La Gorda, and I successfully hide my identity from my husband. To him I am just a woman in love with him, in love with food, in love with lucha. If he ever rolls over in bed, opens his eyes, and finds an empty space beside him, he is confident it'll only be a moment until the bed shifts under my weight again.

These are the good years.

IV

Outside of City of Silver, Guatemalan women and girls die in droves. They suffer gruesome deaths—the bodies, when they appear, are mutilated and disfigured.

Just as El Panzón is known to safeguard his neighborhood's women and girls, the new darkness that's taken over the rest of the city has only feminine targets.

The people name him Cabrakán—after the monstrous Pre-Colombian deity responsible for earthquakes—and the mask they say is his has death written in every seam.

Like El Panzón, Cabrakán never enters the ring, but

popular imagination pits them against each other, and wagers are made.

V

I am at peak weight and in the prime of my life.

I know Cabrakán will not set foot in City of Silver—it is a sign of respect for a worthy opponent. My world is secure, but at its borders, the dark.

I've watched the girls of City of Silver grow up and move to other neighborhoods in the city—places where I can't hear the scuttlebutt in order to come to their rescue. I've watched them leave, and walk straight into Cabrakán territory, and still I bide.

Then it is our Elena who packs her suitcases and heads for an apartment in Zone 1. Her huge eyes land on mine moments before she boards the bus. "Take care of yourself, mi gordita," she says. It is just a term of affection in her mouth, something you might call an overweight sister or cousin, but it sends me to my father's house to stare across the fence at the eucalyptus tree where it all started.

I'm there a long time before I feel a hand on my arm.

"Don't do it, Gorda," El Patojo says.

I turn to look into my husband's lumpy, beloved face.

"I have to," I say after a moment. "I can't stand the thought that someday it could be her broken under Cabrakán's heel."

"One neighborhood is enough responsibility for a luchador," he says.

There is a long silence between us.

"How long have you known?" I ask finally.

"Always," he says. "From the first."

In middle of the night, I leave our bed to put on my mask and outfit. I don't know if my husband is awake or not, and I don't say any special goodbye. No luchador ever does. It's seven blocks from my front door to the edge of City of Silver, and after that, it's up to fate.

VI

The sky tears.
Water falls in sheets that blind and pummel.
The earth bucks.
Stones crack.
Bolts strobe, and turn the scenes unfolding beneath them into a movie.

They say it is this way when the ancient powers walk the same streets. They say it is like this when El Panzón and Cabrakán come face to face.

They say there is no inch of Guatemala City that doesn't run with corn and rubble turned liquid, like blood, on this night.

VII

For a while we are evenly matched—he has his moves, I have mine.

We are of a height, and of a weight—if it weren't for the masks and the colors of our outfits you might not be able to tell one from the other.

He jumps off parapets as if they were the ropes, I dodge and somersault. He propels himself vertical and aims his feet at my chest; I feint away and fall onto him when he's still prone. His elbow to my solar plexus. My knees to his chest.

He draws up and away when one of his strikes loosens the binding on my breasts.

"You are not El Panzón," he says.

"There is no Panzón, just me. La Gorda," I answer.

He spits—not at me but about me.

"Better," he says. "I'll break you exactly as I'd break any other woman."

His attacks turn frenzied then, and after a volley that leaves me with ringing ears and limp arms, I turn myself toward City of Silver and run.

I hear him laugh with delight as he gives chase.

I know there is no safety left in my neighborhood—the respect that stayed Cabrakan's hand at its borders is gone— and still, it is where I head.

I stumble and fall exactly where the stone idol of la gorda was unearthed.

He comes to stand over me, and in that moment looking up at him I notice that the seams of his mask form the outline of a skull.

I hear a low growl as something flings itself at Cabrakán's head. It is El Patojo, in full luchador regalia, and his foot connects with the skull's jaw. Then he's gone, and I hear the distinctive slap of a tag.

I struggle to my feet as El Súper Fly sails at Cabrakán.

They tag in and out as if this were a movie that had been choreographed by a master. El Diablo Colorado, La Princesa, Los Enanitos. El Patojo again.

He tags me.

And then I'm in the ring with them—the team of my dreams, and of my heart.

The people of City of Silver have always had their heroes and their villains in the ring, but they know when the lucha turns real. They come to stand behind us and around us and with us. I hear their roar and feel the trajectory of the clots of clay with which they pelt Cabrakán.

We rout the killer of women. My father gets it on film.

And as the spectators make their way back to their homes, we luchadores and luchadoras limp around giving each other high fives. Then we put our arms around one another and make our way back to my father's house for a Quetzalteca and whatever food I can pull together on such short notice.

There is never an end to evil, so we may have to fight again tomorrow, or the day after.

But that's okay—we're behind the masks anyway.

Home

BY CÉLINE KEATING

Molly was in love even before Billy; she was in love with the way the sand dunes drifted to the ocean's edge, the way the clam and mussel shells crunched underfoot at the shore near the Point, the way her skin smelled after a day in the salty surf, baked in brittle sunlight. But most of all she was in love with the harbor, with the thick coils of rope and the lobster crates massed near the fishing boats, with the stench of dead fish and dried-out seaweed and the flavors of lemon and salt and grease of the fried clams she had every day for lunch at the Promised Land Bar.

"Unload these, will ya?" Phil, her co-worker said, Molly nodded, wiped her hands on her soiled white apron and leaned her weight against the dolly, shoving it with all her strength along the wooden floorboards, her rubber boots making wet, sucking noises. It was heavy, sloppy, exhausting work, but when she left each evening she felt strong and complete, and she slept at night as if she were falling-down drunk. And now there was Billy.

Three weeks ago she hadn't even met Billy; now she was moving in with him. She had never done anything so wild and improbable in her life. Billy came from a long line of fishermen on his mother's side. He worked the charter boats during the season and crewed on a trawler in between. His parents had died the year before, and he had taken his kid brother to spend the summer with relatives in Wisconsin, the only summer he had ever been away. Molly met him on Labor Day weekend, the day before she was due to return home after this, her first job after college. If Molly hadn't met him on Labor Day, she wouldn't have met him at all. *Lucky lucky lucky*, she chanted to herself.

"You look like a madwoman with that blood, and your hair a mess," Vince, the owner, said as she pushed the dolly against the swinging doors into the shop. She laughed, slipping on thick rubber gloves. In the display case, the light caught and reflected the sparkles of freshly chipped ice. She began to lift the fish by the tail and lay them down with expert flips of her wrist. Those for fileting she set aside for Vince, who would soon instruct her in that art. Over the summer she had sold fish and lobster and hauled and mopped and cut. She had learned to gut, leaving on head and tail, learned to scale so skillfully that not a wispy flake remained. But now that she was staying on, Vince would teach her how to make the clean slice under the head, insert the sharp, thin blade, and, with only a few deft motions, remove filets.

She took the dolly out back and left it near the dock, busy with men—for it was only men who worked here—unloading the tuna, thicker than her waist, and recoiling the ropes and emptying the buckets to the plaintive cawing of the gulls as they wheeled overhead and dove for scraps. Rounding the spit of land that poked into Block Island Sound, the Cora Mae, the one Billy worked, was coming in. As she watched it make its stately way, circled with gulls like tiny white flags, like a flock of angels, she felt as if the buoys floating on the water were bobbing around inside her, little capsules of joy.

"Hey, give us a hand?" Phil cuffed her hard on the arm;

she could barely feel it through her thick sweatshirt and slicker.

She took a deep breath, filled her lungs with salty air and pungent fish perfume and, stuffing her hands in her overall pockets, went back inside to work.

———

Billy admired her quietness, her white-blond eyebrows, her tall, strong body. He boasted to his friends how easily she lifted the heavy, ice-packed crates of fish. Billy, too, was big; even stretching herself to her tallest, the top of her head only reached his ear. For the first time in her life—on the docks and with Billy—she felt comfortable with her body. It was as if she'd been living among Lilliputians and only now was in a world properly proportioned.

Billy liked her scruffy from work, sleeves rolled up to reveal bruises, blood under her fingernails. He shook his head at the flowery print dress she wore for their first date and gave her some of his oversized jackets and white shirts, his straight-legged cords. "See," he said, turning her to face the mirror. "You're so sexy when you look tough." She didn't see "sexy," just the contrast of the dark men's clothes with her thick, paintbrush-straight, white-blond hair. Billy liked it when she wore her hair down, and he liked when she plaited it into a long braid he swung like a rope to tease her.

Now he jumped out of his truck and enveloped her, his mouth all over her face like a puppy's. She laughed, pushing him away. He wore a blue wool cap, a cap that contained in its smell the secrets of the sea. His eyes had seen horizons she could only imagine, and his salt-roughened hands, which touched her so gently, had battled with shark and tuna and swordfish and cod.

Molly grabbed her duffel and climbed in, pushed aside the nest of seaweed-encrusted coils of rope, metal buckets, and other gear. The seat springs bit her bottom, as they turned down a rutted road.

"Don't expect too much," Billy said. While he and his brother were away, Billy had rented out his house and only just reclaimed it; Molly was moving in sight unseen.

The road began to wind through forest with taller trees than any Molly had seen before on the peninsula. "Pretty," she said. The light, sifting through branches, was as hazy as gauze.

"It's a bitch to clear through this shit, let me tell you," Billy said as the trees gave way to bramble.

"Jonah knows I'm coming, doesn't he?" A nine-year-old boy; what would a nine-year old be like?

"He's stoked. I told him how terrific and gorgeous you are."

"Oh Billy, now he'll be disappointed."

"You're an idiot, you know that?" Billy said. They took a last turn, and she saw a grassy clearing and a weathered bungalow fronting the bay.

Molly took in the expanse of water, the brackish line of seaweed and shell, the short pier and small boat. "It's paradise!"

"You're sure not going to feel that way when you see the inside." Billy took her hand. "Remember, this was just a fishing shack in the 1920s."

Billy had told her his house was in a small community of fishing families, but she could make out only one house in the distance. "It's so private."

"That's why it's worth a fortune now." He pushed open the door, its screening ripped and sagging, and waited for her to precede him.

Molly took a step back. "You'd never think of selling, would you?"

Billy took a moment to answer. "I guess not. But the money is pretty tempting. The neighbors on both sides are in contract."

"They have to be crazy to give this up."

Billy touched her cheek. "Come." The door opened directly into a narrow pantry and square kitchen. The ceilings were low, the wallpaper a faded flower pattern, and on the walls flanking a tiny porcelain sink were open, wooden shelves. Framed photos were grouped on the wall, faded shots of men standing in or around water and boats. Molly followed Billy into a narrow corridor that opened into a living room and a set of uneven stairs to a second floor. She had never been inside a building so old.

"Jonah, get your ass down here!" Billy shouted.

A pair of sneakered feet came stampeding, and a tall, skinny boy skidded to a dead halt, slipped, and fell. Billy let out a guffaw.

"Billy!" Molly reached out a hand to Jonah. "Are you OK?"

The boy made an indecipherable gargling noise. He had the same square and stubborn jaw as Billy's, but his brown hair was light where Billy's was dark, and his blue eyes were ringed with envy-inducing lashes. He began to pick at a scab on his elbow.

"Stop," Billy said. Blood oozed from the scab. Jonah examined it with satisfaction.

"Would you like to show me your room?" Molly asked.

The second floor was two small bedrooms tucked under dormers with a bathroom in between. Billy's faced the bay, while Jonah's fronted the forested area through which they had driven. Cut-out photos of sharks, dolphins, and whales papered his walls.

"I like dolphins and whales, too," Molly said. "Sharks, I'm not so sure."

"This is a hammerhead," Jonah stroked the glossy paper, "and that's a great white. Did you know they mostly hunt at night? Whales are my favorite. I know someone who saw one from the beach."

"Have you ever gone whale watching? We could do that sometime."

Jonah shrieked and raced back downstairs. "Billy! Molly's gonna take me whale watching!" Jonah wasn't going to pose a problem at all, Molly thought. It's like we're already a family. She wrapped her arms around herself and gave a little squeeze. *Lucky, lucky, lucky.*

————

"I haven't been able to get you to myself since you moved in," Billy said as they sat side by side on the dock a week later, Jonah at a sleepover. Molly had been afraid Jonah would resent her; instead, he couldn't get enough of her. She thought it might be because she could cook. The way he and Billy threw themselves at the food she prepared made it clear how they had been faring since their parents died.

The water was spotted with sunset, the sky pale over rose-tinged clouds hanging just above the horizon. Molly slid her hand through the water, still warm from the day's heat, and tapped her heels against the dock. Billy rested his head on her shoulder. A feeling like honey spread through her body.

"What do you want more than anything else?" she asked.

Billy thrust out his lower jaw in the way he did when concentrating. "Me personally? Not something like world peace?"

"Right." Molly smoothed the wiry black hairs on his forearm that went every which way. He leaned back on his elbows. "What do I wish...I wish you'd come here and let me put my arms around you."

Molly obliged, her back against his chest. He placed his hands over her breasts.

"Holy Mother of God." His breath on her neck was moist and warm.

"Billy, I'm serious."

"So am I."

"Answer my question."

"OK." His hands on her breasts went slack. "I'd like to have enough money, so I wouldn't have to worry."

"That's reasonable." Molly waited for him to ask her. She wanted to tell him how, with him, she had everything she'd ever wanted, especially what she hadn't even known she wanted.

"It might sound reasonable, but it isn't. You think if you work hard you automatically get ahead, but that's a hoax."

"How do you mean?"

"My parents were always thinking, maybe this time we'll get ahead of the bills. But if we got ahead one season, we fell behind the next. The ones born ahead stay ahead. People like us race like crazy their whole lives and barely stay in place." Billy made a sweeping gesture at the opalescent sky. "This is all wasted on us. We're too busy worrying about how we're going to feed ourselves, repair the roof. But if you had enough money, can you see how everything would be different?"

Molly had grown up in a middle-class family up island; she had never known true want. She squeezed Billy's arm. This wasn't the moment to talk about her happiness. She'd keep it to herself, husband it like the conch shell they'd discovered on the beach.

Later, when they were in bed and Billy asked her why she'd asked him such a strange question, she told him she'd been reading a fairy tale, the one where the fisherman catches the golden fish and throws it back in exchange for having his wish come true.

———

By October, tourists had abandoned the area, as had the warm weather. The air drew sharp and cold, and there were two hurricane warnings, Abbot and Becky, neither of which amounted to anything. At the market, Vince told her that they would be cutting the hours back to just weekends until spring. It was what they did every year, but she hadn't known. Seeing her face, Vince kept saying how sorry he was.

She'd talk with Billy about applying to the Kmart for holiday work, Molly thought, though it would mean a thirty-minute commute. When she reached the clearing behind the house, she was surprised to see an unfamiliar car, a white compact, out of place besides Billy's beat-up truck. As she pulled alongside, she spotted a decal for Shore Realtor. Her breath seized.

She ran her eyes over the house, at the curled-up shingles, the mold darkening the top of the door under the eaves where sun didn't reach, the sagging wooden steps. The house canted slightly, but its small proportions were reminiscent of fairytale cottages, dormers like jaunty eyebrows over the windows.

Billy stopped in midsentence as she walked in. A man, dressed in a soft charcoal V-neck sweater, rose, hand outstretched. "Theodore Miloxi." His face was thin and very tan, a few age spots gracing his cheeks.

Molly sat next to Billy. She couldn't read his expression. From outside came the cough of an outboard motor.

"We were talking about your lovely property here," Miloxi said. "Billy tells me you're opposed to selling."

Molly felt her face heat and shot a glance at Billy; he picked up the white rock on the coffee table they used as a paperweight and began shifting it from one hand to the other. Molly turned back to Miloxi. "It's not my call."

"Billy cares what you want," Miloxi smiled. "How can I change your mind?"

"It's been in Billy's family for generations. It's his legacy, his brother's legacy." Her words tripped over each other.

"Ah, sentiment," Miloxi nodded, as if saying, ah, foolish youth. "You could get something far nicer with what I would pay you. A beautiful new home where you could start fresh."

Molly's jaw set. Had Billy told him they had been talking about marrying, even trying for a baby? The motor coughed again, and through the window behind Miloxi's head, she saw a small boat passing by. When she said nothing, Miloxi continued. "My dear, there are very few parcels on the water that will allow me to realize my dreams, and I mean to have this one. I envision a development with a waterside park. It requires that I buy this whole stretch."

"Build around us."

Miloxi chuckled, as if amused by an adorable child. "I don't think so."

Billy stood abruptly. "We'll give it thought."

"The faster you sign, the more I'll pay. Hold out, and it will cost you." Miloxi moved swiftly across the room, shut the door decisively behind him.

"Oh my god," Molly breathed. "He was awful!"

Billy's face was flushed. "He's such a prick I wouldn't sell to him if I had a choice."

"But you don't have to sell, do you?"

Billy ran his hands over his face. "I'm just trying to be responsible. It would be the smart thing. I know you don't want me to."

"Billy, it's not my decision."

"We're together now, Molly. We decide together."

Outside, the boat motor abruptly died.

———

A week later she was slipping a lasagna into the oven as Billy strode in, cheeks raw from the wind. He held his wet boots off to the side as he kissed her.

"Smells wonderful," he pulled out a chair, legs scraping the linoleum. "Listen, Mike is going south next week. Maybe ten days. What do you think?"

"You'd be gone for ten days?"

"Maybe twelve. If it's OK with you."

"I applied to Kmart." When he didn't say anything, she added, "but they didn't call me for an interview yet."

"Maybe they'd let you hold off for a few weeks?"

"I thought you wanted out of fishing." She turned the oven dial and wiped her hands on the dish towel.

"It's a lot of money to turn down."

Only if there's fish, Molly thought.

"If we're not selling, I've got to fish until I figure out some other way to make a decent living."

As soon as Billy left, the weather turned cold. The ferocity of the wind came as a shock. It was an antagonist, a malicious spirit unleashing all its fury. If she forgot a hat, her hair was whipped into a cyclone of strands stinging her face. She tried not to think of Billy miles from shore, pitching on heavy seas, lashed by wind and rain. She tried not to think that it was her fault, because if it weren't for her he'd sell the house and have enough money to get off the water for good.

It got too cold and dark to take Jonah for a walk on the beach after school each day, so they stayed inside. She prepared dinner while he did his homework. He talked aloud as he worked, scrunching his face close over the paper, gripping his pencil awkwardly in his left hand. He talked through dinner, and he talked as they cleaned up, and he talked as she helped him prepare for bed. But then she shushed him and took a book from his bookcase to read aloud. He pressed so close he was practically in her lap, and she breathed his scent of eraser and bubblegum toothpaste. She missed Billy and she knew Jonah did too, but there was something special between them nurtured in the space Billy left behind. Sometimes she lay next to him after he fell asleep and listened to his breathing, imagining she was on the boat with Billy, lying together on the slicked-down surface, staring up at the stars, sharply etched in inky blackness.

All over town scarecrows appeared—an octopus reading a

prayer book on the church steps, a surfer in front of the sports shop. Jonah decided to be the Tin Man. They punched holes in cans and ran fishing line through, and then she stitched the cans to an old thermal shirt. She told Jonah that Billy wouldn't be home by Halloween, wanting it to be a surprise if the boat made it back.

After nine days out at sea, Billy got in touch to say they were heading home; the captain didn't want to take any chances with the impending nor'easter. On TV, the weather map appeared with blue-black Van Gogh swirls. Molly looked out at the bay being whipped by the wind and measured the distance from the shore to the house in her mind.

Halloween morning she drove Jonah to school. He was already dressed in his costume, clanking as she hustled him to the school building. The wind was so fierce she feared it would rip the cans right off. Around them ghosts and witches and Batmen were racing to get inside.

"I'm surprised they didn't call off school," a woman pulled her collar up.

"The school's the shelter," another chimed in. "They'll be safe here."

"It'll stay out to sea," a man said authoritatively. "The usual overhype."

The school doors closed behind the last child. Above, the clouds didn't seem to be moving, but from the direction of the ocean came a low keening sound.

———

Billy was cold and exhausted; his hands criss-crossed with cuts. His share of the take would be almost two thousand, but he'd never do this again, never. He'd had it. Some guys had salt water in their blood. They saved until they could get their own boats, captain their own crews. They loved seeing the sun set over infinity, the thrill of the chase. But it wasn't in him. Or, rather, something else was in him, something that pushed against those things, something he might call caution, or fear, or premonition.

He thought of Molly and Jonah, alone in the house. It was so dark it was hard to believe it was the middle of the day. Overhead was a thick, cottony gray mass; beyond, as if someone had drawn a line in charcoal, solid blackness.

———

As Molly drove home through the woods, leaves rained upon the car, and rain sounded hoofbeats on the hood. The bay was covered with roiling whitecaps, and the wind was so strong she needed both hands to open the kitchen door. She thought of Billy, the boat heaving beneath him, and, feeling herself sway, grabbed the doorjamb.

Water, flashlights, sandbags. She shut all the downstairs windows and then raced upstairs. Looking out at the bay, she was shocked to see the water was already level with the top of the dock. The rowboat!

She grabbed her rain jacket and ran back outside. The wind snapped the hood from her head; rain dripped down her neck. The dock was partially submerged, and the boat strained against its mooring. She should have tied the boat further up the bank. She grasped the rope where it was attached to the dock, and tried to heave the boat back up. She was able to move it a foot or so, but the wind was so strong the boat slid back down. Again she tried, edging backward up the bank, hauling with all her might, slipping into the bay, water up to her knees. The water seemed to be rising before her eyes. With a sob, she let go.

In the tool shed, fifty-pound sandbags listed in a dust-covered stack, but after her summer hauling fish crates, these she could manage easily. She carried them one by one and lined them in front of the house, then stacked two more layers.

Back inside, she piled what furniture she could onto the kitchen table and the living-room couch.

The lights flickered and she held her breath, but they stayed on. She grabbed toiletries and underwear, and stuffed a flashlight in her pocket. She hoped Billy knew the school was the shelter. She hadn't been able to reach him since the storm began.

———

Whipped by the wind and soaked to the skin, the crew brought the boat in on pitching waves. They unloaded the catch—that, or lose everything—then raced to their trucks. Billy turned on the ignition but just sat, shaking with chills. He blasted the heat and held his hands to the vent. The wind shook the Jeep, whistled through the windows. He had been in nor'easters and hurricanes before, but this storm seemed like another beast altogether.

He tried his cell again. No signal. He threw the phone on the seat. He should never have gone on this trip, never have left Molly alone with his baby brother. Rain slashed the windshield, and the inside of the window fogged up. He turned on the defroster, then pulled out, careening around turns, driving as fast as he dared. At the clearing, he saw that Molly's car wasn't there. He fought the wind and rain to the front of the house. The bay waters were already halfway up to the kitchen door. His heart caught in his throat: Molly, his magnificent Molly, had stacked sandbags across the base of the house.

———

They spent the night in the school, bedded down on a wad of blankets, Billy enveloping Molly and Jonah with his body. Every time Molly moved, Billy's arm tightened, as if he were afraid to lose contact. They awoke to a morning clear and windless, with an intense blue sky.

In the morning, after dropping Jonah at his cousin's house, Billy and Molly drove through town, skirting large puddles where the ocean surge had breached the road, and then headed toward the bay. Small branches were strewn everywhere on the dirt road; several times they had to get out and heave off a limb that blocked their passage. When they rounded the bend that opened out onto the clearing, Billy let out a cry. Large pieces of roof dangled over the upper windows. The dock was gone, the rowboat was gone. The front windows were blown out, pieces of glass strewn everywhere, sparkling in the indifferent sunshine.

———

The storm made everything simple.

Billy's parents had purchased flood, but not wind and storm, insurance. Billy filed a claim anyhow, but it was denied. The house would be lost if not fixed quickly, but an appeal would take years.

"There's no other way," Billy said. Molly nodded, pressing her fist into the space between her breasts, pressing the pain back into her body.

While they waited for everything to be finalized, they lived at a motel in town owned by Billy's cousin. Jonah frequently woke Molly with nightmares. She would stroke his forehead until he fell back asleep, then stand by the window listening to the sound of the ocean surf, a sound so different from the lapping of the water by the bay. Billy slept through it all, as if all his cares had been relieved, a weight taken from him.

The amount they got from the sale, though lower than it would have been had they accepted Miloxi's offer, seemed staggering.

"But this is crazy," Molly said. "There's not even much of a house left."

"It was always a teardown." Billy said. "The storm just helped it along."

They agreed to set aside a third of the money for a college fund and a third for savings and the rest to purchase a new house outright, all cash, no mortgage, because Billy's parents taught him that a mortgage was a noose around the neck. With no steady full-time jobs, a mortgage was unlikely anyway.

"I'm sure we can find something on the water," Billy said. But the broker, a local woman, just shook her head. "Not in this price range, Billy." It became clear, as they looked at one listing after another, that they couldn't afford even a distant view of water.

Days went by, weeks. "Stay as long as you like," Billy's cousin said, but they knew come summer she would need the income from the bungalow.

At last they settled on a small house on a slight rise of land not too far from the docks. The back deck looked out onto neighbors' yards, complete with trim lawns and wooden tables, chairs, and umbrellas. This could be anywhere, Molly thought, any suburb she'd ever been.

"You know, with sea level rise, it's smart to be away from the shore," Billy said. "Eventually the water will come to us."

"We should get a boat, then," Molly joked, but the words burned as they left her mouth. They had never found their rowboat, just a washed up piece of the rope where it had severed.

When they brought Jonah to see the house, he took in the close-by houses, the manicured lawns and asphalt, and turned to Molly, his expression troubled. She pulled him to her before he could say anything, and rested her head on his. "I know," she whispered.

They got him a puppy from the Animal Rescue Center, a

little black mutt he named Licorice, and on weekends went for walks along the ocean or in the woods. Billy found a job with a landscaping company, and when it was warm enough they turned a patch of soil for a vegetable garden. They told themselves they would have picnics at the lighthouse come summer and go cranberry picking in the fall. But it wasn't the same, though none of them would say it out loud. As if they had made a solemn oath, they never talked about the storm, or about their old house.

One day, Molly drove back through the woods to the bay. It was early spring, light dappling through trees just beginning to bud. She lowered the car windows and the air rushed in, fresh, smelling of damp soil, reminding her of the early mornings when she would go outside in her pajamas with her coffee cup, the ceramic warm against her hands, the grass cool against her bare feet. But when she rounded the bend to the clearing, an enormous new house blocked the view. A berm had been created fronting the shore, and the ground was covered with bright-white crushed rock. She did a quick U-turn and drove away.

Jonah and Billy were outside throwing a Frisbee with Licorice. The dog leaped high, mouth open, as if hungry for air. She didn't mention where she had gone.

The fish market expanded to four days a week, and most mornings she walked to work along a route linking a patchwork of small open spaces through the residential area. Anticipation built for the moment she would emerge from the clusters of houses to the sight of marinas and boatyards, to men with shaggy hair wearing coveralls and rubber boots, to the reflections of boat masts like ribbons on the water.

In the fish house, she stood inhaling the odor of ice and chill and salt, then took her apron off a hook and slipped it over her head. Fish were waiting, piled in heaps, ready for packing. Their scales were glistening, their eyes searching for home.

Subscription Life

BY MARIE VIBBERT

The worst thing about selling out is liking it. I love my duckie shower curtain and my high-ceilinged apartment with its faux antique fixtures. Everything smells new but looks authentic, not like Mom's Thomas Kinkade Village with the poured concrete "cobblestone." NoLabel put in the work to build a detailed environment. The apartment floors creak like they ought to, (but only in less-traveled areas.) The doors have seeded glass transoms over them. My mailbox is brass filigree, and the front door locks with a real metal key instead of tracking my biometrics. It feels important in my hand, heavy and smooth.

I step outside and there's a man, gaunt and dressed in layers of mismatched clothes. He sits on the stoop next door, wrapped in a comforter, a paper coffee cup in hand. He lifts his cup in toast. "Welcome to the neighborhood."

"You live here?" I ask. I sound stupid.

"Precisely here," he winks.

Of course. NoLabel is an open community. It's why I chose it. No patrolled border, no gate over the entrance roads. Homeless people are safe here. My subscription fees, my life-time contract, pay for that safety. A knot of guilt lets go in my gut. I'm not a traitor to all the people who can't pass the entrance requirements. I'm part of the solution.

He tells me his name is Doug. I tell him I'm on my way to my first day at work.

"All days are the first day; you'll never wake to the same one twice." Doug gestures down the street, like a king preparing the way for his next supplicant.

I feel blessed by his wave. Set off on an adventure. I'm looking forward to spending mornings sitting on the stoop with Doug, trading philosophical thoughts. Maybe if I tell Mom about him, she'll stop saying I'm wasting my degree.

Ruthie's Things is around the corner and four doors down, flanked by other picturesque shops with a single story of apartments overhead. The walk is pleasant. People come and go with pets and strollers. There are young trees regularly spaced with adorable wrought iron fences around them.

Selling out is a privilege. I passed a heavy credit check and had to prove four lines of American citizenship in my family. This is why most people associate Subscription Lifestyle communities with polite-hateful racists. Why I'm still not sure I did the right thing.

The shop has its door open to the street, the big brass bell hanging dormant, so I knock on the frame as I enter.

A slender Black woman, with light brown curls, pulled back in an orange scarf is frowning at a folding card. She waggles her fingers, frowns some more, and drops the card on top of an open box. "Welcome to Ruthie's Things. I'm Ruthie."

"Really?"

She nods slowly, lips rolled in. "They name the store after the manager in every city."

Maybe manufactured authenticity is still, in a way, authentic. "I'm Joan. The agency said you'd be expecting me?"

Ruthie shows me the dishes she is unpacking. The store is intended to feel like a second-hand shop, but all the items are new. The plates are all different patterns, but only three sizes, designed to stack well in the box. The card shows how Ruthie is supposed to set them up on the distressed sideboard. The design looks random. It might be random.

Arranging the dishes is fun, like solving a puzzle.

"I'm leaving the instruction card out," Ruthie says with a fierce smile. "It's a silent protest."

Ruthie's snark adds that touch of realism I was missing. NoLabel welcomes irony at its own expense.

———

At home I have trouble undressing, knowing there are cameras recording me for consumer research. They say they blur the privates automatically, but I still change for bed inside the shower stall.

Yesterday I threw out the last of my old clothes. I can only have NoLabel items in my apartment, in my drawers. I feel silly, like I'm in costume. Like the cameras are inside my clothes. I walk from the bedroom to the kitchen and back in my new yellow nightie. There's no one here. The temperature is comfortable and the nightie slippery. I curl up on the quirky mid-century sofa and open my phone to read the news.

Except I can't find the news sites I like. The social justice librarians working group is a 404. *Marvel* movie gossip is still there. *Open Science* forwards to the *Fox News* science page.

I feel more watched than I did changing clothes.

———

Ruthie is working on inventory from a paper ledger. What an affectation.

"Why did you subscribe?" I ask.

"There's a choice?" Ruthie nibbles a pen with pink feathers dangling from it. She crosses something out.

We haven't had a customer all day. I fiddle with the duster. "As a librarian, I helped people find jobs, take skill courses, fill out resumes. I helped the rare, beautiful enthusiast research a topic. It felt so concrete."

"And now you test-drive toothpastes and next year's fashion colors." She shrugs, flipping the page. "It's concrete."

Ruthie's my boss. I don't want to press the issue. I dust and explore the more interesting items, like the hall tree or the collection of Victorian stereoscope slides. They feel real. I circle back to Ruthie. "It's just… I knew they'd block some sites, like rival companies maybe, but it bothers me I can't get *CNN*."

"They built everything in this neighborhood, and you think they let any information they don't want in?" Ruthie starts muttering about IP protocol and firewalls and other things from her former life as a networking technician.

I should change the subject. Be content with what I have. I asked for it. I do enjoy looking through the cute, kitschy things in the shop. It's novel—for now. Dog-shaped creamers and fish-shaped lamps. A long tray of costume jewelry.

I'm shifting the window display an inch to the left when I see a woman, disheveled, wearing layers of dirty hoodies, creeping along the other side of the street, looking anxiously around. She looks half-starved.

"Hey, Ruthie? Is there any food in the shop?"

The ledger slaps shut. Ruthie comes up behind me. "Damn. Doesn't she know where she'll end up? Damn. Maybe…" Ruthie dashes to the door and freezes there.

A police car has come into view. The fragile-looking woman hasn't seen them yet, but Ruthie and I have. I'm wondering why Ruthie looks so afraid. Would the cops stop us from giving away food?

The woman peers nearsightedly at a selection of event posters stapled to the telephone pole across the street. I hear the car doors slam, and the cops are running, hands on their guns.

The woman drops one of the bags she's carrying as she takes off. The cops give chase. Ruthie's arm is hard across my chest. "Don't," she says. "It's already over."

Ruthie's jaw trembles. I don't understand. "It'll be all right," I say. "We're an open community."

Ruthie looks at me like I said the Earth is flat. "How new *are* you?"

"I picked NoLabel because it's an open community. No locking the world out."

"There's only one community company," Ruthie snaps. "They bought each other and merged, and there is only one. NoLabel is UrbanSophisticate is Calling Woods is Trucktopia."

I don't believe her. She's angry. "I have a cousin in Trucktopia. It's nothing like this."

Ruthie makes a futile gesture. "The same anti-vagrancy laws they have everywhere else apply here." She goes back to the register, muttering, "I wish we'd seen her soon enough to hide her."

My stomach hurts. I'm thinking about the work camps. They say it gets so hot in those tents, and people die waiting for food. I read about it in the news sites I can't get to now.

"Come on," Ruthie says, "We have four more hours of looking busy to get through."

The things in the store are awful, calculated props. The things someone who has never been in a second-hand store thinks a second-hand store would have.

———

I turn the corner onto my street, and Doug is on the stoop next to my apartment's door like usual. He's reading a paperback book. A cardboard "Please Help" sign leans against his leg. Something flat is in front of the sign, bracing the bottom edge. I walk closer, slowly.

A cigar box. Where could a person even get a cigar box in this day and age? I only recognize it from movies. It's the sort of thing you expect the character of the homeless man in the movie to own, but it isn't the sort of thing anyone can actually get.

Doug is absorbed in his book and doesn't notice me staring. I feel like an actor waiting for a cue. I can't bring myself to walk past him.

A police car rolls down the block. I'm angry, watching it.

Angrier when Doug looks up from his book, raises a hand, and the cop returns his wave.

Doug is looking at me now, confused.

I guess that's my cue. I approach.

Doug holds his book closed over one finger. "The neophyte returns. They say work connects a person to her community."

I stand in front of him. I can see he's wondering what's wrong with me. He's also trying to maintain the same aloof, cheerful expression.

I say, "The police chased a homeless woman away from the shop today."

Doug's face is still. I want him to explain. He doesn't. I can't take the uncomfortable silence. I ask, "Where do you live, really?"

"I hope that woman is all right," he says.

"They didn't wait a second to chase her down. She wasn't doing anything. You're visibly panhandling. Cut the bull. What are you? A spy for the company?"

He grimaces. Ducks his head, forcing me to lean close to hear him. "I can lose my job if I break character."

He raises his eyebrows and leans back.

"This is your job? You get paid to impersonate a homeless person? Why? For…for local color? So people like me…"

He throws his hands in the air. "What did I just say?"

The real panic in his voice stops me. I'm not mad anymore. I'm not sure what I'm feeling.

Doug settles back on his elbows. "Here's an ethics question for you: when is it permissible to deceive? For money? For gain? What about for basic survival?"

I wonder where he lives. I wonder if he has stacks of philosophy books and orders to spout wisdom. I walk, silently, to my door. I put the real key in the lock, and pause. I take it out again.

The lock isn't real. The door opens anyway.

———

NoLabel keeps a storefront for customer service on Town Square. It has a funky pink awning with green piping. It could be a cupcake shop. There's a virtual gym on one side of it and a popcorn shop on the other. I dream up a dozen lies. She's my aunt. She's a business client. I invited homeless people to meet me for a photo essay project.

I end up spilling out the truth, in halting, stuttering awkwardness. "Is there anything I can do? There's got to be room for one more Doug!"

The NoLabel rep is a blonde woman, her hair straw-like from too many years of styling. She wears a loose tunic over teal leggings and teaches yoga on Thursday nights at the community center. Her name is Avis. Her concerned face has a blankness to it, like she's waiting for me to finish. When I do, she says, "I understand. It's awful. But where does it stop? One more becomes two more becomes a thousand more, and then our beautiful community is a refugee camp."

"I'm not asking for two more."

"You don't understand. It's like… imagine our community as a person with a gun in each hand. Around us are a thousand other people, each holding a knife. We could reach out, but to do it, we'd have to put a gun down, you see?"

It's the most idiotic bullshit I've ever heard. "I signed my contract expecting an open community. Those exact words were in the sales language."

Her lips tighten. "If you read the contract, 'open community' is defined very clearly." She brings up the paragraph for me. Party of the first part and party of the second part and the parties of the third part...

I have to go over it a second time, like an algebra word problem. "This...it's saying we aren't open at all. It's taking that phrase and making it mean that we're allowed to have registered guests visit."

"It's more than that. We are a permeable community that acknowledges the importance of cross-community ties with *cultural equals*."

She puts so much emphasis on the words they become a euphemism. The silence is uncomfortable. I can't think of anything to say. Avis flicks the text away. "I think what you really need is an altruism outlet. Have you considered volunteering for street cleanup?"

———

I don't have much left after buying a NoLabel wardrobe and furnishings for my apartment. My salary at the store is only a few dollars more than my monthly subscription fee. "Fun money" they call it. It's enough for one meal out or a movie ticket.

I sell my retirement account. I won't need it if I stay with NoLabel for life. I reserve the community center and make flyers and bake cookies, using up my entire month's food coupons. My posters are more polished than the others on the phone poles. If the others are fakes, they are more believable fakes.

My subscription contract grants me the right to host events open to NoLabel subscribers. The community center is on the main square. Picture windows with gold swags look out on couples walking hand-in-hand, averting their eyes when I stare. The only pedestrian to return my gaze is a poodle, soft blond fur and understanding eyes. I get the feeling he would come in, if his owner wasn't tugging him along.

It's a half-hour past my meeting start time. Doug wanders in, takes a cookie, salutes, and leaves.

I watch him walk away across the square. I re-read my notes. Should I have made friends first? I'm still new here. An outsider. I feel clammy. Like my first high school dance. Alone, repulsed by my own repulsiveness.

I'm about to give up when Avis marches in, a folder high in one hand. "We care about your happiness here at NoLabel." She drops the folder on the table next to my pro-homeless fliers. "My superiors have approved a plan I think you'll love."

I don't trust her, but I look it over. I'm too polite not to read anything someone hands me, and my throat is tight with rejection. At least she came.

Avis' plan asks every member of the community to give up part of their grocery ration to serve pasta salad and hot dogs in Town Square on the first Saturday of the month. Community bus drivers will donate their time to deliver visitors from the Westlake Indigent Camp.

It's not a truly open community, but it's something. It's helping people. "You'd do this?"

"Of course! It'll be great for marketing. You'll see our way is both safe and humane. No reason to agitate." She says "agitate" under her breath, like my fliers and cookies are a bomb, primed to go off.

I nod, and thank her. I tell myself the meeting wasn't a waste, thanks to this. It still feels like giving up as I turn out the lights and stack my fliers on top of the cookie box.

Fragile, elderly people step off the bus with wide eyes. I see how beautiful the square is in their faces. I watch until they are all off the bus. The woman I saw arrested isn't there.

"We'll find her," the police chief assures me. He says they keep very good records.

The police help set up tables and walk around chatting. Ruthie donates dishes from the shop, and it's idyllic, everyone eating off bright ceramic plates in the park.

To wash up, we use antique-style wash tubs and a garden hose under the dappled shade of mature oaks. Doug dries his hands on a yellow gingham towel. "This feels better," he says. "I feel better."

I watch the real homeless watch him. He raises a hand, smiles. They avoid him. I feel the pressure to distance myself. "I'd think this would make you feel..." I can't say "obvious."

He drops his heavy hand on my shoulder. "We're working within the system."

It's too much like the accusations I heard from my friends when I signed up with NoLabel. I use putting my stack of dishes down as an excuse to slip out from under his hand.

He sighs. "Don't look like that. I have a degree in moral philosophy. Where else am I supposed to go?"

I want to ask what his dissertation was, but I don't. It might count as breaking character. I wash a blue bowl as smooth and flawless as the sky. Am I happy? Is it okay to be happy?

Doug waits with his towel to dry what I wash. "It might be a soulless corporation bringing us together as a community, but we still are a community."

It's true. Our guests are helping pack up, talking to neighbors I haven't met yet. It looks like a community.

My heart breaks watching the bus leave, but it's a good break.

———

Ruthie smiles beatifically when I enter the shop. "I haven't felt this good since I came here."

I don't want to break her peace, but I've been worrying at a thought like a sore in my mouth. "You said all the subscription companies are one company?"

Her smile intensifies. "Are you thinking what I'm thinking?"

I'm not.

She waves me to the back corner of the shop. Shielded by a Queen Anne hallway tree, she shows me her network connection, news from outside the corporate environment.

As I take her phone to scroll my old sites, she explains, "I've got contacts all around the state. We can get other communities to do the same thing we are!"

There's the headline. "UN criticizes Nest Corporation, owners of Kinkade Villages, NoLabel, and other subscription lifestyle communities, for human rights violations."

I feel nauseous. "Human rights violations?"

Ruthie frowns as I show her the screen. "I...stopped reading," she confesses. "It's too infuriating." She takes the phone back and tucks it in her pocket. "Don't depress yourself. We have a plan, now. It's one company. If one part of it agreed, they all should."

———

The delivery driver thinks it's cute I want to see where the dishes come from. Or he thinks I'm cute. I'm only allowed to see the packing room while he drops off our returned dishes. The packing room is enough. Frail women, mostly brown-skinned, mostly young, dodging around conveyor belts in Department of Corrections jumpsuits. The air is damp with the stink of unwashed humans. They are sweating. I'm sweating. They run like people afraid of what lingers behind them.

The driver returns with a wink and a pop of his gum. "Not very exciting, I told you."

"Why don't they use robots to pack the boxes?"

He shrugs. "Too expensive. Besides, they like saying it's all done by hand. Start to finish." He looks proud. Maybe he's seen this so long that it doesn't feel awful to him.

Dishes and tea towels disappear into identical boxes, some labeled "UrbanSophisticate," some "NoLabel," and some "Trucktopia." I hate that I care about this most benign of the lies, that I had purchased a unique lifestyle. Human feet and human hands on cardboard and concrete make a mingled sound like a swarm of insects walking.

————

Doug unlocks the empty storefront and lets me sit in his room lined in paperbacks. He has a chalkboard listing all the residents and their favorite conversation topics. It adds to the academic air, and the smell of paper dry-rot and chalk softens the new-sawn fiberboard smell of all NoLabel rooms. He kicks back grandly on his sofa, hands behind his head. "You're only upset because you have the luxury to be upset now your own needs are met. Others have suffered for your lifestyle your entire life."

I don't like that he's right. It was a geology professor, of all disciplines, who explained the concept of "energy slaves" to me. Thousands must live destitute lives to pay for the energy consumption of each first-world person. I start to explain it to Doug, but then I remember he has an advanced degree, and I'm afraid I'll sound ignorant. "I want to know I'm causing the least harm."

He wags a finger at me. "Which is itself a selfish desire.

Either the individual matters, or the collective matters. Would you sacrifice the individual? There's only one of you."

"Oh, shut up," I say. I'm reading the titles of his books. More than half are alternate histories about wars, and this makes me feel superior, which I immediately feel guilty for feeling.

Chastened, Doug goes to his refrigerator and gets out two beers. "Don't shoot the messenger. You chose to be here."

"I didn't have much of a choice."

He presses a beer into my hand. "But you did have one. What were you afraid of, what were you escaping, when you signed your contract?"

The library was laying off. A corporation was bulldozing my block. My rent quadrupled to get me to leave. But I had other options. I'd visited apartments in areas not slated for "re-imagining." A second floor of an old house, redolent of burned oil, with the bathroom on a sagging, enclosed porch. Another apartment in a building that had had a fire, charcoal lines drawing the edges wherever the cleaners couldn't reach. I had enough savings, I could afford those places, find another job, work my way up again to a place like I'd had.

I hadn't wanted the struggle and the ugliness. I wanted artisanal cake and my conscience, too. I chose to be here, and now I had no money left for any other option. I sink into a beanbag chair and swig my beer. It's bright and hazy, like a summer day.

"Is it so bad?" Doug resumes his lounging on the couch. "We have art; we have conversation; we have a way to give back. Own your choices."

If I leave, my debt will go to my mother. It will be enough to ruin her. She'll end up sweating in a camp, wearing a jump-suit, no one caring that she has a doctorate in English literature.

If I kill myself...the same thing. I sink into the sofa next to Doug. We drink together, silent. Complicit.

The sidewalks end before the community does. The last two buildings end at the road with no room for a shoulder. I stand on that last sidewalk square, staring at the ugliest part of my community, where the four-story walls open to admit a single road.

The police pull up and ask me what I'm doing. They remind me there is a curfew in NoLabel. That they can't guarantee my safety this close to the unmanaged world. Everything outside the walls feels sucked dry by the life inside them. The pavement is cracked. Not decoratively so. I think about what Doug said. I think about my mother. She said there were still good jobs, that I just wasn't trying hard enough.

"I'm studying the view for a painting," I say, and hold still, concentrating. After the police leave, I step into the road.

I pass an empty building whose windows gape like hungry eyes. In the distance, a wall rises over the crumbling rooftops, separating another closed community. Inside the walls might be painted like forests or meadows or cityscapes. Outside they are gray cinder block. Fortresses unconcerned with their outside image.

It's getting dark and I know I'll be fined for missing curfew. Empty lots dot the landscape like the craters from a slow-motion bombing. A larger open area has turned into a trash dump, sloping down and away toward a stream. A group of people are on the sidewalk near this. They're sitting on overturned buckets, passing coffee mugs back and forth.

I get closer and the mugs are steaming. The people are sipping, talking. They're looking warily at me. They wear dirty white jumpsuits open and tied around their waists. There's a burner on the sidewalk and a giant pot of bright yellow broth. A woman sitting with her knees wide around this pot looks at me. "Sort trash for four hours for soup," she says. "Two hours for tea. We don't have coffee so don't ask."

What I ask is, "Where do you live?"

They study me with closed expressions. One gestures behind himself. There's a cluster of tents and structures in the dump. The shanties are cobbled together, but there is artistry in them. Craftsmanship. I pick out a woman in the group. She's about my height. About my coloration.

"Can I see your place?" I ask. She looks over my NoLabel clothes. I can tell she's wondering if I'm a madwoman or a murderer. I have nothing to offer her. Not on me. "I'm in the market."

I have to sit and talk about old movies for a while before she agrees. The tent is down the slope, along a path that snakes branch-like through mounds of trash and other shelters. The same duckie shower curtain I have is forming one wall. I laugh. I laugh so hard.

My host narrows her eyes. "Fuck you."

"No," I say. "It's lovely. Please." She grudgingly lets me inside. It's tidy, the ground covered in flattened cereal boxes laid in a herringbone pattern. It smells of earth and polyester.

She talks, nervously, to fill the silence. "I collect mylar, mostly. It's valuable stuff. Light. Good for insulating. They used to throw it away on candy wrappers, if you can believe it. I get twenty dollars a bag." She looks around like she wants to pull out a chair or offer a tray of drinks. A plastic milk crate sits on its side, half-full of tattered paperbacks. A Coleman™ cooler with a hand-crank radio on top serves as a bedside table next to a mattress. "So, that's the place. What do you want, anyway? My name's Maxine."

"You'll be Joan, now, if you want to be." I hand her my phone. She weighs it in her hand.

"Serious?" She shakes her head. She hands me her phone. We both realize we can't unlock them and trade them back. The screens light up the small room, making it cozy. Maxine was reading the social justice librarians board. I feel like I'm in a poem.

Maxine wipes her eyes with the back of her hand. "Charlotte runs the Wi-Fi. You'll see her crazy antennas in the morning. Give her any electronics you find. Mark's an artist. He wants dolls, especially garden gnomes. Tell them I'll visit, because I will." She lingers, not wanting to leave. "You're not...you're not doing this because someone is out to kill you?"

"I'm doing it for the Wi-Fi," I say, and she nods like that makes sense. It does. She leaves. Outside, footsteps move by with a rustle like autumn leaves. A child cries and is shushed.

Leash Laws

BY LISA C. TAYLOR

I perch in trees, like a squirrel or woodpecker, always looking over people's heads, spotting a bald spot or the flat part where their hat rested too long, warming the owner's ears. It's not like I'm nimbler than the others, just keener in my vision.

No one knows when his or her tree-time will come. Some folks seem to be glued to the earth with sinews underground like electrical wires. They talk to each other in a way that wastes language, not at all how animals communicate. I speak to Serge by humming even though his room is two doors down. He knows my language, came from a deciduous forest in Maine, and once helped a black bear find a suitable den for hibernation. Because he's mostly human, he doesn't need to hibernate. He used to stay at the St. Francis Shelter when the snows came. Like me, he dislikes human food except for berries and nuts, an occasional bird. Carol brings me granola in a plastic container. Glass is better because it's shiny, but the Strongmen won't allow it. They are used to making the rules, even ones that make no sense like when Carol can visit, and how much time I'm allowed in the sunroom where I can watch the jays raid the birdfeeder, see the cherry trees shriek into blossom. Carol always tells me I'll be home soon, and I think of my favorite maple tree. I don't wound it like the people who insert a metal tap in the tree's torso, hang a bucket to collect the blood. They don't understand that it is the sap that keeps the tree strong. It's important to keep one's fluids to oneself.

"Susan. Time for your pill."

Eliza is a Strongman even though she's female. She wears their uniform of blue cotton with white, whispery shoes. I know she wants to read my dreams so she can understand the language of plants and animals, but I don't let her. I've learned how to stick the pill in my left back molar, the one with a cavity. When I go to the loo, I spit it in the toilet and flush, watch it spiral down into the septic system, but I worry about fish losing their dreams.

I open my mouth like a good robot. Eliza put me on Step Five because I'm one of the well-behaved ones. I don't tie my sheets into knots or spit out mashed potatoes. As long as I can have some nuts and berries, I am quiet as a snake. It is April, and soon they'll open up the courtyard. Carol can take me outside and maybe through the gate to Keeper's Park down the street. You have to be a Six to go there but all it takes is opening my mouth and sitting in the semi-circle when Strongman Dr. Benton comes in.

"Click, clack, click. How do you feel about that, Susan?"

"Click, clack, clack. I feel fine, Dr. Benton."

There's a dogwood sapling outside the window that has been trying to get my attention. She shakes her greening limbs and tells me stories about the vole that lives underground. I promise to save her some water from the pink plastic pitcher by my bed, so her buds will open like promises.

Carol joined the human race when she was seven. She was never one of us, but it's safer that way. She speaks their language, so they let me go places with her. They punch in a series of numbers on the little metal door and then more numbers on the bigger door until it opens to the land of unfenced trees and boxy houses.

"My mother needs fresh air. Do you think I could take her to the park on Saturday?"

"Click, clack, click. Group goals, individual goals, Step Five."

"Great. I know she'll make Six by then. She's so pale, it will be good for her to get outside."

Kurt spoke that language, too. He kicked me out early. At first it felt dark and strange because I didn't fit into his forest, buried my roots beyond the park, next to the hiking trail where Carol got lost one day.

"Susan, why weren't you keeping an eye on her?"

Kurt had a kind face, promised to keep me safe when we met on the bench at Creeley Park. I told him about clear cutting, how they were mowing down my relatives with chainsaws, and he laughed, called me an environmentalist, a *tree-hugger*. He couldn't see the depth of the cuts, the muscles, and all those severed limbs strewn by the path.

"I love how you're passionate about this, Susan. I've met so many people who don't care about the Earth."

I married him because he promised there would be flowers and a trip to see the redwoods in Oregon. We had pink petunias and blue and yellow pansies in ceramic pots so we could plant them outside Kurt's house later. Kurt built me a little wooden bench in the garden, just like the one in the park.

"You can watch your roses and columbine now. You're a funny woman, Susan."

Then he thought I wasn't funny anymore, sometime after Carol was born. Babies can understand all languages. That's why they don't talk; they're too busy listening. Once they start to speak, they become self-absorbed like the rest of the humans. Their words start to click and clack, and they talk about weather and what kind of poison is best for getting rid of dandelions and ants. I wanted to keep Carol away from all that, but Kurt took her from me, put her in the red rectangular building with painted handprints on the wall, and children who brought their lunches in plastic boxes, didn't understand what the trees and dogs had to say.

Kurt doesn't visit me anymore. He married Adrienne, and they moved from the deciduous forest to a place called Stamford. Everything is oblong and gray there. Carol calls it *the city*. She's grown, lives with Seymour, her Irish setter. When I'm on Step Six, the Strongmen will let her bring Seymour to visit me, and we can talk about where he's digging and what the earth smells like in April after a rain. Dogs like to talk about smells since their noses are so close to the ground. If allowed to roam, they reminisce about all the animals that have wandered in their path, and I feel less lonely listening to them. Kurt thought that barking was the dog just taking a breath, a sharp intake of air, but I know better. Barking is conversation, a complicated social network that dogs develop to expand the confines of their yards and homes. Sometimes they escape, arrange to meet by the river or down the street, warn each other about the dreaded animal control officer with his green truck. Leash laws are incarceration for canines. I want to destroy all the leashes and short-circuit the invisible fences.

"I have to get an invisible fence for Seymour. They have a leash law in New Fordham now. A little boy was bitten by a pit bull and now everyone has to restrain their dogs. I know how you hate that, Mother."

Pit bulls are angry because people fear them. They don't want to argue or bite. Little boys and girls tease dogs because they weren't taught to respect animals, and a pit bull is like a wrestler. Broad-chested and muscular, they don't have to put up with anything. Some days I wish I had more pit bull in me.

When I make it to Step Six, they hold a party for me. There are cupcakes with pink icing and nuts and berries. I don't eat the cupcakes, but I drink three cups of a sugary punch the color of cranberries.

When Carol arrives with Seymour, I'm already dressed in my walking clothes, complicated buttons and zippered trousers. It's silly, but I need them to think I know how to look like them.

"You look wonderful, Mother. I like that blue fleece on you. It matches your eyes."

You never hear dogs or trees talk like this. They don't waste language like humans do, saving it to nudge each other or warn of weather or people. Carol drives a red car with gray seats. I buckle my seatbelt even though it makes me feel like the restraints are around me. I know Carol won't drive unless I do this because there's a law. Humans like to make laws about how fast you can go, what you need to do when you get to one of their lights or signs, and where you can park.

When we get to the park, I see all my friends lined up to welcome me. The curly maple has grown taller in my absence. Seymour nuzzles my hand because he knows what it's like to only see the outdoors through a square pane of a window or an electrified plot of land. Carol lets him off his leash, so he can run. He pees on the side of one tree and then another to let his friends know he's been here. When Carol takes out the picnic basket, the one with juice, nuts, berries, and some sort of seedy bread with nut butter, I practice the pill-in-the-molar kind of pretending.

"Delicious lunch, Carol."

"Thanks, Mother. I think you're doing so much better."

Seymour looks at me with his golden eyes, makes a little gurgling sound in the back of his throat and I hum in response.

When I stand up, at least a half dozen trees bend to point out the path ahead. Two red squirrels wait for me by the pines; I saved peanuts and sunflower seeds in my pocket. Now I know why they call these shoes sneakers. While Carol is pulling out the Gala apples, I make a run for it, swooshing over the pine needles and dirt beds, my eye on a patch of sky tangled up in the hair of the Douglas fir trees. The wind gives me a push, and I propel myself faster and faster, watching the smallest squirrel vault from one tree branch to another, poking his head against the bark. Carol is calling me, *click, clack, click, clack,* but it's not a language I understand.

Highwire Act

BY JOEANN HART

The lilting voice that fell like water from the loudspeaker every morning predicted an almost perfect day. "A sky as blue as my right eye," she called it. They have a way of letting us see the world through the odd detail. No matter. It's a blue sky, and I'm an industrious soul, so my thoughts turned to laundry. I'd done the wash days before when it first started to rain, then waited for a dry spell to hang it. And waited. The dome was supposed to be weather resistant but the drains are always clogged, so the weather has nowhere to go but through the wonky seams, and if untreated water touches my clothes, well then, I'll be in worse shape than when I started. The laundry was beginning to smell like a mushroom log but a few hours in the open rotunda would soon cure that.

I grabbed my basket and slid open the glass to the deck. The plexidome capping the rotunda was tinted pinkish-yellow from the sun and it felt good to stand under its glow. I took a cleansing breath in through my nose, then held it for a long moment before slowly letting it out through my mouth. The dome seemed to breathe along with me, expanding and compressing like lungs, as it regulated the oxygen of our living center. The deep vibration of the plexi was a perfect bass note to the piped-in tinkling of chimes. I took one more deep breath and set the basket down before pulling on my gloves. To protect against—what? And there my brain stalled as my healthy-mind kicked in, my years of training falling in step with my breath. Why worry about such things? Worry was a misuse of imagination, as a host once told me. It was best to forget why I should exercise caution when handling laundry, without ever forgetting that I should. We value mindfulness and positivity here at the center. Yes, laundry has to be done, but enjoy the moment. Live in the light, even in darkness. Find joy in your surroundings. Look out over the rotunda, but do not look down. Down is the past. Acknowledge other residents across the wide pit, standing on their decks, assessing the day, testing the air. Nod, smile. Take a breath. Give gratitude for the low volume of particulates in the air. Be thankful the power grid was working, without which we could not view our enlightened master in hologram form twice a day for meditation, but more important, power kept a floor of light suspended over the pit. If the grid went down, the floor disappeared, and the sight was horrific. There is no other word for it. If a blackout was expected to last more than a few hours, a giant canvas tarp has to be manually cranked over the dome to block out any natural light. Turning the rusty gears is not easy, but I crank with all the rest when need be. We put our own selves in darkness, but anything was better than seeing what was really there.

I remembered this guy, a real clown, someone new to the center, who, while we were turning the gears, told us that he thought the blackouts were done on purpose to keep us off balance. We had to kill him. But what was the point of remembering that? I brought my buzzing mind back with a few breaths, then tightened the gloves around my wrists. It was the perfect balance. I could attain equilibrium at will. My mind was my thoughts, and my thoughts created who I was. As the master often told us, "You can decide what to think about. It's all up to you."

It wasn't until I reached for the basket that I noticed Doniker out on his deck, abutting my own. "Oh," I said. "Oh."

He sat so still on his meditation pillow he seemed to be part of the building. Stillness was good. Most predators can not spot their prey unless it moves. They see not the thing itself, but the motion. I hoped I hadn't already disturbed him. His eyes were open as he stared out into the middle distance. He was centering well, but he did not look well. He had developed a bluish cast since I'd last seen him. When was that? When was the last time we could go outside? Again, I sensed my thoughts wandering and brought them back to my breath before I tripped myself up.

In. Hold. And release.

I only wished the weather could stay the way it was so Doniker could sit outside long enough to repair his damaged cells. But there was no point in wishing. It was going to be whatever it was going to be. Worry got you exactly nowhere. A trainer I once worked with taught me that worry was only a way to pretend you had control over what you don't. Amen to that.

I let Doniker be and went back to my laundry, bending with intention as I pawed through the basket. My head was lower than my heart, something we should strive for a few times a day, both physically and spiritually. "Lead with the heart, not with the brain," as the master always says. The plexi flexed and the chimes tinkled, but there was no human sound. All of us seemed as lost in our thoughts as Doniker. It was tempting to just hold my position but there was work to do. The laundry—my best calico tunic, my worst pants, my wool foot coverings, and the fine, impermeable film I wore against my skin—was tumbled together like a single, wet creature. Taking care to keep my spine aligned, I stood up straight, holding a damp foot covering. It was just like the ones on my feet, but clean, washed in the distilled rainwater collected from the dome and pumped right to the tub inside.

It was such an improvement from what it had been like before. What misery that had been, but I did not allow my thoughts to linger in that grim place. It could only drag me down. I glanced over at Doniker and took a deep, mindful breath. I clipped one foot covering on the rigging, then the other. The structural wires crisscrossed the domed rotunda from every one of the hundreds of cubes to another. A beautiful metaphor. "Think of your minds going out on silver cords," the master once said. "If you can separate your consciousness from your body, all your wonderful souls will be connected by energy."

And yet, here we were hanging laundry on those silver cords, because really, what else could we do?

A child warbled, the one who lived on the floor below. One of only two at the center. I got on my knees and squinted between the deck planks to see if the parents might let it out. It was so exciting to see a living, breathing young human instead of the jars some couples kept on their shelves. I wondered if it ought to be in some other, special place, to be on the safe side. For the child's sake, and for ours. A child sighting could trigger all sorts of useless emotions in even the most resolute. It was hard not to think of the future when confronted with the young, making it difficult to tend to the balancing act of the mind. To be wholly in the present. There was nothing to be gained by looking back in nostalgia, and everything to be lost by looking forward with dread. As was stressed in our training, the mind can live in the past, it can project into the future, but it can only process the now. I was here now. I was fine now. I counted my breath to pull myself back to the moment.

In. Hold. Release. Again.

"Mariclaire?"

"Oh. Oh, Doniker."

He did not look my way. I crawled over to him. We were separated by a wall of wire mesh, and I leaned in close and spoke through it.

"Hi, Doniker. It's good to see you outside."

"Mariclaire," he whispered, his eyes still focused on a point in the middle of the rotunda, exactly where the master would appear later for centering down, helping us shut out our worldly cares for the night, complete with sedating incense and the hypnotic hum of chants and singing bowls. "Mariclaire," Doniker said again, and my mind snapped back to the present.

"What is it, Doniker? I'm right here."

"Good-bye," he said, still not looking at me. "I'm dying."

That was a shock. I counted my heartbeats for a full minute before speaking. "We're all dying," I said, forcing a chuckle. "Do you mean to say you're dying right now?"

He didn't answer, nor did he move his eyes or change his focus. He was already far along.

"Should I do something?" I asked, my voice betraying the knot of bile I felt rising in my throat. "Do you want me to help you?"

He did not respond. I looked around the rotunda, but all the people who had been outside just a moment before were gone. Could it be healthy nourishment time already? I hadn't heard the gates open. It didn't matter, there was no way I could leave now. This was my duty. I'd been called upon to spot Doniker, to make sure his transition went well. I began mumbling a mantra that a trainer had taught me long ago: *Panic may cause the situation to get worse. Panic may cause the situation to get worse. Panic may cause...* The prescribed steps came to me, and I lowered my voice. "Doniker, should you go get your MedKit? It can help..."

He shook his head, no.

"You're not in pain?"

He shook no again, and I felt my breathing slow, returning to normal.

"Then you're probably not dying," I said. "Are you concentrating on your breath? That will get rid of any feelings of impending doom."

His head lowered in response, and his gaze shifted down to the hologram floor of the rotunda. He seemed to be seeing right through it. Why would he do that to himself? He was too young. Mid-twenties, at that. He still had his hair. I didn't want to seem judgmental, but he had not rebounded from the loss of his wife the year before. He had not worked hard enough on processing his grief and moving on. I'd watched as he'd tenderly placed her body into the platform chute, the same foul place where our urine-soaked shavings and other messes were swept off each day. He cried openly when she disappeared through the hologram floor, and our eyes locked when we heard her land in the absorbent muck below. He had not really been himself ever since. He paced day and night. It did not speak well of his character or his training. It was a wonder he'd been allowed to stay.

"I'm hanging laundry," I said. "If you want me... If you want me to do anything, anything at all, I'm right here."

I stood up and clipped a piece of impermeable sheath to the rigging, then lifted my tunic from the damp pile, but the fabric began to separate from its own saturated weight. Using my most gentle touch, I tried to extricate it from the tangle of other wet things, but the more I pulled, the more it disintegrated in my hands. I had let it sit too long. The acidity of the water had already begun its work and there was no stopping it.

"Damn," I muttered.

"Don't," whispered Doniker, and he closed his eyes.

"Oh. Sorry. Sorry about that negativity. It was just… It was just that I really liked that tunic."

Doniker groaned, and his chin fell to his chest.

"I know I shouldn't get so attached," I said. "I know that only leads to a world of hurt."

A shadow passed over the dome, a flying, living thing. And then it was gone. Before I knew it, tears burned on my cheeks. Breathe in. Exhale. Hold. Again. Count the breath. Count some more. If Doniker was determined to leave there was nothing to be done. There was no point in focusing on a problem when there was no solution. It was what it was.

"Doniker?" I said, but he did not respond. His color had gotten worse. He did, in fact, seem to be dying in the here and now, not in some abstract future. My pulse accelerated. I had never done this on my own before, assisting in a death-affirming action. It was harder than I could have imagined. I began to sway back and forth, then sideways, a self-comforting trick I'd learned along the way. Maybe I should go inside and get my own MedKit, and find something in it to ease his transition. But by the time I ran in and got it, he could be gone, and I had an obligation to stay with him. That was the most important thing. To be with him now.

The wire fence between us could not be accessed, so I got back on my knees to be eye-level with him and that's when I noticed some corroded mesh. With the clever use of a clothespin I was able to pry apart enough wire for a hole big enough for my arm. After weighing the consequences, and there were many, I removed my glove and squeezed my arm through the opening, pressing my torso hard against the wire, extending my arm until I could touch his shoulder.

"I'm here, Doniker," I said. "It's Mariclaire." My training kicked in and I began to breathe slowly and deeply from the abdomen, concentrating on a long out-breath and letting the in-breath take care of itself. It would all take care of itself. We stayed like that for a good while, his breaths coming weaker and farther apart. I could hear gurgling in his chest. In time, the meditation bell sounded, and gymnasts began swooping through the rigging, each on their own delicate trapeze, signaling everyone to come out of their cubes and onto their decks. Usually we meditated from behind our glass walls, but it was, as foretold, almost perfect weather. Funambulists skittered across the wires with their thuribles of smoke preparing the way for the master. A pinprick of white light began to pulsate under the dome and began to expand, brighter and bigger, filling the center of the rotunda, where the master slowly and completely materialized, a Tibetan singing bowl in his lap. He was rotating a leather mallet along the rim, producing the range of tones needed to restore our vibratory frequencies and bring us into harmony.

With a few breaths of absolute attention to the sounds, I attained the no-mind we all craved, and it was just at the moment I was about to drift off, that Doniker's earthly weight began to tug at him. His realm was shifting. As we had been taught in the rare event we might want to release ourselves from our bodies, he had arranged himself to fall forward towards his open chute, head first. With a blinding flash, the hot-white light was on us, and the master was directing the center's attention to Doniker's journey. "We do not leave this world," he intoned ever so softly. "We only go back to it."

There was an expectant hush. As Doniker slid from my touch, I grasped hold of his tunic, unwilling to let him go, but he continued to fold away from me. The protective film on his shoulder fell, exposing his bare flesh, revealing a tattoo so small only I could see.

Resist.

Oh, Doniker. Poor boy. You spent all your energy with struggle, when, with a little more training, you could have learned to breathe through it. The tunic unraveled in my bare palm as he gently fell onto the chute, a transition of merciful seamlessness. He slid down its short distance, and then, abruptly, went into a stunning freefall, four limbs akimbo. The audience gasped as Doniker disappeared through the bright hologram floor and into the pit, and it was just at that moment our compassionate master clanged sharply on the singing bowl so we would not have to hear him land.

Why Mama Mae Believed in Magic

CYNTHIA ROBINSON YOUNG

Once upon a time not so long ago, when there were good times for white folks and the worst of times for any one of us who were forced to be around them, there was magic. We needed it. We had been captured by a nightmare from which we could not awake. But I brought my magic with me from the Ivory Coast, keeping it close and locked inside where no one could take it away. Not unless I gave it to them to hold. My mother gave it to me in my nightmare, the one I dreamed the first night I knew I was separated from her forever. In the dream she told me sometimes the owner had no control, but sometimes one could chose the magic, and what kind of magic it would be.

When I was on that slave ship, I saw our people flying over the waters. It was when the white men wanted our mothers and daughters, not caring if we were bleeding or nursing or whatever. It was the only time they released us from the chains dragging us down, to drag us up from below to the deck at night. That was when I saw our people flying between the stars, slicing through the blue-black sky. Starlight and moon-light shone on their black bodies and the black sea. I knew where they were going. They were flying back home to their families in Africa. I saw them beaconing me to rise up and follow. Oh, how I longed to join them, to fly away with them, but I didn't have the kind of magic to rise up off of the ship deck to join them. I wish I did.

Before I got on this ship, I was in a room, still in my homeland, still with the rest of my kidnapped people, in a hut that was not a home. All I could see through the window was water and more water, the color of the sky when the sky was blue. It was our holding place until we got on that water that looked like it led to the end of the earth. I wish I could have found a way to release those shackles that connected us to each other. But that wasn't the kind of magic I had either. And now I have left my home, my land, and I am living on this water, moving farther and farther away from what I've always known since before I knew who I was. If I was not below, lying in vomit, in shit, in the shadow of death, a hell on Earth, so unimaginable I cannot bear to bring back the smells, the cries, the heat, then I was on the deck lying on my back, and the men were holding me down, pressing their stinking bodies onto me, stabbing the insides of me. I was only ten years old, not even old enough to bleed. That was when I saw the people flying. Only my eyes were free enough to follow them until they became shadows, and then they were gone.

———

I got to this plantation in 1849, when I was eleven years old. Now it is 1860. I have seen folks come and go, people who acted like family to me, who took care of me, and taught me how to not die inside when that was all I wanted to do. New slaves come and go all kinds of ways. They come in wagons sometimes. Then we know it was probably pretty far away because most times, they came in walking, limping, on blistered feet if they have no shoes, and most times they don't. Why white folks think they need shoes all the time but we don't, when we do way more walking in a day than they walk in a year, I'll never know. Kossula came this way with others from the homeland, not so long ago,

The night before the Lord's Day I always try to soak my feet in jimsonweed and boneset and comfrey I picked from the field right near my cabin, along with some red pepper Anna slipped to me from the main kitchen. Kossula made the bowl I soaked my feet in. That man sure did know how to carve anything out of wood, don't matter what.

After Kossula arrived in America from the same land I was from, he came straight to the plantation where I was in Alabama.[1] So he never left, never got sold, from what I know. We were together from one Easter to the next before I was sold to another plantation. When he came, he didn't know anything except the words he was speaking when they stole him away from his people. He tried to tell me about how he stayed in a hut, and when he said it was "Dwhydah," I remembered the word, and it made me remember everything I had tried to forget and everything I wanted to remember about home.

I helped him with words in America, like he was a bitty baby, but he picked up what he needed to say fast. The folks here? The ones who never saw our homeland because they was born here? They didn't want to give him any credit for really being smarter than them. Here he was, just got here and he didn't know nobody, but now speaking two languages! The others, they laughed at him, said, "You just an African savage! You don't even know nothin' about Easter!" Kossula said he wasn't no savage just because he came from Africa, that he knew about God, just nothing about His Son.

"Specially nothin' 'bout Him rising from the dead!"

But I never laughed because I came from there too. I remember who I am. But the others, they didn't remember much, if anything, about Africa, they been slaves for so long.

But I still remembered home. I think I loved him because he remembered home for me. He was Africa to me.

Kossula helped me remember who I really was; that I was not an animal who had babies just to have them taken away. My milk was for my babies, not the Missus' white ones sucking me so dry my babies could hardly live. And when I had to leave Kossula because back then, Black folks didn't get to choose nothing, didn't really have nothing. So there wasn't anything I could give him except some of my magic, but not directly. It was the only thing that was mine to even try to give, not even sure how it worked. But I believed in the dream. So I told him I would use his name to make it special.

``And how you going to do dat?" he asked me. "You did not even have the power to not be in dis place! I still remember where they hold me and my people. I still remember looking out dat door out of dat door was only water. I think, once we pass through dat door, how we ever gonna return?

"After we bought, they takee away my name. I wanted the white men to callee me de name my mama and my father gave me. But they say my name too crooked. So I say, 'you callee me Cudjo. Dat do.' But in Afficky soil, my mama she name me Kossula."

The name the white folks gave me is Mae. But Kossula, he isn't like me. He told our owner he could call him Cudjo when they couldn't say his name. But I didn't even get that. Why they call me Mae, I don't know. I said, "Kossula, you give the white man what he wants too easily." But all he cared about was going back home. He said nothing else mattered. So everyone called him Cudjo. But I called him Kossula. And he would always cry when I said it, like I was giving him a gift.

"Kossula," I said gently. "Your mama named you a great name. It cannot be for nothing that it means *my children do not die anymore*. I will find a way to make sure your name is something we never forget."

And then I never saw Kossula again. I went to another plantation in Georgia. About five years later, we was told we were free. I wanted to go back to that plantation to find him. But I didn't know where it was or how to begin to get back. I kept Kossula in my heart, but I went on with my life.

I think I was in my early twenties when I jumped the broom with a man named Josiah, a good man who always was looking out for me since the time I got to the new plantation until we was freed from it. And I'm thankful to God that I could finally have my own children and not worry about them being sold, or taken care of by some old gramma on the plantation while I was out in the fields, separated all day from them. I still cry for all my babies who came into this world, saw what their lives would be like, and decided to keep going to Heaven before they got to me. And all of them almost here, but then gone. I tried to hold on to them with the wisdom of the land. I spent my days searching for ways to keep my babies. I found squaw mint, purple plants shooting up to the sky; rue, blue green like the water; and tansy plant, yellow and hopeful. Even the seed and the inner bark of the cotton plant I picked for so many women to increase their milk was my enemy. None of these herbs wanted my babies to live.

I became obsessed with life. And finally my baby, Emmaline came. She stayed with me. I believe that was when the magic came to me—the magic I always knew was there.

All of that was a long time ago. I'm old now. I can forget things—anything I want to forget, things about what happened in slavery. I'm glad them memories are gone. But I remember what I want to remember, like my people flying, and like my promise to Kossula. In my dreams I see him as I saw him the last time, lonely and wishing for home, wishing for his mama, tears in his eyes. In my dreams he wanders through the woods, searching for his family, searching for Home.

I didn't forget my promise. I will never forget. I will keep

my mind on the magic. This is the magic I need to believe in—
to stop being a people who are losing, dying. This is the magic
I choose.

Kossula. Kossula. My children do not die anymore. Kossula.

---

1. In 1860, Kossula, born around 1841 in Bante, home of the Yorubas, was
    kidnapped from the Bight of Benin in West Africa, after the trans-Atlantic
    slave trade was abolished. At that time there were Africans, (Ghezo of
    Dahomey in Kossula's case) who opposed it as well, based on their under-
    standing of internal enslavement in Africa. It was "perceived as essential to
    their traditions and customs...[and gave African kingdoms] wealth and
    political dominance. To maintain a sufficient 'slave supply,' the king of
    Dahomey instigated wars and led raids with the sole purpose of filling the
    royal stockade...reports of his activities had reached the newspapers of
    Mobile, Alabama."

    Source: Hurston, Zora Neale. *Barracoon: The Story of the Last "Black
    Cargo"* (New York: Harper Collins, 2018).

Fourth and Most Important

BY NISI SHAWL

The fourth of the Five Petals of the New Bedford Rose,
Integration, is called by some its most important. Primacy
of place goes to the first petal, Thought, of course—but
linear primacy is deemed by practitioners of the Five Petals
to be overrated.

—From *"A Thousand Flowers of Thought:*
Schisms within the New Bedford Rose"

Willis loved to fly. Zooming on his sister's couch, his phone
tilted against a pillow so his shoulders stayed relaxed, he dived
up, up through the thinning atmosphere. On target? Yes! The
aluminum framing the entrance to his drone's dock sparkled
in the bright sun. The gossamer lines suspending the radio
repeater and dock gondola from Mx. Pickell's weather balloon
shimmered in and out of visibility against the dark blue sky.
They vanished as the drone swooped inside the dock and
dropped into its cradle.

Switching apps, Willis settled down to operating the dock's
waldos. This was nowhere near as fun as flying. But it must be
done; Mx. Pickell maintained this balloon and several neigh-

boring ones at their own expense, and in return for access, Willis and his cohort loaded and unloaded the packages Pickell and their cohort swapped back and forth. And covertly shipped a few other things.

Willis did wish he could see in the dock's darkness. The waldos' grips were Sensitech: they handled the drone's cargo expertly, seizing and releasing it with precision promised to plus/minus three millimeters and/or one gram. But the waldos couldn't tell him what rich people like Pickell were secretly sending each other. Maybe the same sort of stuff as he was, but it would be nice to know.

His crew's more-or-less legal additions to the drone's load came out last: Inca-derived, necklace-like khipus—threads knotted into messages passed between care collectives. The Antitrust Authority frowned on any direct, unlicensed communication between individuals or groups. Also social media posts, even though the computer "virus" SM providers had supposedly disseminated had been proven a hoax; the AA wanted to clamp down on them, too.

The pick-up bay of the dock held a neatly coiled incoming khipu, so he stowed that away first, then extended a waldo arm hopefully toward the transit bay. Empty. "Bloodclot!" He retracted the arm. Nothing to bring to another balloon. No excuse not to come back to Earth.

———

It's always been kind of a dirty word. True, Jung and other psychologists praised integration as a healthy goal. And civil rights activists pushed for racial integration in the 1950s and 60s, but in the 70s black power militants pushed back. Made it synonymous with selling out. In the case of the New Bedford Rose, while there's a whole petal named for it, it's still a problematic area. Integration of what? From what? Into what? How?

—From *"Dissecting the Five Petals of Thought"*

The transmitter was in the attic of his sister Flora's garage, and the driveway doubled as a landing pad. Willis ventured out to retrieve the drone well before she would have to leave for her shift at the plant. He carried the drone to his workbench in the basement. He'd left one in her way once, and Flora never let him forget it. "Almost made me late," she muttered at him every time she passed the couch on the way to shower.

The khipu was mostly gossip. Some clueful guesses about Mx. Pickell's payloads: stock tips, that sort of thing. The business of business is business, as a famous economist supposedly said. Though Willis was pretty sure there had to be more to it than that.

To his left, the steps down from the kitchen creaked under Flora's healthy weight. "Up early?" he asked, as her slippers scuffed across the concrete.

"What do you care?"

A legit question. She'd been instrumental in getting it going, but since the freeze on using her kinetic charging mods, Flora's contribution to the New Bedford Rose was mainly limited to Willis's couch and board. That and his access to her neglected copy of Skye's million-selling *Five Petals of Thought*, and a few other more obscure texts.

"Thought maybe you had time to help set up a cipher for our next message exchange."

"Nah." But his sister leaned over the bench like she was interested. "Stick to your system you got. Less confusing." The system she'd come up with. Flora was hella smart—too smart to be working in a slaughterhouse. But it paid better than teaching.

He twisted the dangling cords of the khipu into a single strand and tied it around his head, over his bandana. Flora watched him closely. "So what's bothering you?" she asked. "Your ex giving you grief for wanting custody of the therapy ferret? She went ahead and had it descented?"

Willis said nothing. Marnee was gone for good. He wasn't going to encourage his sister to talk about her.

Flora shook her head. "Whatever's got you worried, it's been eating at you a while."

Willis slapped his hands on the bench's smooth wood. "You wanna know what's buggin me? Tryin to figure out why all these rich people settin up the balloonnet. What they think they're gettin out of it?"

Flora tilted her head back and smiled at the basement's dusty rafters. "Well. That's a problem so simple it's got two solutions. All you have to do is pick one."

"What's my choices?"

"You could steal a loaded drone. Fly it down here and take a peek inside."

"Uh-uh. Less than zero chance of that. Too easy to be found out." It wasn't just the gossip he'd miss if his collective got kicked off balloonnet. Job postings, client ratings, Dinosaur Fat—the distribution matrix replacing Freecycle. Crucial benefits.

"Second choice is you woman up and demand they tell you."

———

In the US, it's $478,000. Singapore $696,000. That's all you
need to qualify. What's the distinction between being in the
top one percent versus the top five percent? Makes a difference to them but not much to us.

—From *A Young Socialist's Guide to
Understanding Inequality*

Willis picked his most efficient drone for the flight. No
guarantee Mx. Pickell would recharge it for its return trip. He
added his modifications confidently; he knew Pickell lived
within the transmitter's reach because he'd met them on a
regional nature excursion last fall, when the two of them were
assigned the same canoe.

Pickell had steered. Willis had spent as much time looking
back at them as he did watching the descent of the scarlet
maple leaves that matched their skin. Not a natural beauty—
not with all their implants and grafts—but awful easy on the
eyes. Which was a big part of being rich, as far as Willis could
see: never having to be ugly or stick out in any way unless you
wanted to.

So why ally yourself with outcasts like him? Why follow
the Five Petals? What did he and his crew and all the Rose's
other "overconnected" adherents have that rich people didn't?
That they couldn't buy? Because Pickell and their kind could
have hired people to circulate the drones. Volunteers like
Willis weren't strictly necessary. So why use them?

He finished installing the mic and auditory sensors and
went up to the couch to open the control app and enter Pickell's physical address. Along the obsolete freeway, cutting
across the overgrown high school playing field, above the
precariat soy farmers with their bandanas tied over their faces
for practical reasons, not just as a sign of solidarity.

The house was old. Cobbled paths converged on its
sunken patio. Willis circled twice. Between the paths lay green

gardens and trapezoids of bare brown earth, still damp from the morning dew.

He settled onto the patio and enabled the audio packet. The fresh twang of a screen door spring came with a chaser of bare feet rushing down back steps. A human hand darted through his visuals and turned him so he saw Pickell's face. Their lips parted and their eyes narrowed. "Antitrust Authority?"

"No. It's Willis."

The eyes squinted to suspicious slits. "Right. You never come here. Your rule. What's the matter?"

"I was wondering..." He'd made a bet with Flora he would do this. If he lost his nerve at the last minute, he had to ask Marnee for a pity fuck. "I was wondering what you ship. Why you do all this."

"Why I do all...What? Balloonnet? The drone routes?"

"Yeah."

"You sure you're not—"

"Check my load." A click and his belly opened to show them the khipu he carried. Pickell read it by touch.

"All right. The loads are nothing. Sourdough starter. Herbal remedies. The messages are free speech. As for what I want..."

"I'm old." They didn't look it. Money. "This might be my last chance."

"Last chance to..."

"My last chance to what we used to call 'Eat the Rich.'"

On Flora's couch Willis clenched his buttocks, squeezed his phone in his fists. Disconnects always threw him out. He wrestled with the dilemma, tried to grab it by the horns. "But *you're* 'the Rich.'"

"It probably seems that way to you. To me, well, it's normal to own a big house, keep horses, that kind of thing. So many people have so much more than me. *They're* the rich ones—they've got twelve hundred times my income. They're the ones we have to stop."

Willis felt his perspective shift. Pickell had lifted him. The sky wheeled, and the house's spruce-blue walls loomed suddenly nearer. "Long as you're here, can you come inside?" they asked. "I think I figured out a way we could expand balloonnet, make it a better alternative for us than what the AA sanctions."

We. Us.

"What way?"

"There'll be a lot more routes, a lot more balloons. They'll be the fashion. A status symbol. A lot more flying between them."

"My favorite part."

The People's Palace of Glass

BY VERONICA SCHANOES

Once upon a time, there were a king and a queen and a prince and a princess and numerous servants, and they all lived in a gigantic Palace of Glass. Every floor, wall, and ceiling was made of glass. All the fixtures and furniture were made of glass, crystal clear and gleaming, sending sparks of light bouncing in all directions. The palace kept legions of staff busy, as every inch had to be polished free of fingerprints and random debris every morning, on top of the staff a royal family would normally have. So much labor and money went into the upkeep of the glass palace, that it drained the surrounding kingdom dry, and the only source of wealth became tourists, drawn by the warm weather and the illicit opportunities for debauchery made possible by organized crime.

But now the sunburnt tourists have fled, and the waiters and waitresses from the casinos are trembling with fear or excitement or joy or all three. The gangsters who had played hand after hand of cards had seen the writing on the wall and gotten the hell out before anybody else. They had emptied bank accounts and left weeks and weeks ago, their suitcases full of good liquor and fine powders. You don't rule the underworld by hanging around when you know you're both outmanned and outgunned. They had been drawn by the opportunities created by the royal family's need for money, and they knew when their time was up.

The royal family had resisted fleeing. They had not run for any private planes while carrying bags of fancy luggage, even when the cadre of corporate CEOs that surrounded them had done so and begged them to come with them. "The palace will take care of us," the king had assured his friends. "It is enchanted, and it preserves us. It has preserved our family for so long, under glass, safe from the elements, and it will not abandon us now." The royal family stayed in the glass palace. And indeed, the palace kept them safe, as the palace guards fended off the once-beleaguered citizenry turned brave.

But the casinos weren't empty. Not anymore.

The men and women now filling the casinos were clean for the first time in weeks—for some of them, since the campaign had begun. They had showered in shifts, with the majority at any one time ready to defend their locations against any remnants of the royal army.

There were none. The royal army had all fled or been killed by the time the revolutionaries had reached the city. They had been defeated in clash after clash, their ranks depleted by death and desertion, and all the remaining soldiers now wanted was to blend in quietly with the rest of the populace.

A few of the revolutionary generals sat at what had once been a blackjack table, examining maps and other papers. They were sipping from glasses of strong liquor, rum or vodka, just a finger or two each, to celebrate their victory. They had taken the capitol city.

But the Palace of Glass was nowhere to be found.

There was just a massive, blank, dirty hole in the ground where it had once been, and the generals had no way to account for this.

So in between coordinating food and medicine for their soldiers and re-establishing supply lines for the cities and coaxing various government bureaucrats back to their jobs, and doing all the other things you must do after the end of the world to nurture what remains, they searched maps for where the Palace of Glass might have hidden itself. It was enchanted, after all, and surely had such powers. Finally they sent out a search party into the surrounding forests, the forests that had provided cover for them, shade for them, food and water for them. Surely the forests would offer up the palace as well.

Leonardo was at the head of the search party. And he hated it. The night before his way out of the city, when word had gotten around about what his mission was, a middle-aged woman had come to him. All he had wanted had been to get a good night's sleep. But the woman was twisted by worry, wringing her hands, and the lines in her face had become grooves, and the shadows under her eyes were deeper and darker than the shadows he remembered hiding among in the forests.

"You're going to find the palace," she said.

He nodded.

"And the people in it?"

He shrugged. "If they're still there."

"Please," she said. "My daughter—my sister is the palace cook. She brought my daughter there as a scullery maid. Please bring my daughter back unharmed. Please?"

Leonardo thought about what he could promise. He had no wish to harm servants, though servants who had fled along with the royal family and the entourage of corrupt industrialists they had encouraged indiscriminately in exploitation could not necessarily be trusted. But had they fled? Had the palace given this woman's daughter any warning, any time to get out to join her mother? He didn't know. And he resented being put in a position to have to judge.

"We won't harm your daughter," he said. "Unless we have to. I will try to bring her back."

He and his men had been struggling through the forests that surrounded the capitol city for days with no shower and short rations, carrying all kinds of gear and weaponry. They were tired and in pain and that had been one thing when they had been fighting the people's fight against the corrupt royal family and the bourgeois pigs and their flunkies, but was quite another just to search out a glass palace that was probably at this point streaked with dirt and birdshit, either abandoned or housing whatever remained of the royal family and their staff, irrelevant relics of the old world with nothing more to plunder. If they had been out there among people, trying to raise a counter-revolution, he could have understood searching for them then, as well, but nobody had heard anything from the royal family since the Capitol had fallen. Perhaps the wolves had gotten them. Or the tigers.

Screw this, he thought.

And then, on this day when he had come to the end of his patience, as he was about to order a return to the casino-cum-headquarters having found nothing, his comrade, his beloved friend and constant companion, Conrad, put his hand on his shoulder.

"What is that, Leonardo? Do you see? Sparkling beyond the next clearing?"

And Leonardo looked, and he saw the sparkle, so bright it hurt his eyes, which was odd, for very little sunlight penetrated the forest, but there was indeed something there. Something that hurt the eyes to look at.

So Leonardo and his men struggled forward together one more time, once more unto the breach, dear friends, once more, and pushed through the wet bracken and there—

there—

was the Palace of Glass, glittering like a mobster's smile.

No dirt, no dust, no smears, no birdshit, not a scratch, and not a crack marred its surface. It was perfect.

The revolutionaries had their guns at the ready, but no movement came from within or around the palace. It was unnaturally still. Not even any wildlife stirred.

Leonardo and Conrad and the rest of their party advanced further still, and even so there was no other movement, not even when the revolutionaries moved around the glass guards and opened the glass door and entered the glass palace.

Inside they found nothing but glass. The walls and furniture and fixtures were glass, and that was to be expected, but the bedding was glass as well, and the food on the plates and in the kitchen was glass, and even the cook standing over the glass stove was made of glass herself, and she did not move. She was completely transparent, transparent glass skirts falling around transparent glass hips, transparent glass hair pulled back atop a transparent glass head. A glass statue of a woman tending a glass stove. Another glass statue of a younger woman stood over the sink, scrubbing pots. In her face, Leonardo could see the beginnings of the grooves that had lined the face of the older woman who had come to him the night before he left the city. The water coming from the faucet was a frozen shower of glass.

Leonardo became acutely aware of the mud he and his men were tracking into the palace. Not a bird sang.

Gesturing for quiet unnecessarily, for all had been silenced by the eeriness of the place, he and his men searched the palace, and all was glass. The bathrooms were glass with glass plumbing, and the prince sitting on the toilet was of glass. The king and queen sitting at the breakfast table were glass, and the princess still lying abed was glass. A glass nurse tended a glass baby in a glass nursery.

The sunlight poured in around them.

Leonardo wondered what to do. He knew what he should

technically do, what his orders were. He should leave a detachment here to guard the castle, and return with the rest of his squadron to report on its location. But the urge to smash the glass, to watch the cracks spiderweb their way across the walls and furnishings, across the clothing in the closets and glass people themselves was almost overwhelming. He could see them in his mind's eye, cracks reaching up the walls and curving onto the ceilings, spreading across the ceilings and onto the roof, the outer walls, the entire palace collapsing in a heap of sparkling, glittering, murderous shards raining down around and onto them, slicing them to pieces.

He turned to Conrad. "We need to leave. Now."

He ordered the squadron to lower their guns and fall back, moving as swiftly as possible through the glass rooms, the glass hallways, the glass doorways, and the final glass entryway. They moved back around the glass guards. Once the last man was outside, Leonardo and Conrad exchanged looks. "Run," said Conrad.

They ran clear of the glass palace, and while they were running Leonardo wondered what had him so scared, so spooked. Some glass replicas of life? A few glass statues and his courage goes to shit?

A ways from the palace, the squadron stopped running and caught their breath, and Leonardo's mind began working again and he remembered the generals' plans for the Palace of Glass. What if instead of smashing the palace, or allowing it to shatter, the revolutionary government reopened it as a tourist destination? It would be the People's Palace of Glass, no longer a royal palace, and it would bring cash into the local economies, and with no royal family to support, all we would have to do is keep it clean and polished and—Leonardo suddenly had a vision of his children, and his children's children, polishing the glass royal family, wiping them delicately and carefully, every day, tending them as carefully and delicately as they had been cared for in life. He saw them mopping up as tourists trailed mud and debris through the palace, dropping candy wrappers and pissing in the toilets and missing. He saw them treating the glass palace with all the care and delicacy the royal family demanded before they metamorphosed into glass (they weren't statues; he knew they weren't statues; they had never been statues; that poor scullery maid, he thought, that poor baby; but at least now he didn't have to figure out what to do with a scion of the royal family or loyal servants, and he wouldn't have to watch the generals make such terrifying decisions either). And he raised his gun and fired round after round into the glass walls.

The walls shattered. The cracks spread more quickly than in his vision, appearing across every wall in the palace almost immediately, moving like burrowing moles through the palace and leaving glittering confetti-like grains of glass in their wake, as they joined up together and cracked the shards that were all that remained. The sunlight broke against the shattering surface, glinting and refracting, reflecting and spinning out into a million tiny bolts of light darting back out into the forest and illuminating its dark recesses like fireflies.

Leonardo braced himself for the sound of glass crashing in on itself, but heard nothing as the Palace of Glass shimmered—actually *rippled*—in the air and vanished, leaving only the bent foliage and downed trees under it to show it had been there at all.

The birds resumed chirping, the insects whirring, the foliage rustling. And Leonardo and his squadron let out a collective breath.

He met Conrad's eyes again. No People's Palace of Glass. No more lives spent polishing and polishing in the hopes of catching a tossed tip from a tourist. No. "We found nothing," he said.

"We found nothing," echoed Conrad.

"We found nothing," murmured the rest of the squadron.

The Palace of Glass was gone, and had it ever been?

Certainly the generals never found it. It had been a dream. And so was the revolution, Leonardo realized, a beautiful dream. Dreams do not last. Someday the cracks would come for the generals, and perhaps even to him; they would come and spread, and the revolution would become millions of shards, sharp and small and deadly, ready to collapse on the future and cut it to ribbons, unless they vanished as well, to make room for whatever would come next, whatever new dream would arise.

The Patron Saint of Archers

BY TINA EGNOSKI

After his draft number was called, Dixon Matthews took all
the money he had saved from his job at Long's Hardware and
bought a red Mustang convertible. He drove it home, parked
it in the driveway, and never drove it again. For several weeks
in March of 1970, the weeks before he left for boot camp, he
sat in the front seat, smoking. Just sat, a cigarette suspended
between his lips. He was there every afternoon when we
returned home from school, me, Carla, and Dixon's younger
brother Flynn.

Stereo speakers had been propped against the kitchen
window and usually a Rolling Stones song blasted through the
screen. Flynn said his brother was cultivating habits he would
need in Vietnam—patience, stillness, the art of suppressing
fear by smoking—and then he wound a finger around his ear:
craaazzy, man.

One afternoon Dixon actually started the car. We heard
the engine come to life from the corner, but by the time we
reached the house, he had shut it off. He waved to us. He had
on fatigues and combat boots from the army surplus store. His
shirt was unbuttoned, and I couldn't keep my eyes from his
bare chest, bare but for the dark, fuzzy hair.

I was thirteen that year and wanted Dixon's attention, wanted him to notice me not as a neighborhood girl, but in that special girlfriend way. The way I had seen him act with Carla's sister when they dated a year earlier, casually placing an arm around her shoulder, reaching over to loosen a strand of hair caught in the corner of her mouth.

Dixon lit a cigarette. "Everyone smokes in Nam," he said. "Keeps us from getting trigger happy."

"Gimme Shelter" exploded from the speakers.

"What if you get shot?" Carla asked Dixon.

"Don't plan on that," he said.

"What do you plan on?"

"Getting laid," he said.

I thought Laid might be a place, like Saigon.

"That's just the war talking," Flynn said.

Dixon had always been the fun brother, letting us younger kids tag along to baseball practice or a Saturday matinee. That was why his behavior in the weeks following the draft announcement was so puzzling: one day he was friendly and eager to talk, the next he was silent, edgy.

By contrast, Flynn—my age and a good Catholic boy— was studious, stuffy. He readily expounded on the theory of relativity or the political themes in *Richard III*. In fact, he was the one who had explained the lottery system to me: numbers were assigned by birth date, and on December first of the previous year, capsules containing the dates were randomly drawn by the draft board from a kind of spinning game show barrel. Dixon's number was low: five. His birthday was October eighteenth, which I knew because it was the day after mine. He was in the first wave of men called to service.

Carla leaned against the car door and said, "I hope you'll write to me."

I envied the carefree way she moved in her body. Envied her body really, so much like her sister's, high pointed breasts and curvy hips. I was tall and straight and flat. My parents named me after a fruit that wasn't even sweet. If my name ended in an A, like Carla's, I'd at least be Olivia. A pretty girl's name.

Without answering, Dixon brought the cigarette to his lips and took a long pull. I watched the tip burn to ash, the smoke rise and swirl around his face.

————

Each school day morning, my younger sister Bonnie and I stood on the curb outside our house waiting for Flynn and Carla. Even though Flynn went to Saint Sebastian Catholic School, we all walked together.

Across the street, Flynn's mother came out of her house dressed for work in a satin blouse, pleated skirt, and heels. She was a typist for a CPA. A working woman, my mother said with spit on her tongue, not one of the mothers who met for coffee after the rush of getting husbands and children out of the house.

"Morning, girls," Mrs. Matthews said. "Any news yet?"

We shook our heads. Our mother was pregnant, two weeks overdue and under a neighborhood watch.

Mr. Matthews came out next and walked to his car without acknowledging us. He was known for his gruff manner and quick temper, the kind of man who used his belt for punishment. A lawyer, he worked for the largest firm in Florida. There were nights he didn't come home until nine or ten. My father sold insurance, for what he said was the smallest firm in Orlando: a three-man company with an office in a strip mall. Proud of his family, of being able to spend time with us, he was home many afternoons before Bonnie or I returned from school.

A few minutes later Flynn came out of the house. Every morning he and Bonnie performed an absurd kind of vaude-ville routine: Flynn shuffled down the driveway and said good morning to me, ignoring Bonnie. This made her so mad, she punched his arm. At age nine, she was afraid of being left out. Acting surprised, Flynn cuffed his forehead. "Hey, look, Little Miss Invisible, aka Bonnie Cooper. I didn't even see you."

Tall and long-legged, Flynn seemed to be made of pipe-cleaners—he was that wiry. He had a patch of pimples on his left cheek. His dark hair was kinky-curly. He tried to slick it back with some goo his brother used, but on humid days his oily curls sprung loose, like coils in a sofa.

"When does Dixon have to leave?" I asked.

Flynn launched into a sermon about Dixon's plans, saying that he had to report to boot camp in two weeks, but that of course there were ways to get out of going. Not that Dixon would try. He wanted to serve his country. No sweat, he was ready. Flynn spoke with the same cocky bravado I had noticed recently in his brother.

"Some guys, though, pretend to be nuts," he said. "Or they chop off a finger or shoot themselves in the foot."

"Shut up," Bonnie yelled, putting her hands over her ears. For a long time, she hadn't understood the war. But finally my father sat her down at the kitchen table with a mug of hot chocolate for a talk.

Flynn folded his hand into a gun and got right into her face, mimicking the rat-tat-tat of a weapon. His breath made her hair flutter. It looked like she might start to cry any minute.

"Let her alone," I said.

"Okay, okay," he said.

He stuffed the front flap of his shirt back into his waistband. Unlike us, he wore a school uniform: short-sleeve white shirt, navy pants, and tie. In his newly polished shoes, we could see our faces.

"Come on, let's get going," I said.

"What about Carla?" Bonnie asked.

"She'll just have to catch up," Flynn said and took off

ahead of us. His book bag swung at his side, as if it were light as a stick. I knew it wasn't. At his school they had at least two books for every subject. The religion manuals alone would have weighed him down. He often showed me pictures in them: Mary draped in a white gown, her arms crossed tenderly over her chest or Saint Andrew with soft eyes and a knowing smile.

Carla came running up the sidewalk. Her blonde hair was pulled back in a ponytail. She wore blue shadow and mascara on her right eye only.

"You look funny," Bonnie said.

"Yeah, my mother was watching me like a hawk this morning. I didn't have time to finish my makeup."

She never waited to put on makeup until after we got to school, like all the other girls. Instead, she tempted fate, trying to sneak out of the house before her mother caught her.

"You have on too much rouge," I said.

"I'll fix it later, okay? Look at this." She unbuttoned her shirt, revealing a purple halter top. "Wait until Jim Kelleher sees me in this."

"You're wearing that to school?" I asked.

"Just in the halls, where Jim can see me." She re-buttoned.

"Don't you have a dress code or something?" Flynn asked. He couldn't take his eyes off Carla's breasts. "I mean, it looks good and all, but if a girl wore that to my school, she'd get expelled."

We turned the corner across from Saint Sebastian, a serene building, two-story white stucco with blue trim. The fountain out front was a detailed marble carving of jumping fish. A cascade of water bubbled from the center, splashing the rim of the fountain, sending out a spray of holy water on anyone who passed.

"What good are saints anyway?" Bonnie asked Flynn.

"You pray to them is all."

"Do you have to be dead to be a saint?"

"It's the only way I know."

The bell rang for morning chapel and students began filing in. Everyone looked the same, boys dressed like Flynn, girls in plaid skirts, knee socks, and Mary Janes. Flynn crossed the street. He stopped at the front steps and stared back at us, his forehead puckered in worry, knowing we were headed to a place more atrocious than purgatory: public school. I thought of the chaos of Mrs. Tyding's classroom. Kenny Small sticking pencils up his nose, Chad Wilcox burping his way through English, and Laura Bills crying softly in the corner because someone had stuck gum in her hair for the third time this month. It was true, public school kids lacked discipline. Our homework was routinely eaten by dogs. Our skirts were too short, our makeup too garish. We needed the backs of our hands slapped with rulers. We needed our filthy mouths washed out with a bar of soap.

Flynn lifted a hand to wave, and his book bag slipped off his shoulder, spilling pencils and notebooks onto the ground. He bent to rescue them, his starched uniform wrinkling and his hair popping into a lush halo of curls.

———

Five days later my baby sister Haley was born. When my mother brought her home, Bonnie's room became the nursery and she moved in with me. She slept on the top bunk, and once she fell asleep, her mouth dropped open and each breath became a sharp wheeze bellowing from the cavern of her throat.

I got up and tiptoed across the hall to the bathroom, now the only private room in the house. I heard my mother pacing the living room with Haley, whispering, singing, begging her to fall asleep. Her body was tiny and fragile, squirmy. I refused to hold her, afraid that in a split second she would wriggle out of my arms, hit the terrazzo floor, and break into a million pieces.

I sat on the vanity, my feet in the cool ceramic basin. In the mirror, I saw a square, flat face, the skin tanned from the strong Florida sun. I had my father's rich black hair. It hung straight to my shoulders. Carla said my eyes were my best feature: hazel and almond-shaped. My nose, I thought, was hooked and too large for my face. I wanted the delicate features of Saint Agnes, the creamy skin of Mary Magdalene, and a body like Carla's. These conflicting desires scared me. I didn't want to be Sara Price, the girl in 11th grade who got pregnant and sent away to live with her aunt. At the same time, it was no fun to be Plain-Jane, Fair-Claire, Boring-Lori. Why didn't I have the guts, like Carla, to disobey my mother?

Lifting my nightshirt over my head, I studied my chest for signs of growth. The skin around my nipples was tender and underneath I felt oats of flesh. Boys joked that when I turned sideways and stuck out my tongue, I looked like a zipper.

———

One day after school Carla and I stood in front of Saint Sebastian School tossing pennies into the fountain. I had decided the best way to keep my thoughts pure was to trade my off-again, on-again attendance at the Methodist church for the strict regimen of Catholicism, for the pleasure of sitting on hard pews and memorizing catechism. Flynn would be my guide. He could teach me the Latin Mass and loan me a rosary.

"What's the big deal?" Carla asked. "Go to his church on Sunday and take communion." She was impatient with my plan to pump Flynn for information.

"You can't just show up. You have to go to confession first."

Two nuns walked by us, their habits flapping in the wind,

the sound of seagull wings, a sound we knew well from days at the beach—the gulls hovering overhead, inspecting us, and then swooping away.

"Good afternoon, Sisters," Carla said, brave enough to use the word "Sisters."

The nuns nodded and like shorebirds were gone, not upward, toward heaven, but around the corner.

"They don't look like women who would use yardsticks on innocent children, do they?" She took a tissue from her purse and wiped off the lipstick. "I've heard those are no ordinary yardsticks. They make them a foot longer, especially for the nuns."

When Flynn came out of the school and saw us waiting, he said, "Hey, it's my lucky day."

I shouldered up next to him. "I've been thinking, Flynn, about the power of prayer."

He turned to Carla. "What's she talking about?"

"Who knows?"

"I'm just interested in Catholicism. I may convert."

"You have to go to confession first."

"Told you so," I said to Carla.

In the tight, airless confessional booth I would admit, out loud for the first time, that I hated Haley's ear-splitting cry and poopy-diaper smell. That I longed for Dixon to touch me in private places, the places I wasn't even supposed to show when I changed in the locker room for PE.

At Flynn's house, Dixon sat in the car, beating his hands on the steering wheel in time with "Street Fighting Man."

"Hey, kids," he said. His shaggy hair curled behind his ears.

"How come you never drive anywhere, Dix?" Carla asked.

"Drive? Who needs to drive when I have the whole world at my feet?" He pointed to the panoramic view of the Matthews' lush green lawn and yellow split-level ranch. Nodding at the drainage ditch on the far side of the house, he said, "There, can't you see it, the Grand Canyon? It's quite a sight."

"Of course we can," I said. "Can't we, Carla?" I elbowed her.

"Sure, whatever you say."

"Get in, girls," Dixon said, leaning over to open the door. "I'll take you for a trip around the globe."

I climbed in and slid next to Dixon. Carla, skeptical but willing, got in. Rolling his eyes, Flynn said he had homework and went into the house.

I thought Dixon might start the car, like he had a few weeks earlier, and surprise us by driving around town. Instead, he made a noise like the catch of an engine, put his arm around the spine of the seat, and pretended to back out of the driveway.

"And we're off," he said.

He bounced up and down in the seat, imitating the rocking motion of a car with faulty shock absorbers. His arm rubbed against mine, created a spark of friction. Together, we reeled off the names of landmarks seen only in history books: the Eiffel Tower, Big Ben, Stonehenge, the Berlin Wall. The ruins of a rotten birdfeeder became the Great Sphinx, a cluster of rhododendron were the jagged Himalayas. The mix of smells in the car made me light-headed, tobacco with vinyl, damp skin with citrusy aftershave.

Carla, now joining the fun, clambered to her knees, hugging the top of the windshield. She pointed to the house and said, "Look, it's the Taj Mahal."

Dixon fell back against the seat, in awe of this wonder of the ancient world.

"Wow, what a palace," he said.

———

At dusk, two days later, I walked home from Carla's. A smear of dark clouds hung low on the horizon and blocked the setting sun. It was the time when fathers came home from an eight-hour work day and kids returned from an afternoon of hard play and mothers stood at stoves ready to spoon out supper. Our neighbor, Mr. Platt, arrived in his carpool and waved to me.

From my front lawn I heard Haley's irritating cry. I didn't want to go inside. Across the street, through the open dining room curtains, I saw Mrs. Matthews sitting alone at the table, still in her work clothes, smoking a cigarette. I wondered if she counted the days until her son was to leave, if she marked them off on a calendar in red ink, the way my mother had while she was pregnant.

A car came around the corner. It was Mr. Matthews and he pulled into the garage. When he got out, he noticed that his family's garbage cans had been left at the end of the driveway, empty and haphazardly tossed. His stiff shoulders made me shudder. It was trash pick up day. I never gave much thought to who brought in our cans. I guessed my dad always did.

The back door of the Matthews' house slammed, and I watched Mrs. Matthews get up and head toward the kitchen. There was the sound of more slamming doors, something not even allowed in our house. If I got mad, it was best to wait and make a face from the safety of my bedroom. If my parents got mad, they said things like *We're disappointed in you* and that was enough of a punishment.

Shouts, both booming and shrill, both male and female, came from the Matthews house. Mrs. Matthews was not, in my experience, a screamer. It was possible she was at her breaking point. Or was she yelling at her husband for yelling at her sons? Then I heard the eternal parental complaint, one even used by my parents: *How many times do I have to tell you?*

Dixon slumped down the driveway to retrieve the cans. He

didn't even see me—his head was down as he picked them up and carried them to the garage. Other boys from our neighborhood had gone to Vietnam. Three that I knew. Two returned after a year: Mickey Young and Larry Gardner. Larry pumped gas in town, using only his right arm. His left flopped at his side. My mother tipped him extra whenever he was on duty. The other boy, Thomas Foster, the eldest of a family of five—the Foster Five we called them—didn't return. Heir and a spare, I had heard someone say. An heir and four spares.

Inside my house, the kitchen was warm. On the stove, a sauce of chopped tomato and garlic and spices simmered. Bonnie was doing homework at the table. In the middle of the room, my mother tested a bottle on her wrist. My father, posted by the refrigerator, holding Haley, checked the clock.

"Cutting it close," he said.

I should have been home in time to help with dinner. But lately he was loosening the rules, allowing me to set my own schedule to see if I was reliable. Sometimes I was, sometimes not.

Instead of scolding me, my father tickled the baby's chin and said, "Little Haley, you're one lucky kid to be born into this bright bunch of girls."

———

On the last Friday in March, I stayed late at school for math club. Walking home, I saw Flynn sitting alone on the steps of Saint Sebastian, his overstuffed book bag at his feet.

"I stayed to help Sister Bernard clean chalkboards," he said. His shirt was smudged with yellow dust. He nodded toward the school. "You want to come inside?"

Of course I did. "Can we go into the chapel?" I asked.

"Sure, but I'll show you my locker first."

The entrance hall was long and wide. As I expected, it was

the cleanest school I had ever seen, no scraps of paper or lost notebooks littering the floor. I took cautious, quiet steps. Flynn led me to a bank of lockers just outside the main office. "Here it is. She's a beauty," he said.

"It's a locker like any other locker."

On the opposite wall was a larger-than-life oil painting of a man bound and tied to a pillar.

"That's the big man himself," Flynn said.

"You mean?"

"Yup. Saint Sebastian."

His ivory skin was pierced with a rash of arrows, one in his shoulder, one in his calf and another in his chest. One arrow went through his forehead and came out the side of his neck. Blood seeped from each wound.

"Don't worry, those arrows didn't kill him. That's why he's a saint."

"How many days do you think he stayed like that?"

"I'd say six, seven days. It ain't easy being a martyr."

Saint Sebastian's eyes were fixed on heaven. He had a pained look on his face: pained but satisfied. The grace of suffering.

I asked how he became a saint. Hands in pockets, Flynn rocked back on his heels and explained in his most show-offy voice. Saint Sebastian had been a spy, a double agent, so to speak. He joined the army of Roman Emperor Diocletian, even though he—Sebastian—was against killing. What you have to know about Diocletian, Flynn said, was that he hated Christians. So while Sebastian was fighting, he was also curing soldiers of gout, converting and baptizing them. Right under the emperor's nose. All this took place back in the third century, a time I couldn't even fathom.

"I guess he got caught," I said.

A cloth was wrapped around Saint Sebastian's middle, hiding that private area below his navel. But the cloth had slipped so low I could see the nub of each hip bone, the curve of skin that led down, down to the very place that held the secret of my temptation. I let my eyes lag on the tassel of fabric tied loosely there.

"Uh-hum," Flynn cleared his throat. He took my shoulders, turned me, turned me again, and, the way you see in the movies, pressed me back against the lockers. I was dizzy and my feet felt mixed-up, as if my right one was attached to my left leg. I steadied myself with palms against the cool, cool metal.

"I want you," he said, looking like his brother, eyes hard and dark, and sounding like him too, raspy. If I close my eyes, I thought, he might be Dixon, he might want me. With his fingers sunk into the skin on my upper arms, Flynn brought his face to mine, mouth a sneer of hope. Saint Sebastian looked down on us, a disciple of God.

"Devil," I said, not meaning Flynn, but the desire in me that had brought us here.

Flynn dropped his hands and backed away. His face collapsed into a quivering mass. He ran down the hall, his hard-soled shoes chafing the tile, the sound bouncing off the walls, echoing through the hollow tunnel. At the end of the hall, he banked the corner and his footsteps stopped suddenly. I expected him to come back, to whirl around the corner and peer at me with the expression of surprise he wore every morning before school. He would walk up to me and say, "Hey, look, it's Little Miss Tease." Instead, I heard the front door open and slam shut.

———

For the next week, we waited for Flynn each morning, but he never showed. Then I heard a rumor at school, girls in the bathroom talking about how the Matthews kid had gotten into an accident.

"Well, I don't know about accident," one girl said.

"That boy is nutzo," said another.

"If I was going to do something like that," said another, "I'd take a bunch of pills."

I wasn't sure if they were talking about Dixon or Flynn. For weeks, ever since Dixon bought the Mustang, he—the whole Matthews family really—had been the topic of gossip. I didn't stay around to hear anymore, but walked home alone, not even waiting for Carla. I would go straight to the source.

Dixon wasn't in the car. His mother's station wagon was parked next to it, which surprised me. It wasn't even three o'clock. I knocked and Mrs. Matthews answered, greeting me with a distracted hello.

"How nice of you to come by, Olive," she said. "I know he'll be happy to see you."

She sat down on the sofa, knitting the corner of a pillow between her fingers. She rambled, talking to me as if I were an adult, a life-long friend who had just heard the news and came to comfort her. "The thing I can't figure out is why he would do such a silly thing. He knows better than to get into his father's things."

I wondered, had Dixon sliced off a finger?

"He's so young. And such a good boy," she said.

Did that mean she was talking about Flynn? I sat next to her, trying to figure out a way to both console her and coax her into telling me what had happened.

"Well, go on in. Talk to him," she said, patting my knee. "Maybe you can get something out of him."

Sweat slid down the inside of my thighs. I had only been in this house a few times, when I was younger and usually with my mother. The hallway was lined with family photographs, vacations and holidays and studio portraits. The two doors on the right were the boys' bedrooms, Flynn's first. I poked my head around the doorframe and there he was, in bed with piles of magazines scattered over the sheets. He held up his left hand, wrist swathed in a white bandage.

"See, I didn't die," he said. "Must be a saint."

"Where's your brother?" I asked.

"With my dad at the barber shop."

I stepped closer, guilt rising with the question: Was Flynn's *accident* my fault? But what I asked him was, "Did you have to spend the night in the hospital?"

"Yeah. Some guy came and talked to me. Asked me all sorts of questions, like why I did it, how it felt."

I couldn't take my eyes off his wrists, the one ashy and exposed, the other securely wrapped. Finally he asked, "You want to see it?"

"Gross," I said, but my curiosity got the better of me.

He unrolled the bandage, revealing fleshy, purple skin furrowed tight around a dark line of stitches. "Stupid old penknife," he said.

I helped him rewrap the gauze, so thin I didn't see how it would prevent infection. My search for redemption, for discipline, for a savior—the things I thought Flynn might guide me to—was over. We were all afraid. Afraid of mothers who didn't want us to grow up, of fathers who pushed us to grow. Of nuns with four-foot yardsticks. Of the heated need of our own bodies and the small needy bodies of others. But mostly we were afraid of our brothers going to war.

Flynn tossed the magazines onto the floor, said, "Dixon says over there they tie you to a tree and leave you for the fire ants."

———

The morning Dixon left for boot camp, all the families on our street came out to wish him well. The women and children gathered in the yard, the men formed a row along the sidewalk. Carla's mother put her arm around Mrs. Matthews. My mother held Haley, who wiggled and cried softly into her shoulder. Flynn, still recovering, stayed inside.

I went and stood with my father. Dixon was dressed in a suit and tie, his head shaved. He looked older and somehow wiser. Maybe it was the suit or the short hair, or maybe it was the official draft notice sticking out of his front pocket. He went down the line of men, shaking each hand. "Nice of you to come," he said. When he got to me, he took my hand and winked. I saw the return of his boyish features and the restless dance in his eyes.

His father tossed him the car keys and got into the passenger's seat of the Mustang. The engine sputtered, then sprang to life. Dixon backed out of the driveway.

That evening, I locked the bathroom door and sat in front of the mirror. I felt the uncomfortable rumblings of my body. Tremors, like the earth shifting. Stirrings, hovering below the surface, that would leave their mark in the form of breasts and hair between my legs.

I studied the skin stretched taut over the inside of my wrist, prodding the thin blue veins. I made a fist and watched the tendons constrict, release. With my sharpest nail, the thumbnail on my right hand, I drew a line across this tender place. I thought of how the skin splits, shifts to make room for growth, for the damage of a wound, and how the day you are born can determine the day you will be sent to a foreign country, to fight and to die.

Teddy Bump

BY SHEREE RENÉE THOMAS

Down down baby, down down
a rollercoaster
Sweet sweet baby, sweet sweet
won't let you go...

Melanie kicks her skinny legs out. Her ashy elbows and arms pump and pump, ricochet off the cool wintry air. She wears summer clothes, a flowery church dress that billows around her, like a pink upturned umbrella, and cornrows, neat and lustrous, her Easter Sunday best. Melanie swings from a frayed brown rope. Her ankle socks must have looked good in her shiny black Mary Janes, but one shoe is missing. Her giggles bounce off the shards of ice atop the frozen red earth of Miss Dinah's playground. They echo around her, crimson crystals glistening beneath her tiny feet. One shoe on, one shoe off, locked somewhere in an old dusty box, the label is faded, her name long since unremembered, unread.

KeKe blows bubbles in her left hand and waves them around like a magician, pops them like iridescent smoke rings. The bubbles float over her shoulder and drift past the slide that is still and silent for now, then disappear into the surrounding trees. The rusted merry-go-round spins ever so slowly behind her. It creaks and growls like the sound of Miss Dinah's laughter. KeKe sits with her back against a green glacier rock, denim legs splayed out in front of her, like a giant black baby doll. Miss Dinah smiles down at us, then floats from her perch in the willow tree. I shudder then wave from my spot on the prickly grass and hope Miss Dinah doesn't land near me. Melanie laughs and pumps her little legs harder, swinging from the sturdy oak. Even if someone finds the other shoe Melanie is not wearing, somewhere across the red-stained layers of time, as far as the world beyond is concerned, we are all still missing.

The word ricochets in my mind like a stray bullet, and I rub the side of my head. It hurts sometimes to be, just thinking. Sometimes, when the sky is flesh and Melanie's dress flies and flutters like a hollow-boned bird, like the butterfly that once carried me far away from home, I wonder if we are truly missed, missing. Those words hurt, the words Miss Dinah is so careful to never say. When it is cold outside and all the land is grieving, when Melanie is swinging like the first days of Spring, I wonder. Are we missing if no one in the world is looking for us, if we are just another random group of little Black girls lost?

"Halloo!" Melanie cries and leaps from her swing, arcing through the air, a giggling brown grasshopper. "Come on, Ruby, KeKe," she says. "Turn for me?" The rope spins slowly, unseen hands, a question mark waiting in the air behind her.

I groan. I was just getting comfortable. It's not Melanie's fault that she is the youngest among us, that she still finds some joy in this place. Somehow our littlest playmate holds onto hope, but we've been here so long with Miss Dinah, I'm not sure what that means. KeKe coughs, doesn't even look up. Amber, as always, is carving her name furiously in the bark of a tree. What's left of her dress hangs in dark shreds. We pretend like we don't see the wounds beneath them. I pretend the ice on my back is a sailboat. I pretend it will rock me away like a grandmama's arms, like sleep, drifting down through the river of air, spiriting me back to where I belong, fighting my way back to my own tree-lined street, where the sky is Mama.

"Ruby!" Melanie whines, and I can feel Miss Dinah's eyes frowning down at me. Her eyes are so big, they hold a whole river in them. If I knew how, I would climb up in those eyes and kick and swim. If I knew how, I would snatch that rope and find my own way home.

"Leave me alone, ole wor'sem girl."

"I ain't wor'sem," she says. "I'm 'sistent."

"Persistent," Amber says. Her sparkly scrunchie and messy bun dangles on the side. Amber is always whispering in that child's ear, as if new words could change our story. Amber was like a house where the lights are always off. You knew someone lived there, but they were never seen. She carves, destroys whole trees with her big seeking words, hiding in the dark bark of her weird scriptures. As if prayer would save us now, trapped on the other side of Miss Dinah's trees.

"You're too old to talk like that," I say. "Didn't she teach you how to read yet?"

Amber rolls her eyes, brushes away pieces of bark. I watch as she wipes the knife on her bare thigh. I am cold just looking at her. There is no heat from the Jackball sun that spins in the sky above us. It pulses and shimmers, the colors swirling with every move Miss Dinah makes.

Melanie digs her big toe into the hard bright earth, kicks at one of the many weirdly shaped rocks that litter the play-ground. Her head hangs low, lace-white sock buried beneath the ice and snow.

"Be *nice*," Miss Dinah says. Her white teeth glisten like new bones, the words whispered this time, not quite a hiss. Why girls always got to be nice? I huff and puff, and imagine a big gust of wind blows all their asses down, like the house in the story Mama once read to me. I feel my eyes swell up, the pressure behind my closed lids rising, an electric black cloud. I bite my lip hard but as usual I don't taste anything. Not even blood. I don't wanna be, but I'm mad now. Madder than Amber, who is slaughtering another tree. Madder than KeKe, who is always crying and picking at the frayed threads of her jeans, saying how she used to be fine, so damn fine, Teddy Bump fine and pretty. I want to snatch Melanie by her shiny naps, kick Miss Dinah in her sparkly teeth, her dusty shin. Everything was so good, so right before... Why they make me remember? It's cold enough as it is, here. It hurts to remember, and Melanie's little baby girl voice now feels like a cold fire running through my head, burning right into my brain.

"It's alright, Ruby."

Miss Dinah reaches for me with Mississippi Missionary Baptist white-gloved hands. Stiff and clean, she looks like an usher at Granddaddy's old church. I turn and roll over. Don't want her touching me, rubbing her hurt all over me. I trusted her once, Miss Dinah and her Double Dutch lies promising a new way home. *You'll play all the time,* she said. *Never grow hungry, never be cold.* If I could count all the lies a haint told me, I'd be counting forever.

The icy grass stabs and pricks, tickles my belly. Sometimes I envy Melanie. Even if it is just one foot, at least she gets to feel real air, feel real grass tickling her toes, her heel and her sole. The one not wearing the patent leather shoe. Me, I feel nothing but pain. Miss Dinah says she thinks Melanie went missing in her sleep—as if she does not know how. And who does that? Goes missing in their sleep, like a bad dream except when you wake up, you don't exist? Only Miss Dinah would tell a lie like that, sing you a lie and make it feel like truth. But for me, it is always the same. My right pinky toe is squenched up in Emerald's shoes. The black ankle boots are so tight I can almost feel a corn growing. All my big sister's hand-me-downs were too little for me. My too early breasts were too big, crushed inside her too small shirts. My butt, my height, my

mouth, everything too much. Mama called it, "mighty inconvenient." And though my feet hurt and my heart hurt too, I
would laugh, we would roll and gasp together, laughing so
hard I could not breathe. Being a little Black girl can be
mighty inconvenient sometimes. I laugh every time I think
of it.

And that is what I miss most. Not the thinking but Mama's
laughter. She looked so pretty with her eyes all big, not full of
worry, and her perfect, doll-baby lips turned just so. She could
make the biggest hurt sound like a joke, make you laugh so
hard the pain disappeared in your throat. Not like Miss
Dinah. When she laughs, the sound is a splinter in your big
toe, glass in your ears. She is the crow in the tree, mocking us,
each girl one of her shiny things, her own special jewel, a
collection she has picked through the ages.

When she laughs, you want to hide and disappear all over
again. "*I found you,*" she crows. "*No one else did, maybe no one else
will. Remember that.*"

What I remember is Mama's absence. What I remember is
spending my first twelve years missing Mama, missing her
laughter. Mama worked so hard, but when she laughed, you
wouldn't know it. I guess everybody's got mamas like that.
Working so hard to make you the woman they think you
should be, can be, worrying so hard that only a little bit of
them is left. The girl part almost gone, disappeared. But when
Mama laughed there was no more worry. She sounded like
light. And though it never grows dark, night never comes here,
I wonder if Emerald still turns all the lights on, if she still
spends each breath waiting for Mama to come back home,
waiting for her to return from work or sleep. Waiting for the
sun-sound of her laughter, so we could all feel light, pretty,
free, safe.

But we are not free and there is no *safe* here. We just *is*. We
exist, between who we once were and whatever we have

become. I've been here so long I don't know if I am a girl anymore, grown, or something else in between.

"Push me!" Melanie says, her face twisted up in a little brown knot. I want to push her and hold her at once. I want to push and be pushed, to hold and be held. None of that should matter here, but it does. No matter how many scars Amber carves into the tree, no matter how many holes KeKe digs out of her denim pants legs, as long as I've been here, this loneliness, this ache is always here.

I push myself up from the ice-crystal grass. The sound is soft wind chimes in the cold air. I can hear KeKe shivering, sniffling behind me, and Miss Dinah—her cold eyes bearing holes into my back, the top of my head. The Jackball sun is a sickly green, a bruised blue now. Miss Dinah is mad. When she looks at you, you feel like you will disappear all over again, and whatever little peace you felt before her eyes is gone.

When Mama was gone to work, Emerald knew I was afraid, so she pretended she was her. She used to sneak into her make-up drawer when Mama was off to her second shift, and make moon faces in the old-timey mirror. Emerald said Mama ought to throw it out. Get something black lacquer and new. Emerald would say this and then pucker her lips. "Mama got a lipstick mouth," she'd say. "Perfect shape, perfect size for wearing any color she wants." She used to stand in front of Granddaddy's old, green painted dresser and mirror, making faces that looked like her stomach hurt or like she was some kind of strange clownfish. Mama's mouth didn't look nothing like that. It was perfect, like the kind they used for the scratch n' sniff stickers plastered all over my Trapper Keeper note-book, perfect lips that made every hurt feel whole again.

But I don't know if I have Mama's lipstick mouth, or if Emerald's little bitty feet ever caught up with me. I don't know why my Mama named me Ruby but my favorite, favorite color is blue. I don't know when real girls start or stop growing. When the pain ever ends. For Melanie, for KeKe, for Amber and me, maybe Miss Dinah, too, for all of the others lurking behind the trees, crying under the stones, waiting in the river, on the side of the road in a ditch, waiting in a hotel's deep freezer for somebody to come carry us out, every day changes but every night is the same. Nothing grows here, not even our dreams. We are visible and invisible. Just the layers of red dirt, full of time and all of it so full of our tears, the red clay looks like it's crying, like the whole earth bleeding, too.

"You're daydreaming today, better keep up, better keep it lively," KeKe says, mimicking Miss Dinah. She wipes snot from her face with the back of her hand. She talks so funny, half the time I don't even know what to say. She talks like Mrs. Aldridge, KeKe's favorite teacher, the one she used to imitate for us. Said she used to stand in front of the classroom, discussing worlds they had never seen, every detail a new language, then she would weave around the neat rows of their desks, an exotic bird in constant motion. KeKe used to make us laugh so hard, but now she don't talk much anymore, not since she realized Miss Dinah never plans for us to leave here. KeKe just holds herself now, and cries, digging at her denim jacket, her jeans, the last outfit she chose for herself. When she does talk, she tells us about her friends going to the shows, and the cute boys, and the slick girls who smiled in her face and did her wrong, so wrong, and then sometimes, she will tell us about high school.

Mrs. Aldridge sounds nice. The only thing about school I liked was the first day and lunch. But when KeKe talked, she made it sound like some kind of adventure. KeKe is the only one of us to make it to high school, but she missed her prom.

"What is a prom?" Melanie once asked. For a moment, KeKe stopped crying.

"A prom is a promise," KeKe said.

And after she described getting your hair did, the pretty dresses, the decorations, and drinking ice cream punch, she grabbed Melanie and pretended to dance. The only prom I'd seen was in that scary movie when the mean girls covered the magic one with pig blood. Watching KeKe and Melanie dance was one of the few times since Miss Dinah brought her here that I'd seen KeKe look happy. But she don't look happy now.

She has placed snow-covered ice blossoms in the four holes in her matching denim shirt. It looks almost pretty, like her blouse was made that way on purpose. I don't feel like arguing so I just dust myself off, even though I know my parachute pants can never get wet. I'm so sick of them. I wish I could take a knife and rip them up, too. But whatever I do to them, they just turn back the same way they were when I came here.

I can't think of anything more embarrassing than dying in some bright red parachute pants that barely fit, dying in some too shiny polyester nylon that don't even cover your ankles good. Even Michael Jackson wouldn't be caught dead in that. And Melanie might be a wor'sem baby who can't even read, but at least she looked right when she went missing, even with her one little shoe. Me, I am trapped here in Miss Dinah's world looking like Who-Done-It-and- What-For forever. But then I think of Amber. Poor thing. Can't get more pitiful than that.

———

Shimmy, shimmy cocoa pop
Shimmy shimmy down
Shimmy shimmy cocoa puff
Shimmy shimmy break down

"I said, who wants to play?"

"I do!" Melanie raises her hand, hopping around like a cricket. Amber, KeKe, and I just look at each other. "I do," we say in unison but it's not enough. Miss Dinah wants razzle and dazzle, but I feel like my voice has seeped right out of me, or frozen under the ice. I don't feel like playing. I don't feel like singing. I don't feel like...

"Oooh," Melanie says. If her eyes weren't so big, her little hand covering her mouth, I would've thought I'd only imagined it, but the shock on Amber and KeKe's faces says everything: I messed around and said that aloud.

The Jackball sun darkens, and the air feels like fire.

"*I don't understand!*" Miss Dinah roars. "*I do everything for you. I take you from that scary darkness, I carry you in my arms and bring you to the light. I fill your world with toys and games, and none of you can still bring me laughter? None of you can show me gratitude?*"

As she speaks, her ropes hiss and sputter, twisting like serpents. The frayed edges shake with electric flares. Miss Dinah grabs one rope in each hand and begins whipping them in the air, lashing them out right near our feet.

Melanie screams and dives into my arms. I hold her and cover her eyes so she will not see which one of the stone ones, the stone dolls would be brought back to whatever it is Miss Dinah calls our new lives.

Miss Dinah's right rope sizzles and sparks, as she whips it across a small boulder. When I first arrived and crossed over the blueness into Miss Dinah's light, I thought the wet stones were just part of the park. But now I know they had once been little girls, too. Miss Dinah had turned them into stones that remained wet with tears. I once saw her turn a new girl who had never learned to play jacks. She turned another because she could not keep time well. She always stumbled and missed during our hand-clapping games. Clapping when she should've been sliding, stomping when she should've been crossing her heart. I can still hear her screaming.

———

Miss Mary Mack Mack Mack
All dressed in black black black
With silver buttons buttons buttons
All down her back back back

The new girl was still screaming when Miss Dinah's rope hit her and her face turned gray. Her raised palms froze mid-air and her body changed shape. All that was left was her tears on a stone. After that Miss Dinah had us clapping "Miss Mary Mack" so long, it felt like my whole hands were on fire, the skin blistered, red and sore.

To survive Miss Dinah, a girl had to have rhythm, had to have a good memory, too. Little Melanie had neither, as long as she had been beyond the blue, but Miss Dinah kept her anyway.

"All I ask is for a little affection, some cooperation," she says. *"Joy is what we are supposed to be here! Joy!"* The sky roiled above her head, covering the Jackball sun.

"All I ask for is just a little love, a little companionship, a little 'thank you, Miss Dinah,' for all I've done for you, but you have the nerve to fix your lips to tell me what you ain't gon' do, how you feel? Let me tell you about feelings…"

Melanie trembles and KeKe shakes. Amber grips her knife, the blade digging into her hand. The rope writhes back and forth in the air, a spinning cyclone one moment, a whip the next. As it cracks through the air, we wait for Miss Dinah's anger to pass, her black-hole eyes an ever changing storm. She hovers above us, her stained palms raised upward, toward the sky, their redness trembling against the black and blue.

"Fast tailed girls, now you've ruined my gloves."

There is no sound, only the dry rattle of our breath trapped in terrified throats. Our tongues and voices turn back on ourselves. Now Melanie moans. KeKe curses. Amber bites her lip, grinds the blade into the tree's hard flesh. Still the red hands remain outstretched, a prayer or a curse, we cannot tell.

Miss Dinah lowers herself until her bare feet touch the ground. The church shoes now gone, I turn away from the dark, curled nails on her toes. Miss Dinah spins slowly, turning her head to stop and stare at each of us, her wintry eyes great gaping holes of rage, her lips frosted popsicles. She walks stiffly, her long skirt and bare feet dragging in the stiff, frozen grass with a sound that chills me, makes my bones ache. Long toenails scraping across ice.

Melanie twists out of my arms, and turns to face me, her eyes pleading. She grabs my hand. "Turn for me?" she asks. She presses her palm into mine and tries to get me to begin the game.

"*Ruby*," Miss Dinah says, waving my name on the bitter tip of her smile. "*Join the circle or the circle will join you.*"

The rope spins in the air behind her, a warning. It spins then splits into two.

I rise and take my place. The ropes feel like fire in my hands, but I hold onto them. The rhyme is the same as before. Miss Dinah likes the old games.

KeKe bends down to pick up the frayed ends of the ropes from the icy ground. She drops it, as if she is burned. Sucks her fingertips. "Why can't Amber turn today?" she cries. I glance over my shoulder at Amber. She is gripping her blade with two hands, stab, stabbing at the heart of Miss Dinah's favorite tree.

"*You are wasting your time, Amber. That is not where my heart is buried, child.*"

The smile on Miss Dinah's face makes me grip the ropes tighter. "Come on, KeKe," I say. "Begin."

"High John saw the mighty number," she sang. "High John, High John."

"High John saw the mighty number, High John, High John…"

Miss Dinah is a master jumper. No one can beat her jumping. We start off easy then speed the doubled ropes up. She gets real mad if we turn the ropes too slowly.

"High John was a mighty number, High Jo—"

"*Enough of that wearisome ditty. Sing something else,*" she cries.

We are just about to turn the ropes when I hear Amber whisper behind us. We are so astonished to hear her speak, that we let the ropes drop and fall slack. They hiss and groan as they touch the cold ground. The ropes only like heat, they hate the ice crystals prickling their frayed little bellies. The faster we turn, the hotter they get. I hate the ropes. They hiss and move like snakes and shed like them, too.

Miss Dinah whirls, turning to face Amber. "*What did you say, Amber dear?*"

Miss Dinah is trying to resume her nice voice, the friendly voice that comforted me when I awoke to find myself waiting in the dark blue.

Amber takes a deep breath, her eyes intent, her mouth a straight line, unsmiling.

"I said, can we hula hoop here?"

"Hula?" Melanie is confused. We have been jumping rope and patty-caking so long that we barely remember other activities.

"*Is that another way to turn, another way to jump?*" Miss Dinah asks.

Suddenly, I catch KeKe's eye and motion for her to lay the crying ropes all the way down. They hiss in protest.

"Yeah," I say. "Yes," with more enthusiasm. "Can we, Miss Dinah? I haven't hula-hooped in a long, long time."

"It's so fun," KeKe says, finally catching on. She sounds corny as all get out, but she fixes her face to something that looks like excitement.

Melanie hops over to us, her shoeless foot lightly skipping over the snow and ice. "I wanna hula, too! Me, me, me!" she cries, tugging on Miss Dinah's tattered dress.

Miss Dinah narrows her eyes into sharp slits. "*What does this hula look like?*"

"Like a big skinny, hard donut," Amber says. "You spin it around your waist and keep it spinning with your hips. You can spin it as fast or as slow as you want, but you can't let it touch the ground."

"It's so much fun, Miss Dinah," I say, trying to sound bright, light. "And there are songs, too!" KeKe says.

"*Songs?*" Miss Dinah cocks her head like a bird of prey. "*Try me,*" she says, both a warning and an invitation.

Amber walks to the center of the playground, away from the ropes that have finally quieted down. She adjusts the ragged remains of her dress that barely cover her chest, the strips of dark-stained fabric around her waist and begins to sing.

"Hula, hula, now who think they bad?"

"I do!" we all join in.

"Hula, hula, now who think they bad?"

"I do!"

"I think I'm bad 'cause Amber's my name. Yellow is my color don't you worry about my lover, honey."

"*Mmmf,* she think she fine."

"Fine, fine, fine enough, fine enough to blow your mind."

"*Mmmf,* she think she cool."

"Cool, cool, cool enough, cool enough to skip your school!"

"Hula, hula, now who think she bad?"

Miss Dinah's face, first pale with anger, now darkens and shines with pleasure. Her long teeth recede back into her mouth as do her claw-like nails. She turns back into the motherly creature that had come to the blue oneness and smiled and grinned and lied to our face, the haint that claimed us like a fairy godmother in a bad, bad dream.

"*I will get this hula,*" she says and rises to go. Her ugly feet levitate off the ground.

"We need five," Amber says quickly.

"*Five?*" Miss Dinah lowers herself, looks at us, suspicious. "*Why can't we share the one?*"

Amber glances around uneasy. KeKe begins to stutter. I start to speak but then Melanie interrupts me. Any other time I'd be annoyed by that but not this nightday.

"Because I want a pink one with sparkles on it! Sparkles and stars! And Ruby," she raises my hand. "Ruby wants a red one of course."

"No," I cut in. "Blue."

"I want blue," KeKe says, her voice soft, quiet.

Miss Dinah smiles, revealing normal teeth now. "*Yellow for Amber, RED for Ruby, Blue for KeKe, pink for my Melanie, and...and gold for me!*" Delighted, she shoots up into the air like a witch without a broom. She is heading straight for the Jackball sun, the bright, colorful sphere that seems to embody her every mood.

"That's it!" I say.

"That's what?" KeKe asks.

Amber motions at the ropes. I signal agreement.

"I know where she buried her heart." I point up to the fake swirly, swirly nebulous sky, the spinning Jackball where Miss Dinah disappears.

"We've got to get her ropes. Quick, KeKe, I know you hate turning, but we've got to hide them and keep them quiet somehow. Distract her with the new game."

"There are three ropes now. I know just what to do," KeKe says. "I can twist anything, I can braid anything, I just need a little help."

We sneak up on the ropes while little Melanie distracts them and grab them by their tails. Before they hiss and holler, KeKe ties one set of their ends into a tight knot.

"Now turn!" she says.

"Turn?" Melanie asks.

"Not you. Keep watch. Amber, Ruby, help me braid this."

The ropes jerk and yank, trying to get free. They sparkle and sting us but we keep braiding, one loop over the other loop, under the rest.

"It hurts," Amber says. We nod, yes it does—*what doesn't here?*—but keep folding over and over until we are done.

Melanie hops over one of the rocks to us, the little pigtail ends of her cornrows shaking, frantic. "Miss Dinah is on her way back here. She has the hula hoops."

"Back to your places," I whisper. Melanie runs to Amber, then runs back to me.

"What you doing over here?" I ask.

She looks worried. "I don't know how to hula hoop."

"It's easy," I tell her. "Just watch me."

"What if I drop it?"

"Miss Dinah loves you."

Melanie screws up her little chubby face. "Miss Dinah don't love nobody."

Surprised, I think about this as Miss Dinah lands, spinning on one foot.

"*Hulas, hulas,*" Miss Dinah sings. She hands them out, one by one. "*Now let's get started,*" she says.

We sing, each girl stepping into the center of the ring, spinning the hulas, singing of personal glories. Melanie drops her hula many times, but Miss Dinah only laughs and orders us to play again and again.

Finally, when I think I can't sing another note anymore, when I can't think of another boast to share, Amber steps forward to take my hoop.

"One hoop is easy. It's really for beginners and babies," she says, cutting her eye at Miss Dinah.

"*Amber, you know I hate babies.*" Miss Dinah hates babies because babies can't survive here. What would she do with something that needed more attention than her?

"A real master hooper can spin one, two, maybe even three hulas at a time."

Miss Dinah looks curious. *"Are you a master hooper, Amber?"* She is always ready for a challenge.

"I am," Amber says and Melanie gasps. She plops her hand to cover her mouth.

"No, Amber, you're going to drop them," Melanie whines.

"No, I won't, Melanie. Watch me!" Amber wraps her bun tighter in her scrunchie and smooths down what is left of her dress. She adds my red hula and KeKe's blue to her own yellow hula, one by one. She begins to spin around and walk as she hoops.

"Teddy bump, teddy bump! Teddy bump, teddy bump!" she sings as she swivels her hips, the hoops spinning slowly at first, then faster and faster.

Melanie looks like she's thrilled and terrified all at once. Her little eyes are about to pop.

"Oh, you want to try me, I see," Miss Dinah says. She unfurls her razor-sharp fingers, her flat palm up. *"Give them to me."*

Amber shakes her head no. "Miss Dinah, if you think you can beat me, get your own."

Miss Dinah throws her head back, surprised at Amber's tone, her newfound confidence. But she loves a challenge more than anything. What is a game worth if there is no risk? Her explanation for why she mixes danger and pain with all her playground games. But Miss Dinah likes to win every game. The weeping rocks are all that are left of the girls who lost.

Before Melanie can speak, Miss Dinah shoots back up to the Jackball sun. When she returns, she has hula-hoops stacked on her arms and waist. She doesn't even wait to land before she is spinning like a top.

"Hula, hula!" she cries. We cheer her on. "Miss Dinah, Go Dinah, Miss Dinah, Go Dinah!" The more we cheer and clap, the faster she spins.

Miss Dinah spins so fast, she and the hulas begin to sparkle and glow.

She is really showing out now. Doing a little shimmy shimmy limbo shake while she flows.

"Go Dinah, Miss Dinah!" Amber cries, then she nods at me. "Ruby, KeKe, add the heat!"

KeKe and I have unbraided and untangled the ropes. We crack the spinning Miss Dinah Ball like rodeo whips. Miss Dinah squeals with delight at first. "*More! More!*" she cries. She holds herself tightly, spinning as the hula hoops rotate around her. "*Faster, faster!*" The ropes respond, spinning her faster than any top we've ever seen.

"Oooh!" Melanie cries. We crack the ropes harder. They rip through the air like lightning bolts. Miss Dinah's ragged, tattered gown catches afire.

"*Wait!*" Miss Dinah screams, panic spoiling her smile. She tries to slow down, but she can't.

We have her, and we have her ropes.

We lasso her with the remaining hulas, and the Dinah Ball hovers in the air, just a few feet above the ground, crackling and rising the angrier she gets.

"*What have you done?*" she screams and levitates a few feet higher, trying to escape but the hula hoops are weighing her down. She can't go far.

"No!" I yell. "We can't let her get to the sun. If she makes it out of here…" I don't finish. We all know if she does escape, we are all finished. If we lose this game, we will become wet stones, or pebbles, or worse, dust.

"Give me the ropes," I say. KeKe looks confused. Melanie is wailing, and Amber takes out her blade. I think she understands.

She carves a deep groove into her favorite tree. I steer the Miss Dinah Ball with the ropes and use the tree to wrap the ends of the spitting, hissing ropes and anchor myself.

"You are going to have to climb up and ride the ball like a bull."

"Like a skateboard!" Melanie says.

Surprised, now even Amber looks unnerved.

"There's no other way out of here. You'll have to ride her evil tail right up out through the Jackball sky. All of you." They nod, recognition slowly registering in their eyes.

"But what about you, Ruby?" Melanie wails. I don't answer.

"And Amber..." I say, yanking the ropes. "Be still you evil thangs." They sputter in protest.

"Yes," Amber says.

"When you get to the Jackball, to the sun, I need you to carve out the heart she has buried there and toss it down to me. Don't let her get it. Can you do that?"

"Yes." Amber is crying. Melanie is crying, KeKe, all the wet stones, we are all crying. But I know what I have to do. I've seen a lot of movies, and in the movies, folks, especially Black folks, don't always get free. I've been knowing for some time, but hoping all the same. Truth is, I might never see my mama or my sister again. I'd already gotten used to that, but these girls, these plain little Black girls missing just like me, they were the only family I had here.

———

The Jackball pulses, its colors flickering from bright blood-reds, oranges, and yellows, to purples and blues so dark, they look like bruises. Each time Miss Dinah winces with pain, the Jackball changes colors and seems to wince, too. The Jackball is not only where Miss Dinah hid her heart, it is her heart.

I wrap the ropes even tighter around my wrists though it burns, and I scream, "Run, now!"

Miss Dinah has managed to get a few of her bony fingers loose. She's trying to cut through the hula hoops with her nails, but they are too strong. The see-saw, the merry-go-round, the slides on the dark playground are twisting and undulating. Soon the metal will transform, and they will run after the girls, after me.

KeKe takes Melanie by her hand, and they take a running start before they leapfrog onto the Dinah Ball. Amber follows, slips and runs to try again.

"You better stop playing girl," I cry, "and get on out of here!" I don't know how much longer I can hold onto these ropes, how long before Miss Dinah manages to take over the tree.

I yank my arm in a long rippling motion, bouncing the Dinah Ball up, up into the sky, like one of those Atari games. Amber, KeKe, and Melanie are holding onto the hula hoops, clutching them like a ladder. "Now climb!" I say, "climb like they monkey bars!"

Melanie is the first to get free. She pinwheels up and out into the force that circles the Jackball sun. KeKe and Amber follow her. Amber grabs her knife.

"*Noooooooo!*" Miss Dinah screeches, her face contorted, her lips and mouth stretched out like a bottomless hole. "*You can't leave me! Never, never leave me! I cannot bear this place alone.*"

And there it is. Miss Dinah, a creature as powerful as she, is just as lonely as any of the children she pretended to befriend here in the in-between world.

As much as I hate what she has done to us here, I wonder if Miss Dinah was ever missing. I wonder if she is not only a trapper but is trapped here, too.

Amber plunges her blade deep into the center of the Jackball sun. KeKe and Melanie sadly wave goodbye. None of us know what is on the other side of the Jackball sun or the big, wide blue. I do know I will never see them again.

Maybe out there in the blue, there is more than darkness. Maybe in its depths there are more than scary things that just want to run you down. I realize I didn't linger long enough to find out. Miss Dinah had called to me, maybe before anyone else had a chance.

———

When Amber tears the sky in two, and rips the Jackball sun to shreds, Miss Dinah lays in a smoldering heap, and the ropes fall asleep in my hands. The stinging stops, the burning, too. Real light, real warmth returns to the playground. I watch in wonder as ice melts for the first time in what might have been many ages. First the air is filled with the sound of exhalations. Then laughter. The music of little girls awakening from a long, cold nap. Silver and gold rainbow bubbles float in the air above our heads. Then I discover what the ropes can truly do. We each take turns, turning, each take turns, jumping, changing. I reach inside the memory of my oldest girlhood dream, of Trapper Keeper notebooks, scratch n' sniff stickers, new back-to-school clothes, freshly done hair—fried, dyed, and laid to the side—and Granddaddy's old dresser painted green. I hold the rope and remember my sister Emerald and my Mama's face, then I lay the ropes down and skip all the way home, thinking of the color blue.

The Persistence of Memory

BY JAN MAHER

Once you learn you never forget. Marie could hear the voice of her father, encouraging her to pick herself and her new Schwinn bike up from the pavement and try again. He'd refused to put training wheels on it, though her mother had fretted about that. Instead, he'd hold the bike, and run alongside until the speed exceeded his ability to keep up. Then he'd shout encouraging words at his pigtailed and petrified daughter until she fell over. Backpedal! Brake! You can do it! Stop and slide off the seat! Get your feet off the pedals and on the ground!

Bruise by bruise, scrape by scrape, Marie had mastered the art of staying upright, backpedaling to apply the coaster brakes and slow down, sliding from the seat at exactly the same moment the bicycle came to a full stop. She'd even gotten to the point where she could ride hands-free and— inspired by her favorite circus act—sidesaddle. She could balance another child on her handlebars and did so with each of her three younger siblings until they, too, had gotten their own first bikes.

So it was with absolute confidence in her muscle memory and abilities that Marie confronted her great-granddaughter's bicycle, kept in the garage for Celia's occasional visits. She'd been told she was too old to be on the road, and her license was taken away. Not by the state, mind you, but by her own child. Her son Matt had actually hidden it from her. He knew she was too crafty not to have a spare key, and he knew she was a stickler for obeying the law. Without that, she wouldn't dare take her Hyundai into traffic. California had no problems with her abilities: they'd issued her most recent license good through her hundred-and-first birthday.

It's not that she drove much anyway. She just wanted to go down to the Market Cafe to have a little lunch on the balcony with Amy. They had a senior special she'd been enjoying every Tuesday for the past twenty-seven years. Her forays to this favored spot had outlasted even the original owners of the place. A series of new owners had taken it over. Waitresses and waiters had come and gone, menus had changed, but there had always been a senior special at lunch, and she always had it on Tuesday.

Her oldest friends gathered there with her at first, but one by one they shed their mortal coils and shuffled off into the Great Beyond. Marie began eating lunch with their children. Now, she was on her way to meet the newly retired grand-daughter of a woman Marie had called her very best friend in eighth grade. Shirley had married young, bred young, so her daughter Ella had been only sixteen years younger than Shirley. Ella kept the family tradition going and now her daughter Amy was sixty-five with great-grandchildren of her own. Marie liked Amy. She had spunk. It would be fun to see Amy at lunch, to catch up on her plans for retirement. If Amy was a bike rider, maybe they could take a spin now and then together, do a picnic or something.

Matt had come for a few days to visit and talk her into doing things his way. Having secreted her proof of road-worthiness, he insisted she alert him when she needed a ride, so she could see how nice it would be to move into the Living

Well Retirement Home where you never had to fight traffic because they have a little bus that took residents to all the malls and movies. Well, she would be damned if she was going to start acting like some rich woman with a chauffeur just because she was looking at the near edge of a century. And she was not moving. Don't let them carry me out of here, she'd instructed her next-door neighbor, unless they're carrying me to Forest Lawn.

Marie stood for a brief moment contemplating the bike. In her day, you got black ones or blue ones. This bicycle was hot pink and metallic lavender. Her great-grandsons had black, red, silver, or blue bikes. All the fuss over what were boy colors and girl colors didn't make sense to Marie.

She remembered how to tilt it and lift a leg up and through to straddle the center bar. Another thing she didn't understand. Why aren't all bikes this easy to mount? The fellas always have to risk—if not life and limb—something maybe even more important to get themselves all the way up there on the seat, and god forbid they slip off. She remembered Matt's first such mishap vividly, and she bet he remembered it even more.

Taking the helmet from where it had hung on the handle-bars, putting it on, pulling the strap tight, Marie felt ready for anything. She pushed off, wobbled out of the garage and down the driveway. She turned right onto the road. Market Cafe was a straight shot down a mild hill, about a mile ahead, just past the intersection on the left.

In no time at all, she found her secure balance. It was surprisingly easy to pedal. You're right, Pop, she called cheer-ily, picking up speed. You never forget! She rested her legs, letting the momentum of wheels on downhill asphalt take her forward.

Oh, the joy of wind on the face! How long had it been? Decades, but how many now? Matt would have been about twelve when he got too old to want to be seen riding in the company of his mother and father. Then Roger wasn't able to enjoy bicycling anymore because his knee kicked up too much. Marie had given all the bikes away when they moved to their G.I.-loan-backed new house.

At the halfway point, she lifts her hands into the air, just for a second or two. Yes! She can still do it! They want her to move into a home. Pshaw! When she says it in company, they mock her for her old-fashioned speech. Here on the open empty road, she shouts it out. PSHAW! I can take care of myself! She pedals harder, picks up speed.

Her Schwinn was a black 24-incher. She'd begged for it one Christmas and been given to understand in no uncertain terms that it was a luxury the family simply couldn't afford. Yet there it stood, on Christmas morning, the surprise of the century. It had lasted a good long time, too, and a lucky thing. When the Depression hit, she rode that bike everywhere, and having it allowed her to search far and wide for the job she finally found ten miles from home, clerking three days a week in a department store.

She coasts downhill past a clump of serviceberries. She never sees them when she's driving past, but now they jump out at her, inviting her to stop on the way back and pick enough for a jar of jam.

Approaching the intersection now, she backpedals to slow down. The pedals offer no resistance. The bike speeds on. Pop, how the hell do you stop this thing? No pigtails now, just pure panic. And coming from the left on the crossroad, a mammoth semi. On, she zooms, clutching the rubber handlebar grips, unaware that the braking system she so desperately wants is a mere inch from her white knuckles.

If she's lucky, the truck will skedaddle right on through and get out of the way. Then she can survive the intersection and aim for the grass in front of the cafe. That's bound to slow her down at least a little! But the truck, too, is slowing down, preparing to turn.

She barrels on. Dammit, she yells. I want to celebrate my hundredth!

Some ancient part of her mind heeds the call. While her conscious mind holds on for dear life, the feral brain makes a series of crucial decisions. Lean to the left, turn the wheel, register the horrified look on the part of the truck driver, narrowly miss the collision, correct for leaning too far to the left, oh no! Another, steeper downhill now. No one coming? No one coming. U-turn! Stabilize! Breathe!

At last she feels the bicycle begin to slow down. Pedal. Steady. She barks the command at her hands, and miraculously, they obey. Ease over to the edge of the road, ready for one last turn into the cafe parking lot. A car ahead. You can do it. Remember to signal your turn this time. Steady!

She hits the curb and the bike, surprised by the sudden change of terrain, skids sideways and bucks her into the drainage ditch that runs along the driveway, her skirt immodestly askew. The bike falls back into the path of the oncoming motorist.

A crunch. The squeal of brakes, voices shouting, hubbub aplenty.

Her hip hurts, but whose wouldn't? Otherwise, everything seems to be working. The crowd reaches her just as she's about to stand up.

Don't try to move! Stay right there! Hold still! An ambulance is on the way!

Oh, for goodness sake, cancel it, she insists, and hauls herself up out of the cattails, dripping muddy water. The bike, alas, is mangled beyond rideability, but she is miraculously unscathed. No, she is fine, really, and about to be late. The skirt's a mess, but it will dry. She'll take the outside steps to the balcony, so she won't track dirt through the cafe.

After lunch, she calls Matt for a ride home. He bellows and fumes, fusses and grumbles. Could have been killed! Crazy old lady! Retirement home! Blah blah blah blah blah.

Well if you won't let me drive, what choice do I have?

Fine. Fine! If you want to kill yourself, go ahead. Just don't say I didn't try to drum some sense into your ancient contrarian head. He slaps the license down on the table.

The next day, she drives to the bicycle shop to pick out a replacement for the one she totaled. Matt goes along, begrudgingly acknowledging that her skills as a driver are consummate. Well, "adequate" is actually the word he's willing to part with. At least, he grouses, you'll have a seatbelt on the next time you run into something.

They pick out a new shiny bike for Celia, purple and glittery. While she pays for it, Matt browses the accessories, giving Marie an opportunity to chat up the nice young sales clerk. So, sonny, she says, how exactly do you stop one of these?

Lifepod

BY VANDANA SINGH

Sometimes the Eavesdropper remembered being a mother. She would stare at the single empty life-sac and think about the man who should have been lying there in cold sleep, the man who had once been the boy she'd held in her arms. At other moments she was convinced that she had done no such thing, that motherhood had never happened to her, that all she had ever been was what she was now: a traveler on an interminable journey between the stars, afloat in the belly of the Lifepod. At these moments, when even the human sleepers seemed to take on a terrifying unfamiliarity, she would feel as though she were at the edge of some calamitous discovery.

But these hanging, empty moments of anticipation were few. Almost immediately she would be distracted by the thought-clouds, the dreams of the men and women in cold sleep. There were two of them in particular who had once meant something to her: a man and a woman. She returned to their thought-worlds whenever she herself was awake, as though the tattered clouds of their remembrances would bring back to her what she had been. It was rather like eating (she still remembered that, at least) and at the end, still coming away hungry. The life-sacs were filmy, translucent; she couldn't see their faces, only the vague human shape suspended in a watery garden, but she knew them by their thought-signatures, by the worlds of their dreams.

The Man

The man dreamed obsessively of the enemy. Through him she saw the great creatures with their giant, stiff wing (single, like a cloak) folded on their backs, the round, featureless heads swiveling from one side to another, scanning through some invisible means the bleak landscape of his moon-world. The aliens stopped before the broken bodies that littered the battle-field, pausing before human and alien remains, while the young man crouched in the shadow of an outbuilding, trying not to breathe. Through his memories the Eavesdropper saw the long vertical gash on the abdomen of each alien: the lipless mouth open wide into a horrific darkness, the delicacy with which the prehensile edges of the orifice gathered in each body like an embrace and closed around it. She felt the young man's horror, his anger, going through her like a cold knife.

But sometimes he dreamed of a green and primitive place on a distant planet. His childhood: running in a long, green meadow with patches of bare earth and wild tussocks of grass that would make him stumble so that suddenly he would be looking between grass-shoots into an ant's world. And the washer with its arms aloft, swift-walking through the grass, back and forth, making the wash billow out in the constant wind... The mother was holding a woven-reed tray full of yeri grains, shaking it so the tiny winged grains flew up and caught the currents, streaming out in skeins of spotted gold, up the hill to the tanglewood, where the fine nets of the trees would catch them and they would sprout many months later. She did this just for him, not because she needed to; the seedblower had done most of the job already, up high. He watched her brown arms, strong and rhythmic, and the seeds rippling out in wide ribbons, and laughed in delight. She smiled at him. Lying with his face against the ground, the boy saw her as a great tree, her bare, callused toes peering from between the folds of the blue sari like roots that would hold them all to the earth, her head up in the clouds, long black hair turning to gray, loosening from the bun at the back of her neck so that the tendrils were fanned by the breeze...

But what struck the Eavesdropper about this man, this boy, was the way he felt about his mother: she was the bedrock of his world. At these times she felt the shock of familiarity: that she had once been the recipient of such an uncomplicated love. But her memories were unreliable; she recalled things that she had apparently experienced or done that seemed distant, unfamiliar, shocking. She knew for instance that she had herself spent a long time with the enemy aliens, but the knowledge of precisely what had happened—the capture, the incarceration of the humans, including herself, their journey through space in the alien ship in cold sleep, the attack or explosion that had blown the little Lifepod away into space on some random trajectory—the details were blurred in her mind, her personal memory contaminated by those of the others. Whatever she remembered came to her in flashes or glimpses: pungent, warren-like passageways, blind gropings in the heat of a room, the press of terrified bodies, the great silhouette of the alien in the doorway, its mind reaching out to her mind, calming it, telling her what to do (what was it she had been told with such urgency?), and she remembered also sweet hunger, and nutrients snaking out into her in thin, aromatic streams, and the mourning and celebrating of a death...

The Eavesdropper

The Eavesdropper moved slowly through the darkness of

the Lifepod, floating over each womb-like holding unit, tasting the dreams of each dreamer. But what do *I* dream of, then, when I sleep, she thought to herself. She wondered, as she often had, why her own holding sac allowed her to wake and move about, and return to it only when she needed nutrients or rest. Each life-sac was a little ecosystem of alien life-forms: bacterial blooms, algal fans that generated currents of nutrients and harvested waste, the whole maintaining a delicate symbiotic relationship with each occupant. But her sac was unique, larger than the rest, its chemistry adjusted to allow her these moments of wakefulness. Why had she been given this privilege? The vision of the alien in the doorway so many years ago, came to her mind as the answer: was that what it had told her so urgently, to see to the safety of her people, the humans? Why? Where were they being taken before the explosion cast them into space? Why hadn't they been killed? What had been her relationship with the alien? Sometimes she thought of it with simple hatred and fear, the unknown, the monster of nightmare moving across the ruined battlefield; then she would realize that she was seeing it through the eyes of one of the dreamers. When she admitted this to herself she felt as though cracks had appeared in her understanding of the universe, little fissures that threatened to open up and swallow her. She had betrayed her people, these people, in some way. Hadn't she? Else why would she have gotten the privilege (or curse) of wakefulness during this long voyage? Why would she remember the alien with half-buried, shameful hunger (what had they done to her? with her?), with—yes, there was no escaping it—longing, as though the alien had satisfied in her some terrible, chemical need?

Sometimes she thought she saw the alien in the Lifepod. She would feel its presence just beyond the edge of her perceptions, as though it was waiting in the shadows beyond that life-sac or this one. Once or twice she thought she saw its face, so unimaginably strange, yet so familiar, hovering ghost-like just beyond the pale radiance from the life-sacs, or half-concealed among the knotted ganglia of the Lifepod itself. When she approached the phantom or mirage it would dissolve into the darkness, so that in her saner moments she knew it was not really there. At other times she wanted to believe it was there, to know that there was someone watching over her, tasting *her* dreams, knowing *her* thoughts.

And then there were her hands.

They were not as she remembered them; in the half-light, the brown skin was mottled, thickened, her nails grown long. She held the hands before her, floating in a shawl of moisture from her life-sac, and wondered if she herself was the alien in the shadows. She would convince herself very quickly that this could not be so, because the memories she had of being human, even the borrowed ones, were so vivid and familiar. These little debates with herself were a comfort; it was such a human thing to do, after all, to argue with your own doubts and fears when awake in the dark.

But she couldn't come to any definite conclusion because of the voices in her mind. Sometimes something spoke to her without words, deep inside her head. She wasn't certain if it was the alien, the Lifepod in which they were adrift, or some lost memory of her own. It could not be the Lifepod, she reasoned; the Lifepod's mind was barely discernible to her, and what she could read of it was child-like and strange. It had been grown quickly from the body of the alien ship to host the captured humans, and when the explosion blew it away from the ship, it had not had time to mature. It knew how to maintain the environment on which they all depended and to protect itself, and to sing out its name on all permitted frequencies, but it did not know that it was going to die. It did not know that after a certain time it would need to find a mother ship, to dock, to hibernate until it renewed itself for further flight. Here, in this uncharted, empty sector of the galaxy, who would hear it sing? Who would tell it what it needed, how to find it? It was hardly more than a child, singing in joyful ignorance in the dark between the stars.

Then who was it who told her things as she floated in her life-sac at the edge of sleep?

Some of the things she heard were memories, she told herself. She had been incarcerated somewhere in the caverns of the mother ship, among alien bodies, overhearing their conversation. Or it was the alien stowaway, if it existed, telling her all this, opening before her mind's eye the strange vistas of other worlds. Sometimes it would chant to her bits of its own lore, meaningless and frightening all at once, repeating the phrases like a child in a dark room, reciting for comfort. But nothing it said made sense.

To eat and be eaten is to become yourself and another. To eat is to give birth, to see with new eyes. Remember, remember this.

And:

We are separate so the whole may know itself. In eating, we edge closer to the Hidden One. Know this!

But she didn't know anything. Only that she might have been a mother once, and the man who was missing—who should have been in the empty life-sac—was perhaps her son. She knew that she, along with the others, had been captured from their colony on a moon-world. And that she had had some dealings with the enemy, things she would rather not admit to herself. So here they were, blasted away from the ship, adrift in the belly of an infant Lifepod, lost in the sea of night.

The Woman

The other sleeper who had once had some connection

with the Eavesdropper was a woman who hadn't spoken for years, even before the capture. What had led her into silence was not an emotional or physiological condition, but a philosophical one. The Eavesdropper remembered this woman (whether through her own memories or through those of the other sleepers she could not always say) before the capture as a person who liked to be with the others but did little more than smile or nod. The woman liked the physical labor of the research camp; building and repair work, and tending the greenhouses, and when busy in these things she liked to hum strange little tunes, but spoke no words. The Eavesdropper knew that this woman had come to such a state because she had discovered the inadequacy of words. The woman was a scientist-poet whose reality had once been forged of words and mathematics. "Consider that antique concept, force," she had said once, before the silence, "which makes sense at your scale or mine. The ancients built their theories, their mathematics, around that concept. But the moment you enter the sub-atom, or when you begin to examine the graininess of space-time, you realize that the word 'force' has little meaning. You invent the field, another antique concept, and then that, too, fails. You abandon false analogies, then, you take refuge in strange axioms, in your mathematics. But go far enough and even mathematics fails as a descriptive, a language in which to describe nature. What do you have left, then?"

Somebody had laughed. The woman dreamed of a face, sometimes, not yearningly, but with pleasure, and it was the face of the man who should have been lying here in the Life-pod, in the empty sac. "She dreams of my son," the Eavesdropper would say to herself. The man had laughed companionably in the woman's dreams. "When mathematics fails? Then there's only poetry," he had said, smiling—his brown eyes and skin aglow, his black hair so soft and shiny in the light. Only poetry, dreamed the sleeping woman, recalling this, recalling him.

This woman had spent a lifetime studying "the graininess of space-time." She had been part of the first team to map the tachyonic signatures that hinted at the existence of another universe underlying their own. They were only faint trails, like the tracks of ghost crabs walking on a sandy beach ("Ghost," said the Eavesdropper to herself; "Crab. Beach." And she saw a sweep of yellow sand, a windswept blue sky—an old memory, hers or the woman's.) The tachyon trails were regular, their mathematics sublime, their origins mysterious. The woman had lived three hundred and seven Earth-years, traveling on slowships from world to inhabited world, cheating time and death so she could study these trails. "They call to me," she had said defensively to that man, the Eavesdropper's son. "They are the shape of something I do not understand. Something large, complex, perhaps self-aware." "How large?" "Of galactic proportions," she'd said seriously, enjoying his surprise. "Why else would you need tachyons? How else can your brain tell your arm to twitch if it is 400 light-years away?" "You have such ideas!" laughed the man, half admiring, half mocking. "I thought you said last time that the tachyons were evidence of another universe." "I did," she acknowledged, smiling. "It's a matter of words. Whether or not that thing is sentient, it is a universe unto itself."

He was a practical man, an engineer, a pilot, and a poet in three ancient languages, and he kept her sane. "I see a bit here, a bit there," she would tell him, frustrated, after several hours immersed in a holo of her theoretical construct. "But I never see the pattern as a whole, as one complete thing." And he'd looked at her a moment and quoted Kalidasa in the original Sanskrit.

...I see your gaze in the deer's quick glance
Your slender limbs in the shyama vine
Your luminous beauty in the face of the
        moon...
But, oh misfortune! I see not
All of you in any one thing...

Slowly, trying to put together the mathematics of the
tachyon signatures, she had realized that no language existed
—verbal or mathematical—that could describe them. "I must
invent a meta language," thought the dreamer, "a language
beyond words and equations." She became outwardly silent,
although her mind still chattered away in words and equations, but the Eavesdropper sometimes saw great and inexplic-
able vistas in the dreams of the sleeper: vast abstractions,
geometries that defied the imagination, fractal swirls of color
that rose and vanished, and she had the impression that the
scientist-poet was indeed inventing a new language, iota by
iota.

This, then is poetry, thought the Eavesdropper to herself,
and abruptly the memory of the alien would fill her mind.
"Eat," the alien had said to her. "To eat is to become yourself
and another." And the great lipless mouth had opened,
drawing her in, and she could hear herself screaming. With a
great effort she would calm herself, bring herself back to the
dark interior of the Lifepod, and the faint, familiar glow of
each life-sac. And the alien voice in (or out of) her head recited
with childish insistence: "Why do we live? To eat. To be eaten.
And so become closer to the Hidden One."

Sometimes the Eavesdropper talked to the Lifepod. It
understood only a few pictures she sent to it in her mind, and
it seemed to her that the creature resented these interruptions.
It would do as she asked, like a sullen child—once it had
opened for her a round, translucent eye in the wall of the
chamber through which she could see the unmoving starscape

—and as soon as she was done, it would return to its play. In the early months (or years) of this uncharted journey, she had wept and railed at it, asking it to find the way back to their world, but, not knowing what she was talking about (which world? She herself didn't know), it had simply shut her out.

So the Eavesdropper floated through the Lifepod, sipping at the dreams of the sleepers, sometimes going to sleep herself. If she could remember her dreams, if she could be aware of them as she was of the dreams of others, she would know who she was. But she couldn't remember. So she waited, sometimes for death, sometimes for that knock on the door that would signal the return of the lost son, the missing sleeper. He would come back. This she knew about him, he was the kind who never gave up, who came back against all odds. As far as she could remember she hadn't seen him captured. He was on his way to find them. He would knock on the door, she would open it and she would know who she was. She waited for that or for death. Sometimes she couldn't tell the difference.

The Eavesdropper

The Eavesdropper was thinking about the moon-world. Her hands—she saw her hands, brown and fragile against the leaves of the greenhouse: they curled to form a round window through which she could see her world. In the foreground was the leaf, heart-shaped, slightly serrated, with fine white hairs on the green surface, and behind it the transparent wall of the greenhouse, with the familiar view of low, barren hills. Half the sky was dominated by the mother planet, the gas giant with its rings, its phantasmagoria of storm-clouds, the orange glow diffusing into the little room, turning her hands red brown. And the other half of the sky was speckled with stars.

This, she thought to herself, not without a certain incredulity, was a memory all her own: not the view (which was in the dreams of the man and the woman, and some of the other humans who lay sleeping in the Lifepod) but the two hands, and how the fingers had curled around in a circle.

"Look through it!" she had said to someone, a boy who might have been her son. He had peered through the window of her fingers—she remembered glossy black hair that fell to his shoulders and was always getting in his eyes. He had long, brown legs; he liked to run, to chase the other children. He looked through the window and laughed, and ran off on those long legs. Did he understand how moving it was to her, to see that particular juxtaposition of those objects? The moon had been in just the right position for Half-Night, when its night side faced the planet instead of the endless field of stars. In that moment, at that time, the window told all: the sap rising in the green stem, the green leaf opening like a hand toward an alien light, against a partial backdrop of stars. She had been moved to tears.

Remembering, she wasn't sure what had brought her to the middle of the chamber. She had thought she had been sleeping in her life-sac, but here she was, floating in the middle of the Lifepod, surrounded by the other sacs with their sleepers. Their dreams lapped around the edges of her consciousness, but some other feeling was rising through her, overcoming the familiar mental background noise: fear, excitement. She realized that the Lifepod was talking to her —to her, after all this time, communicating something urgently. Between the thick, pillar-like sap-vessels of the Life-pod, a portion of the wall contracted, then expanded into a round window, filmed over with a translucent membrane that slowly cleared. She saw through the window a vista of stars, and a bright, spherical, gray object in the foreground. It had locked velocity with the Lifepod. Memory stirred. A human exploration vessel, a small one that may hold one to three people...

So this was it, thought the Eavesdropper, suddenly light-headed, her heart thudding: this, the moment she had been waiting for all along. He had come, her son, against all odds, following the song of the Lifepod through space.

"Bring me out!" she commanded the Lifepod, pushing off against a sap-vessel so that she bumped gently against the window. She felt herself encased in a thick film of mucosal secretions; a vast muscular contraction launched her out of the window onto the surface of the Lifepod.

She struggled at first with the thick strands of film around her; she couldn't see because the film was still opaque. A jolt of terror coursed through her and then subsided. The film was slowly hardening and clearing—she could breathe, she was atop the Lifepod, poised over a vertiginous emptiness speckled with stars.

She felt it like a rush to the head, the music of the universe running through her as though she were a stream-bed, a cup overflowing. Before, space had been nothing but darkness and stars, something to be crossed so one could get to one's destination. But now she could sense the tachyonic pathways all around her, like fine lacework, like the tangled neural pathways, the guts of some vast beast. The Hidden One, said the alien, exulting, and she looked around for the alien but it wasn't there. Only herself and that strange object motionless above her, round, like an opaque window against the stars.

The rush faded. She saw the small humanoid figure in a space-suit detach from the side of the craft, attached to it with an umbilicus that reeled out slowly as the figure jetted toward her. The light from the craft spilled over her; she saw the surface of the Lifepod, fissured and full of knobs and warts. She remembered something, a fragment of memory that was not her own: a summer hot and breathless, sandy cliffs, and thousands, perhaps millions of the aliens in their summer sleep, their flightless single wings spread to take in the sunlight, to draw in the fuel they needed for the long winter-to-come. It was an image so strange and yet so familiar that she turned around again to see if the alien had somehow manifested in her little bubble, but it was not there. She pushed the image from her mind, stretched her arms out to the descending figure. "My son," she said to herself, her voice catching. Then a jolt of memory: she was standing barefoot in the grass in a blue sari, setting out the washing. The boy was lying face down on the ground, watching ants. It was a green and primitive place on a distant planet; he had been born there, some years before the trip to the barren moon of another world…

But if that is who I am, she thought in sudden consternation, then the man who lies dreaming in the life-sac below my feet is my son. Then who is this?

Or maybe, she thought desperately, the memory was not hers, just as that other memory—with the aliens stretched out like so many flies on a sand dune—that other memory was not hers. She looked up at the human figure in the spacesuit; he was getting closer and closer, decelerating. She could not see his face. Instead she saw the reflection of the Lifepod in the spacesuit's headgear, all lit up by the spacecraft's beacon, and the clear bubble in which she stood like a fly trapped in amber. And she saw what she was.

A half-alien thing: the shape still human but the face so strange! Ovoid eyes, the bony skull sheath jutting over her cheekbones. She held her small brown hands before her and saw the tips curving into hard pincers, transforming almost as she stood there, transfixed with horror and wonder. She looked down at herself in the hard, honest light and saw that the reflection was not false. What am I? she wondered, aghast.

And the alien within answered her, not in words but in a swell of understanding that took her breath away. She remembered what it had proposed, what she had agreed to: the terrifying darkness within its body, her screams echoing in her ears as the thin tendrils inside it wrapped around her, penetrated her skin. After that, the chrysalid sleep as the new bridges between the two of them formed and hardened, as alien transforming organelles coursed through her body, as great, chemical swathes of emotion—pleasure and fear, hunger and sweet, nameless desire swept through her. Then she was lifted from the dead shell of the alien into a brief light, and into the life-sac which eased her once more into the sleep of forget-fulness...

So the Eavesdropper stood before the stranger who might or might not be her son: she a creature not alien, not human, but a bridge, a thing that was new, the first of its kind. He (or was it she?) stood away from her, bumping gently against the Lifepod, the long umbilicus stretching out into the dark like a luminous, flexible bridge. The stranger's hands were as yet empty, but the posture was wary, as though poised to activate the space-suit's weapons systems. She felt some ancient part of her cry out: Do you not know me, son? And something inside her gave way, crumbled like a mud wall before a flood.

I must know, she said to herself. I must know if you are him. She stretched her arms toward him, slowly, saw him tense, then relax. Suddenly she wanted to enclose him in the dark, to exchange blood with blood, to share synapse with synapse, to know him cell by cell, and so become something new. The sharpness of her hunger took her breath away. In that brief moment she saw that the Lifepod itself was her kin, a hybrid of the original alien species and some gravid denizen of a distant ocean world, and its mind was clear to her for the first time. Why couldn't she know the stranger in the same way? No, she said, feeling or imagining the infant mouth straining to open in her chest. That was the alien within, as it had once been, remembering. There had to be some other way.

She opened her hands to show him that they were empty. She put the palms together in the old Indic gesture of greet-ing; then moved the fingers to make a circle, a window through which she could see him against the Lifepod and the infinity of stars. Around her, along pathways invisible to human and alien, sang the tachyons, leaving ghost trails in space-time that the sleeping woman in the chamber under her feet could only imagine. Only the Eavesdropper could sense them, could see where they were leading, to the heart of the great galactic beast, the Hidden One. She saw for just a moment that she had been conceived and forged for a great purpose. But for now she was only a bridge in the darkness between ship and ship, being and being. Through the window of her hands she watched the stranger come slowly toward her.

Portrait of the Terrorist as a Young Suburbanite

BY ANDREW ALTSCHUL

Once upon a time and a very good time it was there were moppy little dogs chasing cars down the lane and a racket of sparrows out the kitchen window. The school bus stopped on the corner and when the child rode in the mornings to the brick schoolhouse on a hill she leaned her cheek against the cold glass and watched the trees curve up into a milk-shot sky and the power lines drooped and rose and drooped and rose and disappeared into green glare spangle.

The gardener came once a week. Out the bay window she watched the truck pull to the curb and the short, gray-faced man went back and forth on the lawn making noise and when he left she went outside and flung fistfuls of cut grass and sneezed. He had a funny mustache and was called Pablo. Sometimes he left a coffee can with new-cut flowers on the doorstep. In summer it was hot and the air rang with insects; her mother made lemonade and brought Pablo a glass which he drank at the bottom of the porch and handed back. She left an envelope in place of the flower can. Pablo never came inside.

In kindergarten you pressed your hand into wet cement—blue for the boys, pink for the girls—and brought home the hard, heavy plate. You built buildings with plastic logs and drew your mother and father in sixty-four colors and each morning you stood proudly with hand on heart and pledged allegiance to the flag. Miss Daniels gave her a cup of chocolate ice cream with a tiny wooden paddle and sent a note to her parents: "She has a sunny disposition and a love of learning, but she is quiet shy [*sic*]."

There was a stream behind the house and neighbor children roamed the woods playing military games. Ash and maple and dogwood, tall ferns and the stink of skunk cabbage. When you rolled a stone the damp dirt wriggled with salamanders. In summer they picked strawberries at Bryce Farm and in winter they sledded down Sam's Hill until Sam's Hill was sold to developers. Soon there were big houses where rich people lived.

"We're not rich," her mother explained. "We're lucky."

Cannondale, New Jersey, sprung from farmland twenty-four miles from the Lincoln Tunnel. The garage door rumbled under the house each night and then her father was home. When they drove into the city she wore a dress and buckled shoes and looked like a real lady. Her brother combed his hair. The car went down through the long tunnel and her father pretended to hold his breath the whole time. Her mother stared straight ahead when the men with dirty faces rubbed newspapers on the windshield.

"Drive away," her mother said.

"The light's red—"

"Just go."

When it snowed, Pablo shoveled the driveway. But then, in spring, a different man mowed the lawn and she asked her mother where Pablo was and her mother fixed her barrette and said Pablo had to go home. In first grade they rode the bus to see Betsy Ross's house and the Liberty Bell. A boy in her class threw up going home and it crept down the aisle and then two more kids threw up.

"She has excellent penmanship," Mrs. Brill wrote. "She always says please."

Her father had a favorite chair and he sat in it each night. Ice made a sudden snapping in his glass. The swim club was down the road and in summer wet feet slapped on the deck and her brother learned to jackknife; orange soda and Marathon bars gave you a stomachache. That winter they took a family vacation on a big ship. Her mother wore a floppy hat. When they came to an island everyone stood at the rail and waved. They threw coins in the water and Black boys leapt from the pier, thrashing in the water and showing their teeth. The child pleaded with her father for a coin and as she pulled back her arm a boy on the pier smiled at her. She wanted him to get the coin. Then there was shouting, many heads frothing in the water and men running down the pier with a cloth stretcher. She would never know if the boy they pulled from the water was the same boy. She would never know if he died.

Miss Gallo had to have her appendix out and the substitute played a guitar and sang a song about answers blowing in the wind. The child lost the spelling bee when she misspelled *tortoise* and she cried in her room and her face was burning. When she came downstairs the tall man was on the television again, the same one every night, with the long, white beard and the black turban. There was a crowd of younger men with black beards kneeling in the street, or waving guns over their heads. Her father looked into his glass, his tie undone, and said, "Jesus, Jesus."

Outside the town library, there was a black cannon on a pedestal overlooking Charlie's general store. Miss Gallo said not to climb on it. The cannon had been there since before there was a town, she said. The mayor set it off each year at the Fourth of July picnic but it fired only smoke. Once upon a time, Miss Gallo said, their grandfather's grandfathers had to defend themselves against enemies. One day they might have to do so again. It was hard to understand, Miss Gallo said, but sometimes when people are lucky it makes other people mad. It makes them want to take what those people have.

"Sometimes we have to protect what belongs to us," she said. "We have to stand up for what's right."

She liked chocolate and strawberry, but never vanilla. She had a habit of plucking the eyes from rag dolls and for a brief period she was fascinated by frogs. She was the first in her class to master long division. She was inexplicably terrified by her grandparents' poodle, Audrey. When her mother was asked, many years later, what might explain her actions, whether anything in her childhood pointed to such tendencies, she teared up, lips tight. There was nothing, she said, nothing —remembering only how lucky she'd once felt. They were a perfect family, she said, a happy family, looking straight into the camera but seeing only the child's clear eyes, doubled in the windows of the school bus, following the power lines as they droop and rise, droop and rise, carrying light into peaceable American homes.

———

She remembers piles of leaves, orange and brown and wet underneath. She remembers the thick, soily smell. Snow days when the lane disappeared and a sea of white becalmed every house. She remembers Miss Moore, her turquoise and feather earrings, remembers when she was suspended for talking too much about Indians. She remembers soccer practice and the Statue of Liberty, chicken pox and sore throats and *Casey at the Bat*. She remembers voting for Jimmy Carter, her mother holding her up in the voting booth to pull the lever that made all the buttons pop back out with a thunk. She remembers times tables and the pyramids of Egypt, a special room full of puzzles and microscopes that the gifted students visited once a week. She remembers Lisa Kim, the Korean girl, her oil-black, fascinating hair in the front row. She remembers the sharp vinegar smell of Lisa Kim's lunch, how the other kids pretended to throw up. Someone said Lisa Kim was adopted; for a few weeks, she decided she was adopted, too.

She remembers the hostages. Every night on TV they told you how many days it had been. Carter tried to save them but it didn't work. The old man with the beard always frightened her, the sound of the word "ayatollah." She remembers asking her father why the old man wanted hostages and her father stirring his drink with his finger. "It's hard to explain," he said.

Her mother turned off the TV and said, "No, it's not."

She remembers Carter losing, after a long day when her mother called every name on a sheet of paper and reminded them to vote. Her father smiled reassuringly and said nothing would change, and it didn't. She remembers the Miracle on Ice. She remembers the morning her mother cried next to the kitchen radio, and the name Mark David Chapman. She remembers when the hostages went free.

She remembers these things during her first year in prison, a frozen stone warren 14,000 feet above sea level. Solitary confinement, only a sink and a pallet, a tiny window, a glimpse of sapphire sky. She walks a butterfly pattern in her cell, two blankets around her shoulders, draped shawl-like over her thinning hair: six steps lengthwise, seven diagonal. She's decided a hundred circuits equals one mile; she walks ten miles a day. Stale bread and cloudy soup comes on a tin tray, if the guards don't steal it first. She eats slowly, despite the foul taste. Her skin has grown scaly with psoriasis, her teeth ache from the relentless cold. She's allowed no visitors, no phone calls, no contact with the embassy, no books. She spends hours at the window, assembling home movies in her mind, sepia-tone fragments, looking for patterns, trying to understand.

She remembers Morning in America. She remembers the Son of Sam. *The Love Boat* and *What's Happenin'?*, the *Electric Company* and the Captain & Tenille. She remembers John

Hinckley, Jr., the scuffle by the limousine. She remembers Live Aid and Abscam. Have It Your Way. Be All That You Can Be.

One night she dreams of the Burned Man: his too-white eyes staring from a blackened face. She remembers shadows scurrying, remembers silence. How she recoiled in the back-seat, pressing up to her brother until he shoved her away. She must have been six or seven—the hot, scratchy feel of tights, her scalp still stinging from her mother's vigorous brushing. They'd gone to see *A Chorus Line*, got lost on the way home: a dark, empty street, girders and ramps criss-crossing overhead. She remembers her mother's agitation. They saw a bright light at the corner, flames flickering out of a trash can. Her father made a high, choked gasp and took off his seatbelt but her mother gripped his arm and said, "Do not get out of this car."

The man was slumped against the building. His hands were black. His clothes and his shoes were black. Tiny tongues of flame still skittered along his pants. The hood of a heavy parka framed his blackened face, but his shocking white eyes stared at her as the car slid past.

"Someone has to help him—" her father said.

"Just go, David. Just get out of here."

She remembers this—his glassy eyes, his swollen black hands—as clearly as she remembers waxy little boxes of chocolate milk and the home phone number her mother drilled into her, as clearly as she remembers who shot J.R. But it never happened—or not the way she remembers it.

"There was something," her mother says when she asks about the Burned Man. "Something in the newspaper, some kids from Long Island did it, I think." She shuts her eyes, shakes her head to dislodge the memory. "I think it happened in the Bronx. They poured gas on him while he was sleeping. Mayor Koch went on TV. I'm surprised you remember that."

But they were there, she insists. She remembers the pained

sound her father made, the look on her brother's face, the long glow of the tunnel when they found their way home.

"What do you think, that I wouldn't remember?" Her mother tilts her head as if she can't recognize her daughter. Her father slumps against the wall of the prison visitors room, face sallow with altitude sickness. "You think we'd just drive right by something like that?" her mother says. "What kind of people do you think we are?"

———

She remembers the first time she heard the term "death squad." Sixth grade, maybe seventh, flopped on the couch with homework. Her father in his armchair, muttering over the newspaper, her brother sprawled on the carpet, mashing buttons on a hand-held football game. Her fingers smelled of formaldehyde from the morning's frog dissection. She remembers the map on the television, the slick, foreign names: Nicaragua, El Salvador. A red-faced congressman slapping the lectern. The US did not belong there, he said. We had no business funding death squads.

"What does that mean? 'Death squads,'" she said. She had a picture in her mind of undercover cops: leather jackets, fake mustaches. Like *The A-Team.*

"Nothing," her father said behind his paper. "Don't worry about it."

"It means we're killing people," her mother said from the kitchen doorway. "It means we help the people we like kill the people we don't like."

"Honey…" her father said.

"Why shouldn't they hear it?" her mother said. "It's on the television."

She turned back to the TV: men in camouflage, dark faces sweaty and unshaven, lying in the dirt; others in neat uniforms, standing at attention on an airport runway.

"Why don't we like them?"

"Because they're poor," her mother said. "Here, baby, have a banana."

She remembers *Fantasy Island*, where rich people got anything they wanted: the beautiful woman, the dead come back to life. She remembers *Sanford & Son*. Helicopters over fallow fields, soldiers with rifles jogging down a beach. She remembers backyard gardens and Catskills summer camps, the mulch of pine needles and dead insects on a creaky screen door. In the military prison, where mice long ago relieved her mattress of its stuffing, she recalls the exact scent of the camp dining hall—peanut spread and industrial detergent—the nightly fantasia of fireflies glistering over the lake. She remembers when they watched *Gandhi* in freshman history: boys in the back snickering at the men in loincloths, whistling at the women with baskets on their heads, the tense, sulky mood that took her when Gandhi was shot at the end.

"It's just a movie," her friend Rachel snorted. "Grow up!"

She came home that night to India on the television: ambulances, dead cows, mothers lying next to their children in the street. Men with bandaged faces, blinded by the chemicals in the air. This happened long before she saw *Gandhi*, but in her memory the two are fused.

"Mom, look," her brother said. Palm trees, soldiers, smoke from a hundred bonfires drifting past the factories of Bhopal. It was people, he said. He turned up the volume and wailing filled the room. "Look, Mom! They're burning people."

―――

The colonel was a handsome man, square-jawed, salt and pepper at his temples. His slow, boyish smile left you with an impression of ease, as if he were slouching, though he sat ramrod straight. He reminded the child, a teenager now, of those senior boys, athletes mostly, whose popularity was so vast they could afford to be nice to everyone. The colonel, proud in his uniform, raised his arm and swore to God and she put down her geometry proofs to listen. He spoke thoughtfully, brow creased with sincerity—he wanted to understand the question, to give an honest answer. She almost sympathized.

"I do not recall," he said. Her mother squeezed her gin and tonic, chewing on the ice. "I do not recall," the colonel said to another question. He whispered something to the man next to him; they laughed and then the colonel turned back to the questioners, a touch of insolence in his posture, and said it again: "I really don't recall."

No one believed him. The child turned up the volume. No one believed him, but he didn't seem to care. This man, Oliver North, didn't expect anyone to believe him. He didn't want them to. He pursed his lips, nodded with great serious-ness, and suddenly she understood: he was humiliating them, daring them to call him a liar, knowing that nobody would. He was demonstrating the depth of their powerlessness, rubbing their noses in it, then offering a sympathetic smile they were also not to believe.

"I believe he's already answered that question, Senator," said the man next to the colonel. Snickers from the gallery, from reporters crosslegged on the floor. She clutched a pillow to her stomach.

"I don't recall! I don't recall!" her mother said. "You asshole."

The facts of the affair didn't interest the child. They seemed too small, like some pathetic sixth-grade cabal. She couldn't take her eyes off the colonel—his easy confidence, the glimmer of his medals. By now she knew what a death squad was. The whole country knew: they'd seen the bodies on television, they'd read about the murdered nuns. Some-thing had happened to separate Cannondale from Paterson, from Managua and Beirut and Bhopal. It hadn't happened by accident. She listened more closely to the words: *freedom fighter, constitution, help me God.* She watched his slow, taunting smile and she started to make connections.

———

"Have you signed your postcard yet?" The voice called through the hot crush of the crowd. "You, with the hair! Sign a postcard, Curly. Let the dictator hear your voice."

She stopped to look for the source of this directive. Rachel and Megan bumped into her from behind, the three girls forming a snag in the human current, the swarming heat of Giants Stadium in June, seventy thousand people smashing their way from hot-dog stand to bathroom to the blazing exposure of seats in the upper tier. She kept one eye on her brother's blue jersey as it winked through the swirl of bodies. Music thudded in the girders and concrete, snatches of melody escaping from the entrances to the stands.

An arm waved at her from behind a table. "C'mere, Curly, help free political prisoners!" Now she saw the speaker: a man in his twenties, feathered hair, a perfect tan.

"Whatever," Rachel said. "Hey, you think that guy in the Zeppelin T-shirt will buy us beer?"

The child angled toward the table and the man tilted his head sardonically. He held up a white card. "Augusto Pinochet?" He had an Australian accent and a chipped front tooth that gave his smile a leering edge. His shirt bore the same logo that was on her ticket and on banners all over the stadium: a lit candle wrapped in barbed wire. Above the candle it read: *A Conspiracy of Hope.* "Y'want to write to him?"

"No," she said, trying to sound flirtatious. She wanted him to call her Curly again.

"Do you even know who Augusto Pinochet is?"

"No."

"Course you don't." He regarded her sadly. "Chile, '73? Kissinger's best friend? He's your man in South America.

Totally psychotic." There were brochures spread on the table, binders full of photographs. Two women stood next to him in tight T-shirts with the same logo, waving at the men walking by. "Alrighty, don't like Pinochet? We've got Deng, Mubarak, Gorbachev. Pick a card, any card. Here——" he flapped a post-card under her nose. "P. W. Botha. Fantastic! Help smash apartheid."

A muffled roar crested around them as Joni Mitchell played her finale, "Big Yellow Taxi." The girl pictured her mother back at the seats, dancing by herself. It was supposed to be her fifteenth birthday present—a daylong concert including U2, her favorite as well as Rachel's and Megan's. For months they'd swapped pictures of Bono, the most beau-tiful boy they'd ever seen; in the parking lot, she'd spent a whopping fifteen dollars on a *War* T-shirt. But so far the day had been boring—and *hot*—her mother singing along with people they'd never heard of: Peter, Paul, and Mary? Jackson Browne? When a salsa band took the stage and her mother started moving her hips, hands in the air, the child's embar-rassment was so profound it felt like vertigo.

"You do know what apartheid is?" the man was saying. "They teach you that?"

She rolled her eyes. "I know what it is."

"Good! Puts you ahead of most of this lot." He slid an open binder toward her. "Did you know today's the tenth anniversary of the Soweto Uprising?"

At first she couldn't tell what she was looking at, the jumbled images, a collage of faces and limbs. Slowly she began to make out bodies heaped on concrete or face-down in the dust, sniffed by dogs, children sprawled on bloody mattresses, strewn like garbage. He turned the pages slowly, as though revealing secret delights. "Happens all over the world. People tortured, raped, buried alive. People like you, your brother, born in the wrong country, under the wrong regime. You know about Steve Biko?"

She slid the binder closer. This photograph was different: a single body on a gurney, covered by a sheet. Only his battered face was visible. The gurney sat in an empty hallway, squalid but clinical, somehow official.

"What happened to him?"

"Torture. Twenty-two hours straight. He was a youth activist, very popular. Until you lot killed him. How do you like the music, by the way? Y'having a good time?"

Behind her, Rachel and Megan were asking for their ticket stubs. Her brother was waiting for his hot dog. But the child, the teenager, was surrounded by empty space.

"I didn't kill him."

He crooked a finger and leaned across the table. "The US is South Africa's number one friend. Didn't know that? Most of their guns, their tanks, you sold to them. It's good business for your arms dealers. Who d'you think makes the decisions, anyway?

"These people wouldn't be in power if it weren't for you," he said. "Pinochet, Saddam Hussein, Shimon Peres. You ought to be ashamed of yourselves. But you're not, are you?"

"I'm fifteen."

"Your mum and dad, then. Didn't know they were killers, did you?"

She could not look up, her eyes drawn to the dead body, its solitude. She suddenly hated the man behind the table, wanted to shove some insult at his smug face.

"What's a card going to do?"

Another cheer went up inside the stadium. The man leaned closer. "Sorry?"

Her face grew hot. "What good is a postcard going to do?"

He pondered this, then shoved a stack of cards at her. "Just send them. Give them to your friends. Maybe they'll let some of these prisoners go free."

"Why would they set them free?" she said. He straightened with a familiar, reluctant insolence, but she would not relent.

"It's just a stupid postcard. My grandmother sends me post-cards every month."

The man sucked his teeth while the women glared. "Look, Curly. Are you planning to start a revolution?" He peered at her T-shirt. "You and Bono? Who are you? Nobody. This is the only thing someone like you can do." He squeezed her hand closed on the stack of cards. "Write the bloody postcard, alright? Tell your father to donate to Amnesty International. Now run on back inside. Y'don't want to miss Bryan Adams."

As she pushed through the concourse, she felt she'd won a small victory. She was pleased with her sarcasm, the anger she'd brought to the man's face. But climbing to the seats, late sun stabbing over the stadium rim, that sense of triumph leached away, leaving in its place the image of the gurney, the dead man's face so small and alone. They'd just left him there, an unclaimed body, a nobody. Already, she'd forgotten his name.

For the rest of the concert she felt dazed, a little out of breath. The space around her felt still and dead. The sky thickened with indigo and the stage glowed far below, across a sea of writhing bodies. Her brother fell asleep with his head in their mother's lap. Megan and Rachel moved down three rows to talk to some older boys. They tossed their hair and laughed while the boys punched each other and passed a joint down the line.

"Are you OK?" her mother said. "You got a little sunburn. Put your sweatshirt on."

Curly's face was tight, her skin tingled. "I'm fine."

In the sky above the stadium, helicopters hovered and banked, spotlights sweeping the crowd. For some time a drum had been tapping out a slow metronome, insistent and ominous. The stage was dark; all the stadium lights were dark. Over and over, the halting drum struck; one by one people lit matches, held up cigarette lighters, until the stands glimmered with thousands of tiny flames.

"You're freezing," her mother said. The thudding drum grew more urgent, and then a low guitar note stabbed into the darkness. It came again, a cruel, droning sound, and then the singer, Peter Gabriel, was alone in the spotlight, his voice nasal, clutched in the back of the throat like a man singing through pain:

Oh, Biko… Biko… Biko.

Her teeth started to chatter. She thought she must have heard it wrong. From the massive speakers the name came again, ghostly and unmistakable, thousands of voices singing along.

The man is dead, he sang. *The man is dead.*

She couldn't sit still. She felt a kind of desperation, a shrinking from that voice and from the galaxy of lights. When she stood she nearly lost her balance. One helicopter sat high in the sky, its silver beam steady and watchful. *Biko… Biko…* The drum held its rhythm, the guitar rang out relentlessly. The sound of bagpipes rose like whirring crickets, fluttering and crackling in the summer air. There were women on stage now, Black women in colorful dresses and head-wraps; their languorous deathwail washed across the sky.

The man is dead, he sang, crouched at the edge of the stage *… And the eyes of the world are watching now.*

She hugged herself, shivering, shook off the arm her mother put around her. The women on stage swayed together, crying their wordless chant over and over. It was grief—pure, liquid grief that crashed in waves all around them. The body on the gurney, abandoned and worthless—it was this body they cried for. When she looked down she saw Megan, the arm of one of the boys around her waist, waving a lighter over her head, and without warning the child burst into tears.

She knew she was ridiculous. Hunched over in her seat, she knew she was exhausted, sunburned. It was all ridiculous: the song, the phony African women, even the photograph— puny and ridiculous and beside the point. She could feel her mother fussing over her. She knew her friends would look at her with scorn and she hated them. She wanted to take Megan's cigarette lighter and burn her with it so she would stop singing—she had no *right*. She shivered and sniffled but she couldn't stop picturing the dead body in the hallway, still there, still alone. And these people singing.

The stage was empty; the women returned to darkness though their chant echoed through the stadium. Only the tap-tap-tap of the heavy drum, receding into the tide of applause. The crowd released itself, returned to plastic seats sticky with spilled beer. She could hear herself sobbing but she didn't try to stop, not when her mother draped the sweatshirt over her, not when the lights came up and Rachel gaped and called her name in astonishment, when her brother roused himself and howled with laughter and announced to their section, "My sister's on the rag!"

———

When she was arrested by counterterrorism forces in August, 1998, she was living in a house in Lima, Peru with between six and nine members of the Cuarta Filosofía, a militant group most of the country believed to be defunct. The Cuarta Filosofía had played a minor role in the decade-long "dirty war," kidnapping businessmen and ambushing patrols in the countryside, targeting politicians for assassination. But its leaders were all dead or in exile; the government thought the group had been neutralized along with its larger, more murderous cousin, the Shining Path. After the military raided the house, killing everyone inside, reporters were shown a cache of assault rifles and grenades, a thousand sticks of dynamite, and blueprints of Peru's Congress, including a seating chart for every member of the legislature. Officials later provided a copy of the lease on the house, which she had

signed, as well as her US passport. She was twenty-six
years old.

According to the government, she and her comrades
planned to invade Congress and abduct legislators. If their
demands were not met, the prosecutor declared, "they
planned to line the halls of government with corpses." When
she was presented to the news media, in keeping with Peru's
counterterrorism protocols, she balled her fists and screamed
at the cameras—red-faced, sweating, an apparition of
unchecked rage. One of her arms had been broken during the
arrest. Her jeans were soaked with urine. "This country was
founded on violence! Built on violence!" she shouted, spittle
misting in the air. Across the country, people recoiled from
their televisions, sickened by this vengeful child. "The wealthy
protect their privilege with violence! Is this justice?" she cried.
"Is it democracy?"

The reporters crowded toward her, they jabbed cameras
and boom mikes in her face. Did she know that her comrades
were murderers, known terrorists? Had she bought the
weapons herself? Had she been sleeping with one of them?
All of them? Why was a gringa trying to restart the war?

The child did not back down. She bared her teeth and
glared into the camera. "If it's terrorism to help poor mothers
and sick children, then I am a terrorist," she screamed. "If it's
a crime to fight for the oppressed, I accept whatever punishment I'm given!"

Her trial took less than thirty minutes. The judges wore
hoods to protect their identities. They spoke through voice-
distortion machines. She had not been provided with a lawyer
until that morning, and she was never to learn his name. She
was never to see the government's evidence or learn who had
testified, what they'd said about her. She was not given
permission to speak. Before she was sentenced to life in prison,
the prosecutor showed the court that morning's newspaper: *¡Yo
soy terrorista!* read the headline, above an image of a

madwoman brandishing her fist. He stood before the judges in their uniforms and canvas hoods and shrugged.

"Señores," he said, "the prisoner has already confessed."

———

The station wagon sped smoothly over the highway, the interior gloomy and sedate as the lights of commerce flashed past. The child leaned her cheek to the steamed window and watched car dealerships and carpet stores and office parks, still seeing her friend Megan dancing, waving the cigarette lighter idiotically, still hearing her sing a name that meant nothing to her: *Biko! Be-caw! Beeeeeeak-O!*

"Quite a day," her mother said, when they pulled into the garage. Her brother ran inside, leaving behind a cool silence, only the ticking of the engine and the scent of gasoline. "Are you feeling any better?"

"I'm feeling fine."

Her mother reached back to smooth the girl's hair and she jerked away, felt the tears coming up again. She was furious with herself, she wished she could wrinkle her nose and transport herself to her room without seeing her father or answering his kind and pointless questions, throw herself under the blankets and howl until her throat bled.

"What's going on with you?" her mother said.

"Have you ever heard of Pinochet?" she asked. This was not the point, and the girl knew it, but she had to find a way to give voice to her wretchedness.

Her mother drew back. "In Chile? Of course."

Something on her mother's face pushed her over the edge. She rocked forward and blubbered helplessly, "Then why didn't you *tell* me?"

For a minute or more she sniffled and hiccupped; she could feel her mother looking at her, feel her gaze go from concerned to perplexed to annoyed. She could hear her brother's careless footsteps overhead, the murmur of her father's voice.

"There are a lot of bad people in the world," her mother finally said. "A lot of ugly things happen."

She looked up in anguish. "But why?"

The killer's smile was fond and unbearable. "That's just how it is."

The child closed her eyes. She felt flattened, her jaw and joints ached. "Nobody does anything. That's why."

"Didn't you see a million people at that concert? Of course people do something."

"Do you?" she said. "What do you and Dad do?"

Her mother pressed her lips together and said nothing. She took the keys from the ignition and stepped out of the car. The pinging of the door chime filled the garage.

"Huh?" she shouted after her mother. "What do you do?"

Out of sight, her mother said, "We live our lives. We try to be good people, raise good children. That's all anyone can do."

"That's not enough!"

After a pause, her mother said, "I know."

The garage door rattled back into motion, thicker gloom descending. She thought her mother had gone inside. But a moment later her voice came through the dark. "Time for bed, baby. It's been a long day. You can't take things so personally." Then the door closed, leaving the child in a restless, cooling car, listening to a creaking house, the receding footsteps and imperceptible mutters of a family on its way to a good night's sleep.

Red Velvet Ant

BY ROBERT V.S. REDICK

We crawled under the juniper and when a branch grazed her temple I pressed my sleeve to the thin line of blood. All better. Nothing to worry about. She looked up at me, weighing my sincerity.

You're barely scratched, I said. Stop worrying.

Who's worrying? said Mattie, terror in her eyes.

We're full of these things, these platelets, I said. They make your blood sticky when it needs to be. Otherwise we'd be dead, wouldn't we? If we cut our little toe it would just run out like water from a bag.

Miss Randolph's my teacher, said Mattie. Not you.

The limbs of the juniper were bleached and twisted like something hauled from the sea. Its limbs nearly brushed the ground but when we crawled under them we were in a hollow where the needles lay in drifts. Mattie checked the hollow space by the juniper trunk where she kept her plastic stegosaurus. Hola Miguel, she said.

You've gotten strong, I told her. You'll be too big to carry soon.

I'm too big now, she said.

Her statement was false. I had carried her that morning.

She would have preferred an argument but I just hitched up my socks. My sister was dear to me that spring because of the dreams in which she died.

It was cool under the juniper. I tried to sleep there once, but the robots and the spotlights kept me up. I don't know who spared the old bush but I was grateful because it had grown right through the fence along the farm's edge, hiding a place where the barbed wire had snapped. If anyone had cared to look they could have slipped into the farm just as we did. There was a lot left to discover when I was twelve and she was six.

But no one ever looked. No one stopped on Loft Mountain Road. The realtor called our house *disadvantaged* because the rare earth operation ran almost to our driveway. From Mattie's window all you saw were miles of pumps and refining crucibles and mole bots grubbing around in the extraction fields and the camera towers and the huge green gumdrops of the wastewater tanks. On busy days the walls of the house would tremble against your hand. I had dreams that I was inside the dishwasher. I still think of that and laugh.

Uphill from the mine was another world, however. Uphill was Loft Mountain, and a great sprawling neglected farm. Dad said the dirty mine itself was why the farm still existed; that no one wanted to cover a mountainside with condos with *all this loud ludicrous bullshit* going on below. I didn't hate the mine like Dad. In fact I never understood how we could be so lucky, how we could have our own secret juniper-door into the lands above, how our good fortune could unspool in this manner, day after day. Sometimes the cameras would change directions and follow you, but did that matter? A camera never hurt anyone, and they lost interest when you got to the fence.

I'm ready, Dyl.

We crawled through, stood up on farm property. Dry grass

high as Mattie's chin. Last year's milkweed, elf ears on stakes. A whiff of honeysuckle. A moth bobbing dazed in the heat.

Bella moth!

Obviously, said Mattie. We'd seen bellas before.

I took her hand and made her run up the slope. It was important, that first run, because it put you out of sight from the farmhouse, which stood below us to the east. The old barn and stone silo looked very far away, but last year the farm manager had spotted us and jumped into his four-wheeler and bounced up the mountainside. We hid in the sowthistle. His tires gnawed up the grass. He didn't catch us—no one ever caught us, and God, how that seemed to matter. That's what passed for scary in the first phase of my life. A phase with just a few hours left.

Half a mile uphill we reached the first of the yellow oaks, and that's where my sister collapsed on the ground. Honk honk, went her breathing. I looked down the mountain: the barn was still in sight.

Your inhaler?

She shook her head. Meaning she wouldn't use it, for reasons I never did understand.

Well, sit up then.

I eased her arms over my shoulders and lifted her and staggered deeper into the trees. She kicked at me feebly. Little toy shoes.

I don't want you to carry me!

(I don't *honk* want you to *honk honk*—)

I slid her down from my back, we were hidden now. I looked away south and saw the fleet of traffic drones lift from the state police building and fan out to manage rush hour. An electric commuter plane, silent, slinking towards Washington. Then a dragonfly—

Dragonfly!

I see it, I see it!

—small and blazing and gone like a flung bit of turquoise,

a benediction Mom would have said. I felt a cold thrill in my chest. I couldn't see the world as Mom saw it, marked everywhere by God's love or fury, a world of endless holy graffiti. *But that dragonfly!* Nimbler than a package drone, silent as a dream. I stood staring between the oaks, willing it to return.

When Mom comes back I get to tell her, said Mattie.

About the dragonfly? Okay.

When is she coming back, Dyl?

I bent and retied her shoes. Amber wing spots, I said. Some kind of pennant. Or maybe a sundragon.

Dad's old *Audubon Guide to the Mid-Atlantic* had a thousand color pictures of birds and animals and insects. When I asked him how many were left he turned his back all of a sudden and stood there breathing funny by the kitchen door. But a moment later he turned to face me again.

Why don't we start counting and see?

Dad's suggestion became our family game, although it tended to make him cry. Not me, though, and not Mattie. We were driven. The dragonfly was the sixteenth kind of creature we'd seen on the farm.

That's what the owners called it, a farm, although they grew nothing and visited just once a year. They lived in Paris and sold the wax and sprays and lipstick you put on dead people to make them look nice underground. They loved Virginia and bought a winery too, and the 1941 Lincoln-Zephyr convertible that had belonged to Governor Darden. Also a brick schoolhouse which they dismantled and shipped to California for someone's birthday but never did put back together because of someone else's divorce. Also the old train station which they turned into a nightclub. They served a drink called the Blue Ridge Tunnel that was supposed to make the lights go out or maybe hit you like an oncoming train.

Why are we standing here? said my sister, munchkin hands on hips.

I had to smile: no more honking from her chest. I'd never seen her recover so quickly.

The next bit is the steepest, do you—

Earthquake! she squeaked.

I crouched over her. It was just your average quake, the kind Dad called a "rare-earth rumble" because there were none before they found yttrium here. We'd felt stronger for sure. But we were under the trees and the cracking was loud and big limbs started to fall. If it got any worse I would lift her and try to run for the meadow but even standing there I kept losing my balance, what if I fell on top of Mattie, fell on her chest?

Dylan. Dylan.

Just hold still.

Down the mountain the gas-leak alarm began to gripe in the extraction field. I heard the howl of the farm manager's dog. Then the earthquake passed and I released her. She was trembling like a fawn.

Are you up to this? I asked.

Shut up, stupid.

You don't have to prove anything, Mattie. We don't have to climb to the Crow's Nest.

Police sirens in the distance. You can't stop me, she said.

———

After the oaks came the meadow with the black locusts and the weed-strangled tractor. No path of course. Her hair and clothes damp with sweat. I stayed behind her so that I could catch her if she fell.

The tractor was a Waterloo Boy with huge wheels of solid iron. People said it had huffed and puffed up the mountain to that spot in 1937 and just died. Mattie couldn't spare it a glance. When I asked if she wanted to play on it she reminded me that she was six.

We pushed on up through the locusts to the flat rock with its vein of milky quartz. With a flourish, I removed a tiny bottle from my pocket and gave it to her. She looked at the label and began, proudly, to read.

Pure Natural Vanilla. Imitation. Net what.

Net weight, I said.

This is Mom's, Dyl. Why did you bring it?

To teach you something. Scratch the bottle with a rock.

This is Mom's, she repeated.

Was, I thought. In fact my lips made a "W" before I could stop myself, and keen-eyed Mattie saw me and guessed the word.

She threw the bottle at my face. I dodged, and she charged at me, screaming.

I hate you I hate you I hate—

I swatted away her little fists. Maybe lying about Mom's return was no way to help her; to this day I'm not sure. When Mattie tried to bite me I swung her around and hugged her, setting my chin on her shoulder to stop her turning her head.

Put it back, she was howling. Put it back on her shelf.

I will. Stop screaming.

You broke the rules.

I have different rules because I'm older, Mattie.

Because you're Mom's favorite, you mean.

I froze. Mattie looked at me over her shoulder, no longer fighting. I *was* Mom's favorite, and clever Mattie wasn't remotely envious. She was scared for me.

Mom had been gone for five months and twelve days. Last September Dad had told her he could put up with just about anything except "the hell and damnation stuff" and Mom had shot back that we'd be putting up with it for eternity unless we got straight with God. After that the fights got loud and Mattie and I spent more time under the juniper. When we'd come home Dad would be closed in his study and Mom took to watching me in a way that made me nervous. One night she slipped into my bedroom after I'd turned off the lamp. She just stood there, a shadow by the wall, and I wondered if she knew I was awake.

We're lucky, she said suddenly, that one man in this house can see things as they are.

I can't see a thing, I said.

She came forward and kissed my cheek. You can, she said. You just don't know it yet.

In those last days Mom spoke to me alone. Mattie followed her around the house, begging for attention, reciting the prayers Mom had told me to memorize (I refused). Poor Mattie never got so much as a smile from Mom, but somehow that just drove her to greater loyalty. Even when Mom abandoned us she rattled off those prayers.

What did you want to teach me, Dyl?

I released her; the bottle of vanilla lay in the dirt. I picked it up and scraped it against the vein of quartz and held it out for her inspection. I told her quartz was hard enough to scratch glass and she said lots of things could.

Lots of things?

A diamond could scratch it.

Well that's one.

Thor's fingernail, she said, a touch of panic in her voice. Also Thor's hammer if he used the edge.

Go on, I said.

She looked around, as though for a tablet or a phone. She wasn't comfortable being caught not knowing something. I considered this a flaw in her character and another day I would have said so. But in my dreams she kept dying and there was no one to laugh or fight with and the things I would never teach her loomed on and on like billboards vanishing with distance so I said *Right!* Thor's fingernail. How do you dream these things up?

Don't make fun of me.

I'm not, idiot. I carried this bottle up here to show you a

trick. For God's sake, can't I just be nice to you once in awhile?

Don't say for God's sake!

No one cares if you say that, Mattie. No one really believes in God.

You don't know that.

Yes I do. And if there's a God-creature up there it doesn't care what we say. You should take some time to reflect on these things.

Stop talking like Dad.

God's asleep at the switch, I said, sounding exactly like Dad. We're not important to it, and the world's not, obviously, it's not watching, we can do what we like here, we could set the whole place on fire.

Are there blackberries? she said.

———

There were blackberries. The bushes started twenty feet to our left. We walked over; the berries were small and dry and already fermenting. I crushed half a dozen in my hand and let her smell them and her eyes went away somewhere dreamy.

How can I tell you about blackberries? The scent like new candy fresh-torn from the wrapper. (Don't look at me that way. I'm not from Mars, I'm just old.) But so much better than candy, sweeter and at the same time less sweet. The stain on my hands a color you've likely never seen. Think of blood close to drying, the last liquid before the scab.

They did something to you, Dyl.

What, the berries?

Mattie was looking glumly at my palm. You have to wash, she said.

It's nothing, it's blackberry juice. By tomorrow the stains will be gone.

It could hurt you. It could kill your skin.

She was threatening a tantrum, so I led her back across the meadow and downhill to the stream. She watched as I bent and scrubbed my hands. The purple lingered, and her eyes welled up. It was astonishing, her collection of fears.

Ask Him to help you, she said.

Now cut that out or I'll get mad.

She ignored me and pulled up her T-shirt sleeve. On her shoulder was a pudgy elephant-god with four arms and a crown. My sister couldn't ride a bicycle but she had a tattoo. Just before Christmas she and Mom had disappeared for a few hours and when she came back it was there on her arm.

What the hell did you do? Dad had whispered, looking at Mom.

Mom smiled and crossed herself. Dad pointed at Mattie's shoulder.

That's a Ganesh, Judith. You're a Christian.

Mom said they were all the same Holy Being and Dad, muttered, How confused can one person get. They had a big fight later on when they thought we were sleeping.

Forget the berries, I told Mattie. Mom and Dad used to eat them, swallow them whole. And they're still alright.

You said Mom was a basket case.

Not because she ate some blackberries. And do you know who *still* eats them? The birds, that's who.

She looked around at the silent woods. There must have been birds hiding somewhere, and it was probably true that they ate berries and such. But a bird is not responsible for its ignorance. Birds don't get alerts from Toxic Watch or the school board or even from their friends. They have no public profiles. You can't share anything with a bird.

———

We followed the stream uphill and cut left through the high meadow and there were the rocks we called the Crow's Nest

above, toothy and gray with the clouds flowing behind them.
The wind was rising, and the tall grass bowed, straightened,
bowed, swept over by invisible boats.

I thought: *My sister's going to make it to the Crow's Nest today.*
There was nothing wrong in the universe. I kissed her forehead, tasting salt.

Mom believes in God, Dylan.

She didn't always, I said. She used to be kind of normal.

And angels too. She says they're coming when the horn
sounds. A multitude.

Do you even know what *multitude* means?

Like a whole sky full when the world is ending. A million
million angels, and God's anger, and the blowing of the horn.

No more God talk, Mattie.

Is that why she blows it so much? When she's driving?

It took me a moment to grasp that Mattie meant the car
horn. That she thought our mother was ready to bring on
Judgment Day to escape a traffic jam. I turned away, fighting
back the giggles. I looked hard at the grass.

And there it was. A scarlet insect, bright as fire. It was
nearly an inch long and delicate and plush.

Bug, bug!

I see it! What is it?

We bent close. In my head I flew through the old stiff
pages of the *Audubon* until the answer leaped to my tongue.

Dasymutilla something. Red velvet ant.

Mattie sat quiet. I guess the ant was so beautiful she forgot
to be afraid. We watched it run into the brown grass, quick
and fidgety, as though ashamed to be seen. She was smiling
and I was grinning ear to ear.

Seventeen creatures.

Say them all, Mattie said.

Earthworm pigeon—

In order! she shrieked.

Earthworm *squirrel* pigeon nuthatch paper wasp blackbird

black ant song sparrow hummingbird chipmunk vulture grackle field sparrow vesper sparrow deer fly dragonfly red velvet ant.

Bugs can sting you, she said.

Only some, I informed her. A whip scorpion is harmless. And a male black widow can't hurt you one bit. This guy has a stinger, though, because a red velvet ant is really a kind of wasp. The males are born without wings.

You're making things up again.

Or maybe the females. It just looks like an ant.

We watched the insect until it vanished. Then my sister rose and started climbing towards the Crow's Nest. I walked behind her, happy about my seventeenth creature, happy at the sight of her little legs powering up the slope.

Race you to the top? she said.

Hell no. You can't run uphill.

Just give me a head start, she said. And don't say hell unless you want to go there.

Hell.

Dylan. Stop.

Hell, hell, hell, hell.

She kicked me and stumbled over and I helped her up. She was praying under her breath like some mumbling machine. *Forgive me my anger Lord this day with Dylan and all my days and nights forgive this sinner and all her failures all the ways she disappoints you all the bad all the terrible—*

I'll count to fifty, I said. But if you don't stop praying I automatically win. Ready, set—

She started puffing up the hill.

———

I watched her, shaking my head. How could anyone move that slowly and still call it running?

Fourteen, I shouted at her back.

I looked again down Loft Mountain, killing time. Beyond the mine stretched a few dead miles where the mole bots fixed themselves and charged their batteries. After that it grew busy. Nirvana Estates, Piedmont Group Homes, MaxFowl Poultry, BioSplice East. Standstill traffic on I-64, a heat mirage over distant Charlottesville. Dad said there was no point in a spring that wasn't divided from the previous autumn by so much as a frost.

Thirty-four, thirty-five.

The interstate was beautiful, though, a cream-colored rattlesnake gliding strong through that disordered land. I wondered if Mom had also found it beautiful, on the entrance ramp in her bad makeup and bangles, trying to thumb down a ride.

Fifty!

I started running, and instantly flushed out a grouse. Just like that: a wild bird rocketing out of the briars, black and gold and caramel, wings booming like drums. (I can tell you don't believe me, but what I can do about that? Such things still happened then).

Bird, Mattie, bird!

She turned and saw it. The grouse labored uphill, flying just a yard or so above the grass, and we both leaped and cheered. We might have been watching a jet fighter at an airshow doing tricks over Norfolk. When the bird noticed Mattie it swerved off to the right into a thicket of mimosa. Gone forever, but we'd seen it. I climbed up to the rocks.

Mattie was bent double, honk-honking of course, but her eyes were all smiles as she returned my high-five. I sat down. The wind was glorious. We stayed there without speaking until the sky was dull orange and the land below filled with lights.

A bug is a cold also, she informed me. Like a sickness. Like a disease.

Correct, I said.

Then what is a Smart Bug?

Excuse me?

It was on the computer. The Smart Bug. It makes you bleed inside. It sprays out when you cough.

I have no idea what you're talking about.

———

Where were you, the day you learned of it? I was on the farm with my sister, with burrs in my socks and the evening breeze cooling my skin. No one forgets. I had a lover once with cataracts like mother-of-pearl. Of course by then there was no treatment for cataracts. (We used to cure it with surgery. I hear you laughing, but it's true.) She couldn't remember being told she would go blind, but she remembered the first time she heard those two words together. Smart Bug. Let's not talk about that.

———

Mom returned in late April, two weeks before the general madness, in a bread truck with a pit bull named Ralphie and a new girlfriend named Fern. She pointed at me and Mattie and made a serious face.

These two came from my womb.

As if Fern couldn't work that one out. It made us all feel weird but that was Mom's special talent—discomfort, followed by dread. Everyone was quiet until Mattie said *Well duh* and Fern laughed and I liked her. Dad offered breakfast. Mom turned and looked me up and down.

How's your soul? she asked.

I shrugged, hoping to annoy her. She had new strength in her shoulders. She had tied back her hair with baling twine.

The truck was crammed with dry food and solar panels, spools of razor wire, handguns, shotguns, grenades. Also fifteen laying hens and a rooster. And fifty pounds of beef jerky. And bags of musty, mouse-chewed paperbacks and board games that Fern said had come from her basement.

The adults slept every night by the windows. We were safe for a long time because the mine hired private security. Big guns on the wastewater tanks.

————

I'm not a liar, Mattie said.

I never called you a liar. I just said I don't know what you're talking about.

Ask Dad. Smart Bug was on the computer.

But I'd lost interest already.

When we grow up, I said, this can still be our place. Not just the farm. These rocks. The Crow's Nest.

The juniper's closer to our house, said Mattie.

The juniper might be gone, I said. Even the house might be gone, or sold to someone else. But the rocks will still be here. This is the spot, Mattie. Our Asgard, our Fortress of Something or Other. Can we agree on that?

She nodded, so serious it was funny. Then she pointed at the sky.

First star.

No, Venus comes first. That's Mars, because it's red. Venus must be hidden in the clouds.

You don't know everything, Dyl.

I do, pretty much. It's not a star, either, it's a planet. We sent ships there, with robots and cameras. Even a mini helicopter. We landed a drone on that little red light.

You make things up, she said.

————

In August her sickness advanced. Whole weeks in bed, coughs too deep to come from her tiny body, days of nausea and stabbing pains. When those came she'd scream so hard Ralphie whined and tucked his tail.

It wasn't the Bug of course but her private hell, the auto-immune mystery ailment that had been building for years. But the timing was vicious. The rest of us were just holding on. Days of fear, nights of gunfire, a pit beyond our swing set for the corpses. I was afraid to shut my eyes. If I slept, her screams became a mass of demons with human faces and the bodies of worms, filling the house like a liquid, climbing the stairs to her room.

But at summer's end she started feeling better, and by Halloween she was cured. As in perfect, as in reborn. She chased Ralphie. She played a plastic flute that made him howl. Something in the food we ran out of, was Dad's theory. Some contaminant, some poison. Something we were too goddamn stupid to stop putting in her mouth.

Mom had other ideas. We had witnessed a miracle, she decided, and she was never one to let a miracle go to waste. Long before Mattie turned the corner, Mom went to work on me with a furious will. Day and night, whispering, warning. Didn't I love my sister? Was I deaf to those screams? And humanity, why exactly was it dying? What was the meaning of the Bug, if not to scare us straight, to punish the faithless once and for all?

You're her favorite. Mattie had seen it: the danger, the menace of my closeness to Mom. I was her favorite; I was the one who could be saved. These days I can't help speculating. What did Mom notice in me? Some hairline crack she could pry open, with the aid of Mattie's screams? Or was I bound to shatter anyway? Was I broken from the start?

What's certain is that I began to feel it. I knelt and whispered to the shape on Mattie's shoulder, I touched the crucifix and wept. Perhaps I bargained with the darkness, offered myself in exchange for my sister. Perhaps I called the darkness God.

By then I had seen quite a number of things. In June an old woman came to the door selling jars of colored paste. It looked a lot like Play-Doh mixed with something oily, but she said the blue paste would protect you from dysentery and the green would give you such happy dreams you'd smile for a week. She didn't smile much herself. The next week someone came selling strings of chicken feet. On July 4 a security guard took the last working mole bot for a joy ride under the interstate and made a hundred yards of it collapse.

In August a man leaped through our window with a machete. I stood up from the loveseat with a shotgun and fired and the blast made me sit down again. He did not look surprised or even angry, just disappointed in himself, look before you leap. I was calm as the others ran in shouting, calm as they dragged the body outside, calm as I swept up buckshot with a magnet before Ralphie could start licking the floor. I slept well that night. I was not yet thirteen.

But Mom knew better. Inside me it was not all ice. She could see how I melted when I dared to think that Mattie might live. Like the mole bots, she grubbed and grubbed, drilled and drilled.

Prayer is power, my darling boy. Turn to Him, talk to Him. He loves your sister too.

The slaughter lasted two years in that part of the country. When it ended, Mattie was alive and I was a believer. Mom had suggested the terms of the holy bargain, and in the depths of that black tunnel I'd agreed.

So out we stepped, Mom and Fern and me, into the charred, reeking remnants of Virginia, preaching Deliverance, weighed down with guns. It's a scouting trip, Mom promised. A month from now I'll have you home.

Just a month?

Or a little longer. If folks are open to the faith.

We snuck away in the dawn light. I stepped over my sleeping sister in a way I'd practiced for some time. In the driveway, Mom took my hand and said, You're a warrior, Dylan Salinger, Child of God. Now don't let Him catch you looking back.

And I didn't.

It was faith that lost me my family. Not the Smart Bug, or Mattie's sickness. God whipped me out the door and down Loft Mountain Road. Heartsick for a couple miles. Dragging my heels, not joining in my mother's songs. Then needing someone to smile at me I joined the chorus and Fern ruffled my hair. By midmorning I was walking ahead of them, still singing, face lifted to the sun.

I was still marching strong when they grew tired at dusk. I marched for three proud, trembling, terrified decades of belief.

Faith only released me when Mom did. She'd left Fern for a bald marine called T-Rex who wore a sword through his belt and never forgave me for giggling about it. One day I woke up and they were gone in Fern's truck and though I went on believing six more wasted months that was the end of Mom's place in my life.

I made my way home, then. Too late. The yard was sopping with what smelled like charcoal lighter and soon enough I found the bullet holes in the wastewater tanks. We'd spray-painted them long ago:

Not Gasoline. Contaminated Water. Useless.

For a few years it had worked.

Inside, there was not much left. A dictionary. The torn cover of the *Audubon Field Guide*. A jar of yeast in the pantry. But on the wall of my sister's room I found words in magic marker, scrawled in her hand:

Race you to the top?

———

I am fifty now. I have stopped hawking miracles, dropped the burden of those dreams. But hope is another matter. The world is healing, the Bug has burned itself out, the poisons are fading from the soil around the tanks. I have lived to see a sky dark with blackbirds, honey bees swarming from one skyscraper to another, foxes prancing on the interstate's broken spine.

The farm is history, the forest burned twice over and struggling to regrow. Nothing we saw from the Crow's Nest is the same, Mars excepted. But the rocks themselves are still here, waiting for her. And so am I, each spring.

———

We sat with our backs together. Did we sense an ending out there, waiting to pounce when we returned? Did we know that the afternoon's small miracles would have to sustain us for the better part of our lives?

Let's go, I told her. It's late. Dad's certain to fuss.

Five more minutes, she said, leaning back against my knees.

Not as if *you'll* get in trouble, I said.

All the same I was content to stay awhile. Her voice was fearless, and I could walk that mountain in the dark.

Ember Heats in Ashen Bodies

BY CHARLES PAYSEUR

The woman collapses into a pile of ash while we're both waiting at the bus stop. In the distance, a police siren cuts over the city noise, the rumbling engines of the cars, the muffled curses of a hundred thousand people caught out in the sharp cold of the early winter morning. We all look up at the distant wail, as if to dispel the fear that knocks hard against our ribs that it's us, that our whispered hour has arrived and the cops in their warm blue wools are finally set to take us off to the Gaol.

I hear the smallest gasp, and it pulls enough of my attention that I see when it happens. The bloom of orange that spreads up the woman's uncovered neck and into her face. It strikes me as I see the color flare that she must have been sweltering, pretending to need the coat and the hat and the gloves. And then she's crumbling, the orange deepening to red and I hold her gaze that moment when she realizes what's happened. Shock, her mouth rounding into an O, unable to speak. But also…relief.

And then her skin flakes, and it's as if she's letting out one large breath that rises as smoke into the air. A pile of dusty clothes are all that remains as the rest of us take a step away.

Sorry.

The only respect we can pay her. Until the bus comes, and we all get on.

Later, on the bus, I think I might have grabbed the clothes, which must have been fire-resistant to withstand the heat of what happened. It would have been too small for me or Gabe, but I could probably have sold it for something.

On the street, windows are boarded and people don't wander. Each person moves with purpose, not wanting to be seen as loitering or plotting. They wrap industriousness around themselves like it's proof against the cold, shrugging when they arrive at locations suddenly closed and vacant, knowing better than to ask why. Police wagons are the only things that linger, weaving ponderous routes through the city, always from west to east, from the factories to the government center, where the Gaol sits like a gravestone.

———

Work is life; work is service; work is the feeling of being squeezed, a little tighter each day. I keep my eyes on the papers in front of me, an endless stream of black and white forms. I can feel eyes on the back of my neck, know that if I look behind me Georgina will be there, lips a line so thin they almost disappear from her face. So I don't look behind me, don't flinch when Keagan walks briskly down along the aisle, pausing every now and again to peer at the paper we're working on. Sometimes, he'll touch one of us on the shoulder and we'll have to stand as he takes the paper and inspects it. Sometimes, he'll shake his head, and the guards by the door will approach and lead someone away, and the next day there will be someone new on the line.

I work quickly, in part because it's not hard. We have acquired the pensions of the United Forge Workers, and our job is to find reasons to discontinue the payouts. No one expected it to fail, to collapse, to be shattered in a single strike of the High Court's gavel. But it was, it is, and there are ever so many reasons to discontinue the pensions, as they were illegal all along. So easy that we aren't allowed more than five minutes on any single form. Skim, stamp, and set aside, marring the neat black lines with the great red X.

My eyes skim as I work, and my body stiffens as I study the latest form for continuance. I can almost read the pain beneath the lines. Disabled in the line of work. A thirty-year veteran of the Central Forge, with two kids to support, and a second pension drawn from their wife, killed while working. But the disability pension started six years ago, one year too long ago to be covered by the terms of our acquisition, and we have no obligation to pay out pensions for dead workers. I can feel the seconds tick away in my head as I stare, my hand hovering over the stamp. Keagan's boots ring on the floor behind me.

I reach for my pen instead. The motion is similar enough to what I'm supposed to do that I know Georgina won't see it, and I have ten seconds before Keagan reaches the end of the line and turns. I smudge the date for the disability incident up two years and then slide the document into the tray for accepted claims. Only three there today, and still hours to go in the shift. If we pass more than five in a shift, someone new will be in our spot the next day. Or if we pass five too often. I've already stamped two more applications by the time Keagan walks behind me again.

————

Gabe curses as he enters our apartment, and I'm on my feet in time to see him drop his sign as if bit by it.

"Fucking cheap cardboard," he says, glaring at the NO BREAD NO STEEL sign on the floor. A dark handprint smolders on one corner.

"Are you——"

"Okay?" Gabe asks, kicking the sign further into the apartment, slamming the door. "What do you think?"

Guilt runs hot through me, tickling the back of my throat. "I think you could probably use some water," I say.

Gabe grunts and heads into the tiny kitchen area, grabbing a bottle of vodka.

"I need something a little stronger than that, after today."

He takes a deep pull from the bottle and holds it out to me. I don't even hesitate, just take it and drink. In my stomach, the heat radiates outward, into my chest and arms. When Gabe takes another belt I can see his veins blaze orange before fading back.

"Have they agreed to meet with you?" I ask.

"The only meeting they're eager to initiate is between their bullets and our bodies."

"They *shot* at you?"

"They claim they shot *above* us," Gabe says. He puts the vodka bottle back and holds onto the counter with both hands. I wince as I see the cheap plastic surface blister. "But when we ran, there—two people were on the ground. I—I don't know…"

I wrap my arms around his body. The heat doesn't come as a surprise, but it still takes effort not to pull away. Instead, I hold him tighter and pull his hands away from the counter.

"I probably just need to sleep," he says, seemingly unwilling as I try to tug him toward the bedroom.

"I think you need something a little stronger than that, after today," I say, and finally he smiles, resistance melted under the heat of our touch.

"Tristan," he says. A rush of steam. A promise.

In bed we trace fire along our veins, down our throats and chests and lower still. We are a furnace burning hot, hotter, and when we come it is a volcano erupting, striking out against the winter, the world, every ugly thing.

Despite the extra we've spent on flame-resistant sheets, we

wake to the scream of the smoke detector, a smoldering fire threatening to spread from Gabe's pillow. I immediately try to swat it, smother it, but the heat from my body only makes the fledgling flames angrier, alive. Gabe acts smarter, grasping the burning mass and rushing it to the shower, dousing it. His body glows in the steam as the water overcomes the flames, and in his face I can see the computations. Cleaning the smoke damage. New pillow. The strike showing no sign of ending in anything but blood.

"At least we save money because we don't need to heat the place," Gabe says.

"Until the next law passes stating that we have to run it anyway, so landlords don't have to worry about their pipes freezing."

Gabe laughs and after a mute moment I join him, a broken sort of keening noise. We won't be surprised when it happens. Perhaps it already has... Our bodies glow in the darkness. We can save on lights, too.

———

"Someday that'll be us," Gabe says, nudging me as he points at a couple going into one of the wedding tailor shops.

I can't help but flush, the heat rising from my chest and pooling in my face, intense and bright. With Gabe's job at the Forge and my new job in a new notary house, we might finally have enough to pay for the rings, the taxes, and for the small event we want. And yet even as my heart leaps, I try to hold it back.

"Pretty sure the landlord would just use it as an excuse to increase our rent," I say.

"That's ridiculous!"

"You haven't heard about the latest High Court case, then?" I ask.

"I remember the one about the Gazette," Gabe says. "High time, too, someone took the media to task for the garbage they print."

The sky overhead is bright but for wisps of gray clouds, and I worry that despite the forecast it might rain in full sunlight.

"Not that one. There was a case where a landlord was charging more for married couples because they were more likely to have children, and couples with kids were more likely to damage the rentals. The couples challenged, but the Court upheld. 'Owner rights' are their two favorite words."

"That's hardly going to be an issue for us, though. One good thing about being…unconventional."

True enough, with no chance at biological children, and no plans to adopt.

"You think landlords will make a distinction, after how long it took to prevent them from denying us housing altogether?" I ask.

Gabe blows a raspberry.

"Can't you just enjoy the nice day for once?"

I keep my mouth in a flat line and a different kind of heat blossoms in my chest.

The streets hold a tension like a lit fuse, and everyone walks hunched as if the walls are about to come tumbling down. Maybe they are. News from the picket line isn't good. The military is being called in to back up the police and end the strike. Even the police wagons are moving faster, empty as they course west, full as they stream eastward. I watch them as the bus navigates, hoping that Gabe hasn't already been taken into a wagon's belly, isn't already waiting in chains in the Gaol.

At work I stare at paper after paper and wonder if the people I try to help are even alive any longer. Even after we sneak through those few approvals, they have to be checked against a list of "agitators and dissidents" for additional screening. My pen hovers over an unchecked box, knowing that if I fill it in the application can be approved.

There is a tap on my shoulder.

People describe freezing in place as a physical cold, as though all the blood drains away and the body braces, holding back its warmth until the blow strikes and it knows how to respond. But I don't feel cold. I don't move, don't flinch. Instead, I see orange curl beneath the skin of my arms all the way to my fingertips. I am heat. I am fire, and I wait to fall to ash.

But I don't. I stand without speaking and step to the side of my desk. Keagan nods and leans over, inspecting the paper and the pen I haven't bothered to hide. The rest of the line keep on working, none of them willing to look. Only Georgina, in the back, watches me as I stand.

Keagan hums, and I watch out of the corner of my eye as he picks up the pen. With a flick, he checks the box, then nods, straightens, and returns to his pacing.

I swallow. Inside me it's as if a length of molten steel has just been quenched—all that dissipating heat—I'm surprised to find no steam rushing out my ears and nose and eyes. I sit back at my desk, slip the application into the accepted tray, and pull out the next from the stack, red stamp already raised.

———

Home in our apartment I watch the sky. Smoke trails up in snaking tendrils. I put a record on, something loud, to cover the sound of distant shouting, possible gunfire, sirens everywhere. I wait for Gabe to return. Eventually, I'm surrounded by darkness, the only light rising from my body. I feel the heat crawling up my neck, see its reflection in the window's glass. It stokes higher with each breath, with each beat of my heart.

Below, figures move in the twilight, and I can see sparks of color moving. Flashing lights of police moving toward the Great Forge, east to west. Snatches of orange and red as people run the opposite direction, fleeing whatever is happening there. The record player is replaced by the radio's

static, interrupted by official warnings to avoid rebel broad-
casts. I lean against the wall near the window. At some point
the color creeps back into the sky without Gabe returning.
The record must have finished, because there's only silence. I
think I cry, but all that comes from the corners of my eyes is
hissing steam.

In the morning I go to work as normal, as if nothing is
different, because I don't know what else to do. The buses
seem to know the new detours, the checkpoints, know where
to avoid the rubble. The building isn't even singed when I
arrive. Even as the sky to the west is so dark with smoke it
seems like a storm is rolling in.

But outside, the police are waiting. Keagan sits on the sidewalk, hands cuffed behind his back. One of his eyes is swollen
shut, and there is blood on his shirt. No one else looks at him
as they enter the building, and if I join them I wonder if I'll
be able to keep my eyes from stealing a glance. From searching
his face for the answer to the question that is burning in me.
Has he told them about me?

It feels as if I'm stuck in cement. My feet won't rise, my
body won't move. Work is life, work is service. Work is safety.
That's what I've told myself. Work is safety for me, for Gabe.
Food on the table, a place to live. My vision flares orange, as I
feel the heat inside me stretch to the top of my head. I exhale
steam, everything in me dry, thirsty.

The wind shifts, picks up, and I am sprinkled with ash that
swirls around me and away. I shake my head, and bits of it fall
free. Were they buildings, I wonder. Or people? I remember
the woman at the bus stop. I lift my hand to catch a speck of
ash like a child would catch a snowflake. Only this doesn't
melt, doesn't disappear. It remains, a gray memory of something lost.

I turn away from the building, away from Keagan on the
sidewalk, away from the cops. I face the darkened sky and I

start walking west. Somewhere in there Gabe is fighting, or running, or dead. And work will not protect him, or me.

————

The government building is decorated with scaffolding, crowned with caution warnings. Construction rings through the city like bells, and the city is out in celebration.

"It doesn't feel like a reason to celebrate," I say, but Gabe takes my hand and leads me to a stall selling meat sticks.

"It'll mean a lot of iron," he says. "Work for a long time to come. Job security, right?"

Every so often the sun manages to pierce the clouds, and light catches his smile in a way that sends a wave of warmth rushing through me.

"A jail, though," I say. "And so... big. We've never needed a jail that big."

"It'll probably sit empty most of the time," Gabe says. "It's just a way to get the economy moving. Create jobs. It's a symbol."

We walk around the artist's rendition of the proposed building. The Gaol. One enormous eyesore, a slab of concrete and metal.

"A symbol of what?"

————

I move through the streets toward the Great Forge and fall in stride with others in the march west. House cleaners and clerks, nurses and grocers. The smoke grows thicker but we keep moving, the heat of our bodies joining together in waves. Everything is noise, shouting, the wail of sirens and the sharp punctuations of gunshots. But we don't turn back. I think of Gabe's smiling face, think of the relief in the expression of the woman at the bus stop. The heat rises and I feel the stone of the road blister under our feet.

Ahead, the street opens into the chaos of the Great Forge. Soldiers and police stand their ground before the approaching crowd, weapons drawn, aimed. There is a crack as they unleash.

No one falls. We walk through puddles of liquid metal falling harmlessly to the ground. Tanks begin to roll forward, then stall screaming as their treads melt, as people throw themselves out before they're baked inside. Across the square, the forge workers are waiting for us. Gabe is waiting for me.

We meet, hands grasping, that heat like a gift we pass between each other. Something that alone would have reduced us to ash. But together…I press my lips to Gabe's and taste fire. We are more than ember hearts in ashen bodies. More than a forest of people burning down to fuel something that seeks to own us. And all around us people are turning, bodies pointing east, toward the monolith of the Gaol. Together, we are fire itself, and there is so much left to burn.

About the Editors

Julie C. Day (Series Editor) is currently at work on her mosaic novel *Stories of Driesch*. Her dark fantasy novella, *The Rampant*, was a Lambda Literary Award finalist. She is the author of the genre-bending collection *Uncommon Miracles* and editor-in-chief of the charity anthology *Weird Dream Society*. Day has had over forty stories published in magazines and journals such as *The Dark Magazine*, *BlackStatic*, *Podcastle*, *Interzone*, and *The Cincinnati Review*. With an MFA in creative writing from the University of Southern Maine's Stonecoast program and MS in microbiology from the University of Massachusetts at Amherst, all research is now in service of her stories and her rabbit-hole curiosity. You can find Julie online at @thisjulieday or on her blog at www.stillwingingit.com.

Ellen Meeropol (Guest Editor) is the author of the novels *The Lost Women of Azalea Court*, *Her Sister's Tattoo*, *Kinship of Clover*, *On Hurricane Island*, and *House Arrest* and the play *Gridlock*. Her dramatic program telling the story of the Rosenberg Fund for Children was produced five times between 1997 and 2013, featuring Ossie Davis, Mandy Patinkin, Ed Asner, Danny Glover, Pete Seeger, Harry Belafonte, Bill T. Jones,

Angela Davis, Eve Ensler, and Howard Zinn. Recent essay and short story publications include *Ms. Magazine, Lilith, Guernica, Lit Hub, Solstice,* and *Mom Egg Review.* Her work has been honored by the Sarton Women's Prize, Women's National Book Association, and the Massachusetts Center for the Book. A founding member of Straw Dog Writers Guild, Ellen coordinates their Emerging Writer Fellowship program. Find her online at www.ellenmeeropol.com.

Carina Bissett (Assistant Editor) is a writer, poet, and educator working primarily in the fields of dark fiction and fabulism. Her short fiction and poetry have been published in multiple journals and anthologies including *Upon a Twice Time, Bitter Distillations: An Anthology of Poisonous Tales, Arterial Bloom, Gorgon: Stories of Emergence, Weird Dream Society, Hath No Fury,* and the *HWA Poetry Showcase Vol. V, VI,* and *VIII.* She has also written stories set in shared worlds for RPGs at Green Ronin Publishing and Onyx Path Publishing. In addition to writing, she co-edited *Shadow Atlas: Dark Landscapes of the Americas,* which was a winner of the Colorado Book Awards. Carina also teaches generative writing workshops at The Storied Imaginarium and works as a volunteer for the Horror Writers Association (HWA). In 2021, she was acknowledged for her volunteer efforts at HWA with the prestigious Silver Hammer Award. Carina's work has been nominated for several awards, including the Pushcart Prize and the Sundress Publications Best of the Net. She can be found online at www.carinabissett.com.

Celia Jeffries (Assistant Editor) is a writer, editor, and teacher whose work has appeared in numerous newspapers and literary magazines including *Solsticelitmag, Puerto del Sol, The Writer's Chronicle,* and *Linea,* as well as the anthology *Beyond the Yellow Wallpaper.* She holds an MFA from Lesley University and an MA from Brandeis and teaches online workshops through Pioneer Valley Writers Workshop and Straw Dog Writers Guild. She is currently at work on a triptych memoir, as well as a series of micro memoirs. Her work has taken her from North America to Africa, and many places in between. *Blue Desert,* her first novel, was a finalist for both the Independent Publishers of New England literary fiction award and the May Sarton Award in historical fiction. Find her online at www.celiajeffries.com.

About the Contributors

Andrew Altschul is the author of the novels *The Gringa, Deus Ex Machina,* and *Lady Lazarus,* and of short stories that have appeared in *O. Henry Prize Stories, Best New American Voices, Best American Nonrequired Reading,* and many journals and magazines. A former Wallace Stegner Fellow and Jones Lecturer at Stanford, he has received fellowships from the Rockefeller Foundation Bellagio Center, the Fundación Valparaíso, and the Ucross Foundation. Altschul is the Director of creative writing at Colorado State University, in Fort Collins, and a contributing editor of *ZYZZYVA.*

Joy Baglio is a speculative-literary fiction writer and proud Leo living in Northampton, MA. Her short stories have appeared in *Tin House, American Short Fiction, Conjunctions, The Missouri Review, The Iowa Review, The Fairy Tale Review, Gulf Coast, TriQuarterly, New Ohio Review,* and elsewhere. She has received scholarships, fellowships, and grants from Yaddo, the Bread Loaf Writers Conference, Sewanee Writers' Conference, Vermont Studio Center, The Elizabeth George Foundation, and The Speculative Literature Foundation, among others. Baglio holds an MFA from The New School and is the founder of the literary arts organization, Pioneer Valley Writer's Workshop. She is at work on a collection of short stories and a centuries-spanning novel about ghosts. Find her online at www.joybaglio.com and Twitter @JoyBaglio.

Breena Clarke is the author of three novels. Her recent novel, *Angels Make Their Hope Here*, is set in an imagined mixed-race community in 19th-century New Jersey. Clarke's debut novel, *River, Cross My Heart*, was an October 1999 Oprah Book Club selection. Her critically reviewed second novel, *Stand the Storm*, is set in mid-19th-century Washington, D.C. Clarke's short fiction has appeared in *Kweli Journal*, *Stonecoast Review*, *Nervous Breakdown*, *Mom Egg Review*, and *Catapult*, as well as, *Like Light: 25 Years of Poetry & Prose by Bright Hill Poets & Writers*. She contributed an essay to *IDOL TALK: Women Writers on the Teenage Infatuations That Changed Their Lives* and was co-editor of *Chicken Soup for the Soul: I'm Speaking Now: Black Women Share Their Truth in 101 Stories of Love, Courage and Hope*, to which she contributed two personal narratives. Clarke has been a member of the fiction faculty of Stonecoast MFA in creative writing since 2013. Two new books are forthcoming: another story collection, *Fruiting Bodies*, in Fall 2022, and in January 2023, a middle-grade historical fantasy novel, *Speculation*. She is co-founder and co-organizer (with Cheryl Clarke and Barbara Balliet) of The Hobart Book Village Festival of Women Writers, now entering its ninth consecutive year of celebrating the work of women writers in Hobart, New York, despite the challenges of the global pandemic. Two new books are forthcoming: another story collection, *Fruiting Bodies*, in Fall 2022, and in January 2023, a middle-grade historical fantasy novel, *Speculation.*"

Zig Zag Claybourne is the author of *The Brothers Jetstream: Leviathan* and its sequel *Afro Puffs Are the Antennae of the Universe*. Other works include *By All Our Violent Guides*, *Neon Lights*, and

Conversations with Idras. His stories and essays on science fiction, fandom, and howlingly existential life have appeared in *Apex*, *Galaxy's Edge*, *GigaNotosaurus*, *Strange Horizons*, and other genre venues, as well as his blog *42* on his website www.writeon righton.com. He is the 2021 Kresge Foundation Literary Fellow. He grew up watching *The Twilight Zone* and considers himself a better person for it.

Tina Egnoski is the author most recently of the novel *Burn Down This World* and the story collection *You Can Tell Me Anything*. Her work, both fiction and poetry, has appeared in a number of literary journals, including *Flying South*, *Green Briar Review*, *Gris-Gris*, and *The Masters Review*. She leads community-based writing workshops and has been an instructor with Grubstreet Providence. Along with writing, she's a papermaker and bookbinder.

Cai Emmons is the author of seven books of fiction: the novels *His Mother's Son* (winner of the Oregon Book Award), *The Stylist*, *Weather Woman*, and *Sinking Islands*, as well as the forthcoming *Unleashed* and *Hair on Fire* (working title). Her collection of short stories, *Vanishing*, won the 2020 Leapfrog Press fiction contest. Emmons's short work has appeared in *The L.A. Times*, *Ms. Magazine*, *TriQuarterly*, *Narrative*, *Arts and Culture*, *The Santa Monica Review*, *LitHub*, and *Electric Literature*, among others. Before turning to fiction Emmons wrote plays and screenplays. She has taught film and fiction at various universities, (most recently the University of Oregon), and is now a full-time writer.

JoeAnn Hart is the author of the memoir *Stamford '76: A True Story of Murder, Corruption, Race, and Feminism in the 1970s*. Her novels are *Float*, a dark comedy about plastics in the ocean, and *Addled*, a social satire. Her short fiction and essays have appeared in a wide range of literary publications, including

Orion, The Hopper, Prairie Schooner, The Sonora Review, The Woven Tale, and *Black Lives Have Always Mattered*. Her work, which also includes photography and drama, often explores the relationship between humans and their environments.

Ava Homa is a writer, journalist, and activist specializing in women's issues and Middle Eastern affairs. She holds an MA in English and creative writing from the University of Windsor in Canada. Her collection of short stories, *Echoes from the Other Land*, was longlisted for the Frank O'Connor International Prize, and she is the inaugural recipient of the PEN Canada-Humber College Writers-in-Exile Scholarship. *Daughters of Smoke and Fire*, her debut novel, won the Nautilus Book Award for fiction.

Céline Keating is an award-winning writer of fiction. She is co-editor of *On Montauk: A Literary Celebration* and the author of two novels, *Layla*, a featured title in *The Huffington Post*, and *Play for Me*, a finalist in the International Book Awards, Indie Excellence Awards, and USA Book Awards. An excerpt from her novel-in-progress, *The Stark Beauty of Last Things*, won the first-place fiction award from the Tucson Book Festival in 2021. Her story "Home" received the first-place 2014 Hackney Award for Short Fiction. Other short fiction has been published in *Appearances, Echoes, Emry's Journal, Mount Hope, The North Stone Review, Prairie Schooner*, and the *Santa Clara Review*. Keating lives in New York with her husband, Mark Levy, and is on the board of environmental organization Concerned Citizens of Montauk.

Innocent Chizarama Ilo is Igbo. They are the winner of the 2020 Commonwealth Short Story Prize [African Region] and an Otherwise Award Honoree. Their works have appeared or are forthcoming in *Granta, F&SF, Strange Horizons, Fireside, Escape Pod, Reckoning Press*, and elsewhere. Innocent currently lives in Lagos, Nigeria, but dreams of exciting lives in far-flung places.

Aimee Liu is the bestselling author of the novels *Glorious Boy, Flash House, Cloud Mountain,* and *Face,* as well as the memoirs *Solitaire* and *Gaining.* Her work has been published in more than twelve languages. She lives in Los Angeles.

Jan Maher's novels *Heaven, Indiana; Earth as It Is;* and her short fiction collection *The Persistence of Memory and Other Stories* have each won Kirkus "Best Of" designations. Her stories and poems have been published regionally in *Meat for Tea: The Valley Review,* and *Compass Roads: Poems about the Pioneer Valley.* She is currently working on a third novel set in the fictional town of Heaven, Indiana. Her documentary stage play *Most Dangerous Women* celebrates with word and song a century of the international women's peace movement. She leads three online programs for The LAVA Center in Greenfield, MA: a poets & writers café, a playwrights circle, and a book club. Maher is a member of the ECHO Greenfield project team, a local history project that encourages people to uncover the hidden histories of their communities and to recognize themselves as history makers. Her website is www.janmaher.com.

Usman T. Malik's fiction has been reprinted in several year's best anthologies, including *The Best American Science Fiction & Fantasy* series. He has been nominated for the World Fantasy Award and the Nebula Award, and has won the Bram Stoker Award, the Nebula Award, and the Crawford Award. Malik's debut collection *Midnight Doorways: Fables from Pakistan* has garnered praise from Brian Evenson, Paul Tremblay, Karen Joy Fowler, Kelly Link, and others, and is available through his website at www.usmanmalik.org. You can find Usman on Twitter @usmantm.

Benjamin Parzybok is the author of the novels *Couch* (a two-time Indie-Next pick) and *Sherwood Nation* (chosen for the Silicon Valley Reads program). Among other projects, he founded *Gumball Poetry*, a literary journal published in gumball capsule machines; co-ran Project Hamad, an effort to free a Guantanamo inmate [Adel Hamad is now free]; and co-runs Black Magic Insurance Agency, a one-night, city-wide, alternative reality game. Parzybok also provides guidance to a number of projects such as Street Books, a bicycle-powered library for people living outside, and the *Between the Covers* podcast, a literary interview series. He lives in Portland, Oregon with the artist/writer Laura Moulton, and can be found at www.levinofearth.com and on Twitter @sparkwatson.

Charles Payseur is an avid reader, writer, and reviewer of speculative fiction. His works have appeared in *The Best American Science Fiction and Fantasy*, *Lightspeed Magazine*, and *Beneath Ceaseless Skies*, among others, and many are included in his debut collection, *The Burning Day and Other Strange Stories* (Lethe Press 2021). He is the series editor of *We're Here: The Best Queer Speculative Fiction* (Neon Hemlock Press) and a multiple-time Hugo and Ignyte Award finalist for his work at Quick Sip Reviews. He now reviews short fiction at *Locus Magazine*. When not drunkenly discussing Goosebumps, X-Men comic books, and his cats on his Patreon (/quicksipreviews) and Twitter (@ClowderofTwo), he can probably found raising a beer with his husband, Matt, in their home in Eau Claire, Wisconsin.

Robert V.S. Redick is a novelist, teacher, editor, and international development consultant with thirty years experience in the Neotropics and Southeast Asia. His debut novel, *The Red Wolf Conspiracy*, was a finalist for the SFX Novel Award and received a special commendation by the 2010

Crawford Award Committee. He is the author of *The Fire Sacraments* epic fantasy series, including the recently-published *Sidewinders*, and *The Chathrand Voyage Quartet*. He is a winner of the New Millennium Writings Award, and a finalist for the Booknest Award for Best Novel and the Thomas Dunne Novel Award. Redick lives with his partner, Dr. Kiran Asher, in Western Massachusetts.

Veronica Schanoes is an American author of fantasy stories and an associate professor in the department of English at Queens College, CUNY. Her novella *Burning Girls* was nominated for the Nebula Award and the World Fantasy Award and won the Shirley Jackson Award for Best Novella in 2013. She lives in New York City. *Burning Girls and Other Stories* was her debut collection.

Nisi Shawl is best known for fiction dealing with gender, race, and colonialism, including the Nebula finalist novel *Everfair*, an alternate history of the Congo. Their story collection *Filter House* was a winner of the Otherwise Award, formerly the James Tiptree, Jr. Award. They're the coauthor of *Writing the Other: A Practical Approach*, a standard text on inclusive representation, and a cofounder of the Carl Brandon Society. Their criticism and essays appear widely, including as introductions to a volume of the *Library of America* and to a new edition of Octavia E. Butler's last novel, *Fledgling*.

Shawl edited *New Suns: Speculative Fiction by People of Color*. They co-edited *Strange Matings: Science Fiction, Feminism, African American Voices, and Octavia E. Butler*; and *Stories for Chip: A Tribute to Samuel R. Delany*. Awards recently received include the World Fantasy Award, two Locus Awards, and FIYAH's Ignyte Award. Two new books are forthcoming in fall of 2022: another story collection, *Fruiting Bodies*, and a middle-grade historical fantasy novel, *Speculation*.

Vandana Singh is a writer of speculative fiction and a professor of physics at a small and lively public university near Boston. Her critically acclaimed short stories have been reprinted in numerous best-of-year anthologies, and her most recent collection, *Ambiguity Machines and Other Stories* was a finalist for the Philip K. Dick award. A particle physicist by training, she has been working for a decade on a transdisciplinary, justice-based conceptualization of the climate crisis at the nexus of science, pedagogy, and society. She is a Fellow of the Center for Science and the Imagination at Arizona State University. Singh was born and raised in India, where she continues to have multiple entanglements—both personal and professional—and divides her time between New Delhi and the Boston area. She can be found online at www.vandana-writes.com.

Lisa C. Taylor is the author of two poetry chapbooks and two full-length collections including *Necessary Silence* and *The Other Side of Longing* with Irish poet and writer, Geraldine Mills. She is also the author of two short story collections, most recently *Impossibly Small Spaces*. Taylor's honors include the Elizabeth Shanley Gerson Lecture at University of Connecticut (with Geraldine Mills) in 2011; writing residencies at Vermont Studio Center, Willowtail Springs, and Tyrone Guthrie at Annaghmakerrig in Ireland; a spotlight feature in Associated Writing Programs (AWP); the Hugo House New Works Fiction Award; and Pushcart nominations in fiction and poetry. Her work has been in numerous anthologies and has been taught in college classes in New England. She was a two-time mentor with the AWP writer-to-writer program, and she taught creative writing at the secondary and college level for many years. Taylor holds an MFA in creative writing from Stonecoast, University of Southern Maine. She recently moved to a small town in the mountains where she offers workshops and private writing consultations. She is the fiction editor for the online magazine, *Wordpeace*, and a book reviewer for *Mom Egg Review* and other publications. She is online at www.lisactaylor.com.

Sheree Renée Thomas is an award-winning fiction writer, poet, and editor. Her work is inspired by myth and folklore, natural science, and Mississippi Delta conjure. *Nine Bar Blues: Stories from an Ancient Future* is her first prose collection. She is also the author of two multigenre/hybrid collections, *Sleeping Under the Tree of Life*, longlisted for the 2016 Otherwise Award and honored with a *Publishers Weekly* starred review, and *Shotgun Lullabies*. Thomas edited the World Fantasy-winning ground-breaking Black speculative fiction anthologies, *Dark Matter* (2000 and 2004) and is the first to introduce W.E.B. Du Bois's science fiction short stories. Her work is widely anthologized and appears in *The Big Book of Modern Fantasy*. She is the associate editor of the historic Black arts literary journal, *Obsidian: Literature & the Arts in the African Diaspora*, and is the editor of *The Magazine of Fantasy & Science Fiction*. Thomas also writes book reviews for *Asimov's*. She was recently honored as a 2020 World Fantasy Award Finalist in the Special Award Professional category for contributions to the genre and is the co-host of the 2021 Hugo Awards Ceremony at Discon III in Washington, D.C. with Malka Older. Thomas is the Guest of Honor of Wiscon 45 and a Special Guest of Boskone 58. She is a Marvel writer and contributor to the groundbreaking anthology, *Black Panther: Tales of Wakanda*. She lives in her hometown, Memphis, Tennessee near a mighty river and a pyramid.

Marie Vibbert has published over seventy short stories, including eleven appearances in *Analog* and three in *China's Science Fiction World*. Her debut novel, *Galactic Hellcats*, is about a female biker gang in outer space rescuing a gay prince. Vibbert played women's professional football for five years

with the Cleveland Fusion. By day she is a computer
programmer.

Sabrina Vourvoulias is an award-winning Latina news
editor, writer, and digital storyteller whose work has appeared
at *Guardian US*, PRI's *The World*, *Inquirer.com*, *NBC Philadelphia*,
and *Philadelphia Magazine* and other English- and Spanish-
language publications.

An American citizen by birth, she grew up in Guatemala
during the armed internal conflict and moved to the United
States when she was fifteen. Her journalism and news editing
have garnered an Emmy, and an Edward R. Murrow award,
as well as multiple José Martí, Keystone, and New York Press
Association awards. In addition to short speculative fiction,
Vourvoulias is the author of *Ink*, a near-future, immigration-
centered dystopia which was named to Latinidad's Best Books
of 2012. In 2020, she wrote a middle-school nonfiction
anthology, *Nuestra América: 30 Inspiring Latinas/Latinos Who Have
Shaped the United States*. Vourvoulias lives in Pennsylvania with
her husband, daughter, and a dog who believes she is the one
ring to rule them all. Follow her on Twitter @followthelede
and online at www.sabrinavourvoulias.com.

Cynthia Robinson Young is a native of Newark, New
Jersey, but after thirty years in the San Francisco Bay Area, she
now lives and writes in Chattanooga, Tennessee with her
family, which includes eight children and seventeen grandchil-
dren. She is the author of the chapbook, *Migration*, which was
named Finalist in the 2019 Georgia Author of the Year Award
for chapbooks. Her work has appeared in anthologies
including *Across the Generations, vols. I and V*, and in journals and
magazines, including *The Ekphrastic Review*, *The Amistad*, *Mantis*,
The Writer's Chronicle, and *Sixfold*. She is currently working on a
novel.